ALSO by JUDITH A. BARRETT

DONUT LADY COZY MYSTERY SERIES

MAGGIE SLOAN THRILLER SERIES

GRID DOWN SURVIVAL SERIES

RILEY MALLOY THRILLER SERIES

SWEET DEAL APPEALED

Donut Lady Cozy Mystery

Book 4

Judith A. Barrett

SWEET DEAL APPEALED

DONUT LADY COZY MYSTERY, BOOK 4

Published in the United States of America by Wobbly Creek, LLC

2020 Georgia

wobblycreek.com

SWEET DEAL APPEALED is a work of fiction. Names, characters, businesses, places, events, locales, and incidents either are the products of the author's imagination or used in a fictitious manner. Any resemblance to actual persons, living or dead, or actual events is purely coincidental.

Edited by Judith Euen Davis

Cover by Wobbly Creek, LLC

ISBN 978-1-953870-01-8

DEDICATION

SWEET DEAL APPEALED is dedicated to challenges, seeing what is there, and the colors of imagination.

CHAPTER ONE

I woke and swung my feet to the floor. Before I could rise, I almost collapsed from an overwhelming feeling of dread, and I broke into a sweat. The dark, gloomy shadows in the doorway scattered when my gray cat, Mia, darted out from under my bed, hissed, and arched her back.

I relaxed as I sat on the side of my bed until Colonel, my German Shepherd, whined from the kitchen. I slipped on my shoes and waved away the shadows as I hurried down the hallway. When I flipped on the light, Colonel barked at the back door.

"What is it, boy?" I cracked the door to peer into the dark, but Colonel growled and barked as he barreled into the backyard. A raccoon jumped the fence, and shadows slipped between the houses on the other side of the alley. I turned and glared at my house shadows as they swirled in the kitchen and under the pantry door.

Colonel patrolled the perimeter of the fenced yard before he joined me on the porch. I wrapped my arms around his neck, buried my face in his thick fur, and shuddered.

"Something's wrong. I don't know what it is, but it's bad."

Colonel licked my neck.

"You're right. We'll face it together." I rose, and Colonel followed me into the house.

* * *

When we reached the Donut Hole, Colonel hopped out of the car, and I picked up Mia's carrier. Andrew came out of the shop and hurried to my car. He was stocky and wore his Donut Hole ballcap and apron, oversized black Bulldogs T-shirt, and jeans pulled high on his waist.

"Can I carry Mia?" As he reached for Mia, his pale hand shook. "Ms. Tiffany is mad and throwing things. She yelled and scared me. I don't know what I did wrong." He hugged the carrier to his chest. "I don't like loud noises."

"Do you want to stay out here a minute with Mia?"

"Yes, Miss Lady."

The bell jingled when I opened the door. Tiffany had crammed her ballcap tight onto her head, but her black hair sprung out around the cap. Her back stiffened as she measured flour into the mixer.

"Good morning." I hurried to the storeroom for my apron. As I tied the apron strings, I glanced at Tiffany, and her brown eyes flashed anger as she scowled.

"Do you plan to apologize to Andrew now or wait?" I asked.

"What are you talking about?" Tiffany growled as she slammed the wooden spoon onto the table.

I filled the large coffee maker with water and measured coffee into its basket. After I made coffee in the smaller pot, I loaded the utility cart for the pink meeting room.

Tiffany hadn't budged.

"When I arrived this morning, Andrew said you were mad and scared him. I'm happy to listen if you ever want to talk, but Andrew thinks he did something wrong, and I don't want him to spend the morning outside alone and afraid."

Tiffany marched to the front door and slammed it so hard behind her that the bell fell to the floor. Andrew was near the window, and he backed away from Tiffany. She relaxed her tight shoulders and clenched fists, and Andrew smiled as she spoke to him.

I mixed the dough for the first batch of donuts. After I covered the bowl for the dough to rise, I mixed the dough for scones.

Andrew rushed into the shop and washed his hands before he peered at the rising dough. "Thank you for starting the donuts for me, Miss Lady. If Ms. Tiffany feels better, she can take over the scones."

"What's our plan for today?" I asked.

"We have the Methodist men today." Andrew mixed his second batch of dough. "Woody and I decided they need a surprise, and we planned rocky road scones and a dust to dust donut."

I snickered. "How do you make a dust to dust donut?"

Andrew covered his dough to rise. "Woody made it up. Classic glaze with a dusting of cocoa powder, and our second donut is frosted maple. Ms. Tiffany said it would be fun to add chocolate sprinkles and call it decadent maple."

"She's right. I'll get busy on the rocky road scones. While the scones bake, I'll record our specials for the day on our board." I hurried to the pantry for miniature marshmallows and chocolate and grabbed chopped nuts from the freezer.

After I popped my scones into the oven, I pulled out my folding ladder and climbed up to mark the board. *Rocky Road Scones. Decadent Maple and Dust to Dust Donuts.*

"Ms. Tiffany doesn't need the ladder." Andrew folded the ladder and hung it on its hook. He hurried to join me at the counter as I admired the board. I held up my hand, and we high-fived.

"Back to work." Andrew strode to the fryer to begin his first batch of donuts.

I pulled my scones out of the oven and mixed the next batch before I decorated the batches of donuts and scones that had cooled.

When the Sheriff stepped inside, he kicked the bell, and it skittered across the floor. He stared at me as he scanned the shop.

I smiled. "Good morning, Sheriff."

"Oh, good. I was afraid it wasn't safe to come in. Tiffany growled when I said good morning to her." He scooped up the bell as he beelined to his seat, but I beat him to the counter with a cup of coffee for him.

He set the bell on the counter and blew on his coffee. "Why is Tiffany outside?"

"She's in timeout," I said.

"Yes. Timeout," Andrew echoed.

Sheriff drank his coffee while he read the board. "I need one of each. I've started the search to replace Roger. I might need more donuts later this week. Are you making termite donuts anytime soon? Might as well give them the acid test."

I snickered as Andrew plated the sheriff's pastries before he returned to his fryer.

The sheriff broke off a quarter of his decadent maple, shoved it into his mouth and chased it down with a swig of coffee. "Methodist men meet this morning, am I right? What time? I might rearrange my schedule to stop by."

I refilled the Sheriff's cup. "They'll be here at eight. I hope the mayor comes today. We're a trifle shorthanded."

"According to the folks at the gas station, he'll be here, and they aren't wrong very often."

"Good." I hurried back to my scones and my decorating.

"Your bell must have fallen, Donut Lady. Shall I reattach it for you?" Sheriff asked.

"Yes, please." I brought him a screwdriver from the storeroom.

"Five or six batches of donuts today?" Andrew asked as the sheriff rehung the bell.

"Let's go with six today." I slid two more trays of scones into the oven.

"You got a feeling, Karen?" Sheriff returned the screwdriver to my office.

I bit my lip. "Thanks for fixing the bell, Sheriff. I have a feeling, but it's not a good one. More of a foreboding than a feeling. I woke up with it."

Sheriff frowned as he poured himself more coffee. "Want me to assign a deputy to the shop today?"

"No, Andrew, Mayor, Colonel, and I can handle anything."

"Colonel is brave. I get scared," Andrew said.

"Would you be too scared to call Ms. Tess, Andrew?" Sheriff asked.

"No. I like Ms. Tess. She knows how to help."

Sheriff nodded. "Might be smart to get Andrew his own cell phone, Karen. Do you mind if I take care of that? I'll clear it with his folks first."

"What do you think, Andrew? Could you be brave and call Ms. Tess?" I asked.

"Yes. Woody can teach me."

"You're right. Woody is a good teacher, but he's in school. I'll teach you."

Andrew turned his attention to his donuts, and the sheriff grinned as he winked. "Call me or Tess if you need me. I'll be back later."

After Sheriff left, Tiffany opened the shop door. "Andrew said I could come in when I could be nice, but I don't have to talk."

"I think that's a good rule," I said.

She washed her hands. "I'll finish up the scones. I am not marrying Roger. I am canceling the wedding."

Wedding is ten days away. Just about right for pre-wedding jitters. I poured myself a cup of coffee then sat at the counter and waited.

Tiffany placed the last two trays into the oven and decorated donuts. "He said I can't work after we move to Savannah. I can't marry a man who makes rules about my life."

I blinked. *Wonder what Roger really said?* "Does he know the wedding's off?"

"He should. That was a rotten thing to say. I told him we'd just see about that."

"What did he say about your engineering classes?" I asked.

"That has nothing to do with anything." Tiffany added chocolate sprinkles to the last batch of maple donuts.

The bell jingled, and I poured Shirley's coffee. Tiffany set Shirley's to-go sack on the counter next to the register. Shirley wore a black skirt, a white blouse, and her signature red jacket, but her cheeks were tear-stained with mascara.

"Can't stop to chat. I'm showing two houses this morning and a third one this afternoon. Did you hear the thunder earlier this morning? I think the storm went north of us, but there's another band of rain headed our way. I encourage buyers to look at houses when it's raining because it gives them a chance to see if the yard floods or the roof leaks, but some folks cancel because of rain."

Her shoulders slumped as she sat on a stool. "I realized I'm not cut out for this foster mother business. Woody told me this morning that none of his friends has a mother with white hair. When I told him my hair is blond, not white, he said blond and white are the same. When I told him he was being rude, he told me it's a free country, and I didn't understand fun. Can you believe that?"

She brushed away the tear that had slipped onto her cheek. "I told him I was the most fun person he'll ever meet and grounded him. No electronics for two days except for schoolwork under my supervision. He's not speaking to me. After I dropped him off at school, I contacted my parent support group. They said I did the right thing, but I don't think he'd be mouthy if he had a good foster mother."

"Only a good foster mother would care enough to set limits," I said. "Go into the bathroom and wash your face. You've smeared your mascara."

Shirley rushed to clean her face.

"Better?" she asked.

"Much."

She grabbed her sack and coffee on her way out.

"Woody's being ornery," I said.

Andrew carried donuts and scones to the display case. "Yes."

Tiffany glowered and put her hands on her hips. "Well, I think—"

I raised my eyebrows and glared at her.

Tiffany bit her lip. "Woody needs to be respectful."

"You are smart, Ms. Tiffany," Andrew said.

The mayor hurried into the shop at seven forty-five and read the board. "For the Methodist men's group, right? I love my job."

He chuckled on his way to the storeroom for his apron and ballcap. While he was setting up the pink meeting room, a crash of thunder shook the windows, and the door flew open as the Methodist men hurried in to get out of the sudden downpour. The first few stopped and read the board, so that the men behind them collided in the rush to get out of the rain.

"Coffee's in here, gentlemen." Mayor waved from the door of the meeting room and smiled as he stood back to avoid the stampede. The men jostled into the room, and Tiffany hurried to deliver two more carafes while Andrew carried in the platters of donuts and scones.

Mayor quieted the men then announced, "Today you face a Rocky Road on your path to the Decadent Maple, and your final destination? Dust to dust." The men applauded and whistled as Mayor closed the door.

Tiffany giggled. "The mayor could be a preacher."

I smiled. "Or a storyteller."

Sheriff came into the shop. The dark look on his face startled me. "Karen, where can you, Tiffany, and I talk in private?"

I led the way to the storeroom that doubled as my office.

Sheriff closed the door behind him. "Please sit. Both of you."

Tiffany's face paled as she sat on the old counter stool. I sat at my desk and turned my chair to face Sheriff. *This isn't good.*

"Gee and Isaiah picked up a load of merchandise early this morning, and on the way back, a tractor trailer jackknifed on the road when the car in front of it spun out on the wet pavement. Isaiah managed to control his truck and avoided the big rig, but a moving van behind him couldn't stop and slammed into him. Isaiah's truck flipped and rolled over at least twice, but bystanders extricated him and Gee."

Tiffany swayed, and the sheriff steadied her. He moved her to the desk chair, and I slipped out and returned with a glass of water.

She held the cool glass with both hands and sipped. "Such a shock. Are they okay?"

"Gee was badly injured, and the ambulance rushed her north to the Macon trauma center. Isaiah had minor injuries, but the contents of the moving van burst into flames, and two cars that had crashed into it caught fire. Isaiah and an off-duty firefighter pulled out all the occupants of the burning cars, but both of them suffered severe burns and were flown to the Burn Center in Florida."

"I'm going," Tiffany said.

Sheriff cleared his throat. "I've given Roger time off to go with you."

Tiffany frowned, and Sheriff raised his eyebrows. "Is there a problem?"

Tiffany nodded, and I said, "Pre-wedding jitters."

"Yes, pre-wedding jitters." Tears slipped down her cheeks. "I can't go to both hospitals at once. How do I choose? What about the thrift shop? What about the donut shop?"

"Blow your nose, Tiffany. We'll handle everything here. Sheriff, someone needs to talk to Isaiah's girlfriend, Tammy."

Tiffany grabbed a tissue. "I forgot about Tammy. She'll want to see Isaiah. I should go to Macon to be with Aunt Gee. I'll pack a few things."

When Sheriff opened the door, Roger was waiting. He was two inches taller than Tiffany, and his brown skin was not quite as dark as hers. His adoration showed in his eyes as he gazed at her. "Tiffany, I have the hospital phone numbers you can call for information, and I've packed for five days. Where do we go first?"

"Macon," she said. Roger put his arm around her, and they hurried out together.

"Wedding crisis averted or at least postponed," I muttered.

"How will you cover the donut shop and the thrift shop at the same time?" Sheriff asked.

"The gas station."

He frowned. "I'm sure the gas station has already—oh, I get it."

The mayor carried out two empty carafes. "Why were Tiffany and Roger in such a rush?"

"I'll fill the carafes and refill cups," I said.

"There's been a bad crash. I'll explain," the sheriff said.

When I carried the carafes into the meeting room, one of the men rose. "I'll take that, Ms. Donut Lady. We'll pass it around for refills."

Andrew was scrubbing pans at the sink. After he rinsed them and set them in the drying rack, I told him about the crash and explained we'd run the shop together while Tiffany was gone.

Andrew nodded. "We can do it."

I removed the grounds and filter from the large coffee maker, and Andrew carried the large stainless-steel container to the sink. After he cleaned it, he refilled it with water for the next large pot.

Darlene Rothenberger rolled in with the aid of her walker. She wore lime green slacks, a pale-yellow blouse that strained across her ample bosom, her pearl necklace, and sturdy, white shoes. She adjusted her glasses and smiled as she read the board. "Dad would be tickled to see the life and creativity you've brought to the old donut shop."

I poured her a cup of coffee, and she continued to the counter and eased onto a stool.

"I heard about the crash and realized how I can help our town's small businesses. The best fit for me is to cover Gee's thrift shop. I'll never be the keen negotiator that Gee is, but no one will get the best of me, and I'll protect her interests. I'll need someone strong to move and deliver furniture, but I can manage everything else."

"You're not interested in filling in here after all the years you worked the Donut Shop with your dad?"

"Heavens to Betsy, no. I could never be on my feet for hours at my age. I can rest from time to time at the thrift shop."

"Makes sense. Thank you, and I'll find someone to work with you. You can decide what hours you want to work and post a sign on the window. I'll give you my key, and I'll ask Tiffany to drop hers off with me."

"Perfect plan. Tell Tiffany we have everything under control."

I gave Darlene my thrift shop key, and she bustled out. I texted Tiffany and asked her to drop off her thrift shop key at the donut shop. Colonel nudged me, and I scratched his ears then hugged him.

My phone rang. *Tiffany.*

"Miss Lady, we'll drop off the thrift shop key on our way out of town. I talked to Tammy. Her cousin from Valdosta will go with her to Gainesville. I'm relieved she won't be driving by herself or be alone in the city."

"I'm glad to hear that. Darlene Rothenberger volunteered to keep the thrift store open. She said to tell you we have everything under control."

"Wow. Darlene is the perfect fill-in for Gee. See you in a few minutes."

The mayor returned to the meeting room with a full platter of donuts and scones. A few minutes later, he brought out an empty platter. "I can be here every morning for the club meetings, Karen. "

Amber came into the shop and kissed her dad on the cheek before he returned to the men's group. She had piled her dark hair on top of her head in a messy ponytail, and she wore jeans and a burnt-orange Auburn T-shirt. My eyes widened.

"Ms. Amber, is your Bulldogs shirt in the laundry?" Andrew asked.

"No, and orange is not my color."

"Not mine either," Andrew said.

I poured her coffee, and she sighed as she sat at the counter.

"I lost a bet and have to wear this T-shirt every day this week that I'm not in court. I offered to cover preliminary hearings for other lawyers, but they've already heard about my bet with Alfred, and the traitors have sided with the banker. But that's not why I'm here. I need coffee and—"

She chuckled as she read the board. "Decadent maple and a rocky road scone, and I'll take a dozen dust to dust to go. I have some papers to drop off at the courthouse. Maybe I'll find someone willing to throw me a court appearance or two this week."

Andrew served Amber her donut and scone, and she smiled. "Thank you, Andrew." She bit into her chocolate-sprinkled maple donut. "This is good. Karen, I got an email early this morning from the court in Ohio. Someone blocked our appeal for your felony conviction, and our appeal was denied. I was shocked. Our Ohio lawyer had the judge ready to sign. I'll follow up, but who on earth would block your appeal?"

I shook my head. "I can't think of anyone except maybe Terry's brother, Lloyd. I was the sole beneficiary of Terry's insurance because Terry didn't change his policy after we were divorced. Lloyd spoke at the trial and said I had murdered Terry and didn't deserve the money. I don't remember much of the trial, but I'll never forget the hate-filled evil in his face as he spoke about me. He argued that the insurance money should revert to him as Terry's closest relative. Lloyd never forgave me for giving the insurance company the documents that Terry had created to prove he was the biological father of his girlfriend's daughter."

Amber narrowed her eyes. "I'd forgotten about that. I'll do some digging, but we may have to start over. After I get my copy of the appeal proceedings, I'll have a better idea of what our course of action will be."

I rubbed my forehead. "I'm sorry this is such a mess. It's been over eighteen years since Terry died. You'd think Lloyd would have moved on by now, but he always was vindictive."

Amber polished off her donut and scone, while Andrew boxed up the donuts for her. She hugged me before she left. "It's been a rough morning for you. I'm sorry."

Jack held the door for Amber as she left. "I just heard about Gee and Isaiah. What's my assignment?"

I poured his coffee, and Andrew plated two donuts and a scone.

"Darlene Rothenberger offered to take over the thrift shop, but she'll need help. She can't unload stock or deliver furniture. Isaiah's friends can pitch in once in a while, but she needs someone there she can count on at least part of the day."

"Thanks, Andrew." Jack bit into his dust to dust donut. "Bittersweet. Perfect. I can help Darlene, Karen."

"Thank you. I gave my thrift store key to Darlene. Tiffany's dropping off her key as a backup for me and should be here soon. Would you mind making a copy for yourself?"

"What about Mandy and Sandy? Will they stay at the thrift shop?" Jack asked.

"I'd forgotten all about them." I frowned. "Sandy won't mind staying at the shop, but he still must be fed. Mandy can be at the shop during the day. Maybe I can pick her up and drop her off at the shop in the mornings. I'll talk to Darlene—"

"Why don't you let me take care of all that?" Jack put his arm around me, and my shoulders relaxed.

"Thank you. I don't know if there's something I'm forgetting, but for now, we have the most critical items covered."

The mayor followed the Methodist men as they filed out of the meeting room. After they left, he said, "One of the men suggested we set up a fund to help with extra expenses like Tiffany's and Tammy's hotels and food and, of course, the out-of-pocket medical expenses. I'll talk to Alfred this morning to see if we can set up a fund at the bank and whether he's willing to find someone to manage it."

"That's brilliant, Mayor," Jack said. "Darlene's taking care of the thrift shop to keep it open. We can post a notice there for donations."

Roger ran into the shop. "Here's Tiffany's key, and thanks to you, Ms. Karen, we're talking through our different expectations. Tiffany said to tell you."

Jack left with the key, and Andrew and Mayor cleaned and straightened the meeting room. After the room was clean, the mayor left.

Jorge, the gas station owner, came into the shop, and my eyes widened. *It's a miracle Jorge wasn't trampled in the stampede of Methodist men vying to be first at the gas station.*

"I'll take all the donuts you have to cheer up the gas station guys. Josh and the mechanics are moping over this morning's crash. Not that I blame them."

"They're on the house. It's my chance to show my appreciation for the services you all provide to the community."

Jorge smiled. "Thank you. I'll tell the guys what you said. That will perk them up. I hear the bank will set up a fund for medical and other expenses. We'll have a jar at the gas station for it. Too bad Woody got himself grounded. He could have made a nice poster."

After Jorge left, Andrew swept, and I cleaned the counter and stools. The sheriff tapped on the door, and grinned when he came in. "Sun's out, Karen. Your day will be brighter. Andrew, I have your phone. I bought it at the computer store from the new owner, Audrey. If you take it to her, she said she'd teach you how to call nine-one-one and text Ms. Karen and me. I gave her our numbers."

"Ms. Audrey is nice."

After Andrew left, Sheriff said, "Karen, I didn't want to say anything in front of Andrew, but your neighbor behind you reported that a man ran from your house then through her yard early this morning. Did you see anything?"

I frowned. "Colonel whined to go out this morning. When I opened the door, he barked and chased off a raccoon. I thought I saw something between the two houses behind me, but with the pale moon, it was hard to tell if it was a shadow or a person."

I checked the back door before Colonel, Mia, and I headed home.

After I released Mia from her carrier and let Colonel out back, my phone rang. *Jack.*

"What are you doing for lunch? Ms. Darlene is working me into starvation. She said to tell you that I'm the slave drive, not her. Did I tell you I'm not allowed any privacy either? Ouch. She smacked me. Would you care to join us for lunch? We'll let you pick it up from Gus's Sandwich Shop. Darlene already ordered our lunches and yours too."

I snickered. "You are such a smooth-talker. After Colonel takes his break, we'll pick up our order."

"Darlene says I'm not allowed to tease you, and I have to tell you she already paid for it. She's no fun. See you soon."

I watched Colonel as he checked his yard. On a whim, I strolled to the alley to check for footprints. The alley gravel and sand were smooth from the heavy rain. I snorted. *Glad I didn't announce my plan to find footprints in the sandy alley after a downpour.*

Colonel accompanied me to Gus's. When I walked into the shop, the pickup line snaked from the pickup window to the front door and snaked toward the order window.

Gus caught my eye and winked. "Donut Lady. Order up!" he shouted. The dishwasher appeared from the back of the shop and grabbed the three sacks and four drinks.

"I'll carry these out for you," he said. When we reached the car, he scanned the lot. "Ms. Darlene told Gus to give you the lunch when you showed up. I think there's something going on between them two old people because he jumped right to it."

He set the lunches on the passenger's seat and the drink holder on the floorboard.

"Don't tell Gus I told you about him and Ms. Darlene." He patted the car roof twice before he hurried back into the shop.

"Did you hear that, Colonel?" I snorted. "I think it's more likely that Darlene knows where some skeletons are hidden."

When we reached the thrift shop, Colonel whined to get out, and Gee's collie, Mandy, and Jack's chocolate lab, Roxie, bounded to the car door. I opened Colonel's door, and he and the girl dogs raced inside. *Darlene must have found Gee's stash of dog snacks.*

Jack and one of Isaiah's friends, Thomas, were loading a large sofa into the back of Jack's truck. After they were satisfied the sofa was secure, Thomas loaded the matching recliner into the pickup, and Jack closed the tailgate.

I carried lunch into the shop and paused to enjoy the familiar setting.

Takes me back in time. This furniture could have been in Grandma's house. I inhaled and breathed in the familiar, musky aroma of old wood and aged furnishings. I smiled at the idea of the long-gone owners lovingly guarding each piece, shook off my fanciful thoughts, and joined Darlene at a Formica-topped kitchen table. Jack and Thomas followed.

Darlene handed Jack and Thomas their sandwiches, and the men helped themselves to sweet tea. Darlene had ordered a sandwich and a salad for the two of us to split. While she cut the sandwich, I divided the salad onto the paper plates Darlene had set out for us.

Darlene winked. "Karen, you gave me the short end of the stick when you pawned off Jack onto me. He's hard of hearing and bull-headed. Won't do a thing I tell him, and when he does, he doesn't do it right."

Jack snorted. "You wouldn't believe the difficulties we've suffered working with a woman who can't make up her mind, but she's promised to double our pay. Right, Thomas?"

Thomas peered at Jack. "She bought me lunch. You sure you want to drag me into this?"

Jack burst out laughing, and Darlene chuckled.

Thomas rolled his eyes. "Ms. Lady, this is what I put up with all morning. Don't you and Andrew have some donuts you need for me to remove from the shop?"

I chuckled. "You all are a riot."

After the two men finished their lunches, Darlene gave each of them two of Gus's cookies.

As he munched his second cookie, Jack said, "Karen, our delivery is in Conway. Can you stay with Darlene while we're gone? Not that I think anybody would dare bother a cantankerous woman, but she and Sandy argue if there's no one around for her to pester."

After the men left, I picked up our trash and tossed it, and Darlene sat on a soft chair and pulled a footstool close to prop up her feet.

"I really like that Jack, Karen. You got yourself a keeper. He's as kindhearted a man as I've ever met."

A couple came in to browse, and Darlene smiled and gave them space to come into her lair. She was on duty. I slipped to the back. I pretended I was searching for what might replace the sofa and chair on the display floor, but I snooped to see what was there. *This is dangerous. Gee has a flair for finding the unusual, and I really don't have room for anything else.*

The couple purchased a fine old pecan wood dining table that had four mismatched chairs. They said their son and his friend would pick up their purchase in an hour. Darlene printed SOLD on a large yellow card and set it in the middle of the table as a centerpiece, and the couple beamed.

After they left, Darlene headed toward the back until a man entered the shop.

"Nice place," he said.

I dropped onto a trunk and shook as the hairs on my arms rose. My heart pounded, and I couldn't breathe. *I know that voice. Terry and his brother, Lloyd, sounded just alike. Slimy and smooth.*

"You know Karen Ahrens? She might go by O'Brien."

I held my breath.

"Can't say that I do. You looking for anything special?" Darlene asked.

Lloyd glanced around and pointed at a small table. "That. How much is that little table?"

"You have a discerning eye. That's the finest piece of furniture in the house. Go ahead. Guess how much."

Lloyd had always prized himself on being able to judge the value of items. Terry told me once it was because Lloyd was a fence. I snorted. *Terry lied about so much, may or may not be true.*

"I'd say three-fifty retail, but I bet you're willing to let it go at three hundred."

Darlene adjusted her glasses and nodded, and I covered my mouth to keep from snickering. "You are right on the money. Cash or credit card?"

"Cash," he said.

She pulled out the receipt book and wrote out a receipt for three hundred dollars. "Who shall I say is the buyer?"

"Lloyd Ahr—Erhart."

"Is that E-r-h-a-r-t?"

"Yes." Lloyd removed his wallet from his back pocket and peeled out three hundred dollars from his bundle of twenties. Darlene smiled, but I knew she counted the money along with him.

"You are a shrewd buyer, Mr. Erhart. Did you want us to deliver? Delivery for this table would be free."

CHAPTER TWO

"Thank you, no. I'll take it with me. Oh, about Karen Ahrens. She'd be middle-aged now. I haven't seen her since we taught school together in Ohio. She's much shorter than you are but not as classy in how she dresses. She would have moved here in the past three or four years."

Darlene removed her glasses and held them high as she examined them. "Dirtier than I thought." She rubbed her glasses on her sleeve and put them on. "No. Can't even think of anybody new who came to town since Clarissa showed up in 1997 with a baby and no husband, or was it 1987? The years just run together sometimes, don't they?" She chuckled. "We appreciate your business. You can sign up for our newsletter to hear about our new, old items." She tittered. "I love saying that. If you sign up, you're also entered in our monthly giveaway of binoculars worth five hundred dollars."

"Hate to pass on that, but I'm traveling for business over the next few months." Lloyd picked up his table and swaggered as he left.

Darlene wandered around the showroom and continued to face forward.

When she paused near the back, I said, "You are awesome, Darlene. That table has been in here for ages. Gee was asking thirty-five dollars but told me she'd take thirty." I laughed, and Darlene smirked.

"Who is that guy who's looking for you?" she asked.

"His name is Lloyd Ahrens. He's my dead ex-husband's brother."

"Piece of work, if you ask me." Darlene headed to her preferred spot in the front. "You calling the sheriff?"

"Yes."

"Sheriff, I'm fine. Everybody's fine. I'm at the thrift store with Darlene. Lloyd Aherns, Terry's brother, came to the shop looking for me. Darlene pled ignorance, but it's just a matter of time until he goes to the gas station or a diner. He's asking for Karen Aherns or Karen O'Brien."

"Most of the town knows you as Donut Lady. He might be slowed down for no more than a day, but I think you're right. Why do you think he's here?"

"I don't know. It doesn't make any sense. Lloyd always wanted Terry's insurance money, but Terry blackmailed his girlfriend with a fraudulent birth certificate and other documents that named him as the biological father of his girlfriend's daughter. I used those documents as proof that the insurance money belonged to the girl, but that was before I went to prison. It's been almost twenty years ago. Amber said the judge in

Ohio was prepared to sign the appeal that overturned my felony conviction on Terry's death, but someone blocked it. I think it was Lloyd; Amber's checking."

"What about the little girl? Were there any stipulations in the insurance that it reverted or something when she reached a certain age or died? How old would she be now?"

"She was ten or eleven, which means she'd be in her late twenties. It was boilerplate insurance. Nothing special. I think Terry intended to fake his death and collect his own insurance maybe through his supposed daughter. He was grooming her to be under his complete control."

"If this is about revenge for his brother's death, he's a little slow. Why such a huge time gap? The cop in me wonders if he's been in prison all this time?" Sheriff asked.

"It's a possibility. I'll list all our questions and theories and give them to Amber. Something might help her in the new appeal."

"It will be interesting information, but I don't see where anything could be helpful in an appeal," Sheriff said. "This needs to go to a good detective."

I nodded. *Project for Monica.* "Where does that leave us?"

"I'll see if I can find any outstanding warrants."

We hung up as three women came into the shop. Darlene's face brightened, and I grabbed a notebook and slipped back into the storeroom.

I sent Monica a text. "Call me."

My phone rang. *Tiffany.*

"We're here. Aunt Gee is still in surgery. I don't know the extent of her injuries, but the doctor told me she's stable. After she goes to recovery, I can go in. Only one visitor at a time in recovery."

"Sounds encouraging."

"Yes, it does. I'm glad I'm here, though. I talked to Tammy. She has less information than I do. She said the doctor told her Isaiah was alive, but they needed to complete their assessment of his injuries. He has to be more stable before she can see him, but it might not be until late tonight or tomorrow. She said she doesn't understand half of what they said because she's scared for Isaiah. The nurses and her cousin want her to check into the nearby hotel and get some rest. The nurse promised she'd call Tammy when she can see Isaiah. I told her I understood because I couldn't think straight either if it was Roger."

"Sounds like Tammy's having a hard time."

"That's what I told her, and she said as soon as she gets Isaiah back in Georgia, they are getting married. When I asked her if Isaiah had proposed, she told me to stop being so picky. When I laughed and told her she was back to her feisty self, she said takes one to know one." Tiffany chuckled. "I feel better too. Roger and I are in Georgia and have our marriage license."

My eyes widened. "Does that mean—"

"It means you know nothing, old woman." Tiffany snickered.

I laughed as we hung up.

Colonel flopped down next to me, Mandy dropped next to Colonel, and Roxie leaned against me. Gee's black cat, Sandy, darted past us into the showroom.

"Hi, Colonel. I know nothing." I stifled my giggle in case anyone in the showroom heard me. *Never had the chance to say that before.*

Colonel peered at me with a soulful look.

"It's a reference to an old television show that's about a prison, and there's this sergeant—oh, never mind. Now I'm not sure why I thought it was funny, either."

My phone rang. *Monica.*

"What mischief do you have lined up for us this time, girlfriend?"

I chuckled. "You know me well, but to be fair, I'm the hapless victim. What are you doing for supper?"

"Hapless?" she snorted. "More like formidable. I'm stopping by Ida's and picking up some victuals to bring to your house at six o'clock. What are you doing?"

"Fixing sweet tea. See you at six."

After we hung up, I said, "Everyone needs a magical friend, don't they?"

"Yes." A soft voice drifted from the showroom. I glanced up, and the shadows danced in the doorway.

What are you doing here?

The shadows slid away, and I hurried to the showroom. The shoppers had left, and Darlene was slumped in a chair at the front of the store.

"Darlene." I rushed to her, and her eyes opened.

"Sorry." She yawned. "The looky-loos left a few minutes ago, and I thought I'd close my eyes for just a minute. I've always been able to catnap at a moment's notice."

She stretched. "What time is it?"

I dropped into the nearest chair, and my heart rate slowed to normal. "Four-thirty."

"Let's call it a day." Darlene pulled herself up with her walker. "Bank closes at five, and I'd like to drop off our deposit."

"I'll lock up and wait for Jack and Thomas. You go on."

Darlene slipped the day's receipts into an old bank bag, gathered her things, and left.

After I locked the door, I dragged a chair from the back to fill one of our empty slots. Colonel joined me in the back room as I searched for the right table and replaced the small table with one of similar size.

"Darlene will rearrange it tomorrow, but this gives her a start."

I glanced at the clock and frowned. "Wonder where—"

Jack pulled in front of the store, and Thomas hopped out and rushed to his truck.

I unlocked the door, and Jack wheeled in the dolly.

"Everything go okay?" I asked.

"Of course. It was Thomas and me; you're the one who has adventures. Everything okay here?"

I told him about Lloyd and caught him up on Gee's and Isaiah's conditions.

"I should have been here except it wouldn't have been fair to make Thomas do that run by himself." He sighed. "What are our dinner plans?"

"I am having dinner with Monica. She's picking up two meals from Ida's and will be at my house at six."

He snorted. "No way are you two plotting without including me. I'll give Ida's a call and meet Monica there."

"You are supposed to give me space," I growled.

He held up his hands. "You can have all the space you want, but I'm part of the team."

I glared. "What team is that?"

"The Donut Lady Investigative Team." He smirked. "You can't deny it."

I blinked to hold back the rising giggles, but it didn't work. When I snickered, he laughed as he hooked his thumbs in his jeans and swaggered away to clean Sandy's box and to feed him.

I called Monica. "Slight change in plans. Jack invited himself to the Donut Lady Investigative Team meeting."

Monica burst into laughter. "He's quite creative for an engineer."

"I suppose. Don't ever say that in front of him. He's full of himself as it is. Come straight to my house. He's taking charge of the order at Ida's."

"Got it, Boss. See you at six." She chuckled.

When Jack returned to the front, I said, "I called Monica. She'll come to my house at six. You can change the order at Ida's and pick it up."

Jack smiled. "Touché. If the dogs ride with me, I'll drop them off at your house before I go to Ida's."

Jack and the dogs stepped outside as he called Ida's. I checked the back door, turned off the lights, and locked up. By the time I was outside, the dogs were in Jack's truck. I rolled my eyes, and Jack grinned. When I pulled away from the thrift shop, he followed me to my house.

I unlocked the front door. "You aren't fooling me. You wanted to check the house before you went to Ida's. Those fickle dogs were easy to entice into your truck, weren't they? I know you carry dog treats in your glove compartment."

Jack smirked and brought in Mandy's food bowl. After he checked the back door, he left for Ida's. I locked the door behind him before I fed the dogs. The dogs roamed the backyard while I made a fresh pitcher of sweet tea.

I jotted the last of my notes into my notebook as Monica tapped on the door with her silver pen, and it opened. *I know I locked that.*

Monica winked. She wore a neon green blouse with red ruffles on the sleeves, bright purple leggings, and deep pink ballerina shoes. She had wrapped a long, gauzy orange scarf around her waist and stuck a feather into her short, coal-black hair. Her dangly silver earrings jingled like tiny fairy bells when she moved.

"Whatcha got there, Donut Boss Lady?" She pointed at my notebook with her silver pen, and her metallic bracelets jangled.

"Facts and theories that I jotted down." I handed it to her, and she jingled and jangled as she sat cross-legged on the floor.

While Monica read, she mumbled under her breath, and I went out back to give her space and to spend time with the dogs.

I raised my eyebrows when I stepped on the porch. Mandy and Roxie sat at the corners of the back fence and faced opposite directions. Colonel stood on the porch near the steps. When I sat on my chair, he glanced at me but didn't change his stance. *Colonel's Security Team is on duty.*

Monica called from inside the house. "Jack's here."

Roxie and Mandy raced to the door; when Monica opened it, they rushed inside. I hurried to follow them, with Colonel bringing up the rear. Roxie and Mandy danced around Jack as he made his way to the kitchen table to set down his sacks.

"The special tonight was oven fried chicken, scalloped potatoes, green beans, tossed salad, and cherry pie for dessert. Do we have ice cream?" Jack asked. "I should have asked earlier. I could have picked up some."

"Always." I poured three glasses of sweet tea and popped our slices of pie onto a cookie tin, covered them with foil, and slid them into the oven at a low temperature. Monica emptied the sacks and put the three portions of meal and salad next to our places at the table.

Monica had set the table with silverware, napkins, and plates. Roxie and Mandy flopped down on the kitchen floor and faced the back door. Colonel trotted to the living room and lay down near the front door.

As we sat at our places at the table, Jack said, "Did you notice we have guards? It's amazing how quickly Mandy joined the pack."

"Smart dogs," Monica said.

After we ate dinner, I asked, "Pie now or later?"

"Now," Jack and Monica said in unison.

Jack jumped up and pulled out the ice cream, and I plated our pie while Monica cleared the table.

"Where do we start?" Jack asked as he ate his last bite.

"I have some thoughts. Pie first," Monica said.

Jack took the dogs out back while Monica and I finished our pie.

"I brought you a pen." Monica rose and cleared our dishes then reached into her pocket.

My eyes widened. *A silver pen.*

"It doesn't have the features that mine does, but it's calming." Monica eyes twinkled.

I held the smooth, silver pen in my hand. The cool metal reminded me of a bicycle's handlebars on an early frosty morning. I clipped my pen onto the neck of my shirt when we moved to the more comfortable seating in the living room.

Jack sat next to me on the sofa, and Monica snuggled into the ugly chair. She patted its arms. "This is a gorgeous chair. If I'd seen it before you did, you'd have a plain, boring chair and never know what you missed."

I gazed at Monica. *Never know what I missed. I'm missing something.*

Monica winked and nodded.

"Did I get left out of something here?" Jack stared at us.

I frowned. "Lloyd may show up at the Donut Hole tomorrow."

I unclipped my pen and rubbed with my thumb.

"You're holding your pen like it's a worry rock. Remember those?" Jack asked.

"Worry stone, but you are right." I smiled.

Monica's head tilted. "Click it again."

I clicked it and felt a small vibration and the temperature of the pen shift from cool to warm. "Oh."

Monica nodded. "You weren't quite as focused the first time."

I returned my pen to its position on my shirt. "Focus is exactly what I need. Thank you. What else do we put on our radar?"

"I've got an entire nation of librarians on standby for research," Monica said. "We want to know where Lloyd Ahrens has been the past twenty years. Was he in prison? What else?"

"Terry told me Lloyd was a fence. He carried a wad of cash and played the big shot at the thrift store, but he didn't know anything about antique furniture."

"Maybe he worked at a pawn shop," Jack said.

Monica nodded. "Sources of employment over the years. We'll take that."

"Amber will review the court proceedings for the appeal. I have all of Terry's documents—the original insurance policy, the insurance policy in force at the time of his death, our divorce papers, and all the phony documents he had to prove his legal paternity of his girlfriend's daughter. I still hear from Victoria from time to time. She was the only one who wrote to me while I was in prison. I was pleased when she sent me Bria's high school and college graduation announcements. When Bria was named the Teacher of the Year in Cincinnati six years ago, Victoria sent me the newspaper clipping. I think I was almost as proud as she was."

"I can review all those documents. Contracts are my specialty," Jack said.

I frowned. "You two have your assignments. What's mine?"

Monica snorted. "You are the spider, Donut Lady. Weave your sweet web and catch that stinkin' fly."

I snickered. "I like that much better than being the bait in a trap, which is what I was thinking. Thanks."

Monica rose. "We all have our assignments. Shall we schedule our next team meeting for Thursday? Here at the same time? I'll deliver next time. I know a budding personal chef who would be excited to show off her talents."

I nodded, and Jack rose to accompany Monica to the door. After Monica left, Jack returned to sit with me on the sofa.

"Are you worried, Karen? I am." He frowned.

I patted his hand. "I was until you and Monica stepped up to help. There's just something about dividing up all the scattered pieces that makes it more manageable for me. Does that make sense?"

"Sure does."

Colonel scratched on the back door, and Jack rose. "I'll let the dogs in."

Colonel dashed into the house and leapt onto the sofa next to me, and Roxie and Mandy trotted to the front door.

Jack chuckled. "It appears it's time for us to leave too. Are you sure you'll be okay here? You, Colonel, and Mia are welcome to come to my house. Lloyd isn't likely to find you there, and you can get a good night's rest."

"Normally, I'd say no. Can I have some time to think about it?"

"Yes. Shall I wait, or do you want to call me? This isn't a stalling tactic, is it? Just to get me out of your house?"

I snorted. "No. My version of a stalling tactic would be to say no."

"I knew that." Jack smiled and opened the door for the dogs. "Call me either way?" He strode back to the sofa and kissed my forehead before he hurried out. "Lock up," he called after he closed the door.

Colonel followed me to the front door, and I locked it. I checked the back door to be sure it was locked. Mia slipped out of the pantry and stalked the house for Roxie and Mandy. When she was satisfied the canine intruders were gone, she stalked the ugly chair before she leapt into it and curled up in the corner. I brewed a cup of tea, picked out a book to read, and settled on the sofa. I snickered when I realized I held my nature book on predators. When Colonel joined me, he put his head on my lap, and I propped my book on his back and read.

After I finished the first chapter, I called Jack. "I'm staying here. I'll sleep better, and I have an excellent guard dog and alarm cat. You have to promise me you'll sleep at home not in your truck."

"I will if you'll promise me you'll keep your phone close."

I smiled. "Fair enough. I'll call the sheriff and give him a quick update."

After we hung up, I called the sheriff. "Everything's okay. Monica, Jack, and I got together this evening." I gave him a quick summary of our tasks.

"I'll keep my cell phone close," Sheriff said. "Is Jack sleeping in his truck behind your house again?"

I smiled. *Sheriff knows his regulars.* "He promised to sleep at his house if I promised to keep my phone close."

"Well played, Donut Lady. See you in the morning."

I searched the index of my book on spiders to read about their predatory practices. After I finished the chapter, I rubbed Colonel's ears. "There are three major types of spiders, Colonel. My choices are hunter, web-spinner, or ambush. Hunting spiders have excellent vision. That's not me. Web-spinners have poor vision but rely on vibrations. That might be me. Ambush spiders hide and wait for their prey. Nope. I used up all my patience long ago. I'm a web-spinner. Let's go to bed."

The shadows followed me down the hall on my way to bed. Mia raced to my bedroom and scattered the shadows in the doorway before she slid under my bed. After Colonel completed one last pass through the house, he joined me in the bedroom. The shadows lingered on the ceiling in the hallway.

"Goodnight, everyone."

* * *

I woke when Colonel snuffled and whined in his sleep, and I checked the clock. *One-thirty. Too early to get up.* I rolled over until the alarm woke me. *Four o'clock comes earlier some days than others.*

I hurried to the kitchen and made coffee. While it perked, I let Colonel out. After the coffee was ready, I took my pen and my cup out back. While I rocked, the neighborhood birds sang. Mia slipped out of the house and jumped up on my lap. I stroked her back, and she purred. Colonel trotted to the porch and lay at my feet. I finished off my coffee and carried Mia inside, and Colonel padded in with us.

After I dressed, I set Mia's carrier by the door, and she darted to the pantry. "See you later, Mia."

When we reached the donut shop, the lights were on. Colonel and I went inside, and the distinct aroma of the rising yeast dough greeted me.

"Hello, Miss Lady." Andrew wore his pink-sprinkled donut ballcap and apron. He added flour to the mixer bowl for his second batch.

"You're here extra early. We have something special going on today?"

Andrew filled the large coffee maker with water then made coffee in the smaller pot. I measured ground coffee for the large coffee maker.

"The executive boards of the radio-controlled planes, boats, and cars are meeting," he said.

"I never thought they'd agree on a day to meet. It's a red-letter day."

Andrew cocked his head and stared at me.

"It's an old expression. It means really important. We used to have calendars with the important days like special holidays printed in red. It started in ancient Rome."

"We can have a red-letter day." Andrew grinned. "Raspberry red scones. Strawberry lemonade donuts. Classic vanilla glazed with a side of red hots."

"Perfect. Should I run to the store for red hots?"

"No, Miss Lady. We have some in the storeroom. Woody buys extras like red hots for specials. He keeps his list in the freezer. He said that was what Mr. Otto did."

"I'll get busy on the scones. Do you have everything you need for the donuts?"

Andrew nodded and hurried to the storeroom for his ingredients.

After I decorated our first batches of donuts and scones, Sheriff Grady strode into the shop. "Red letter day? What's today?"

"Tuesday." I poured his coffee and wiggled my eyebrows. Andrew snickered.

"I walked right into that trap, didn't I?" Sheriff laughed.

I served him a plate with one of each pastry.

"Raspberry scone. Strawberry and something donut, but how does the classic glazed fit in?" he asked.

"It's strawberry lemonade as a new twist, and we also have—" I reached under the counter for a paper condiment cup. "Red hots are optional with the classic."

"I was thinking about your theory of Lloyd visiting the shop today." Sheriff ate his white glazed donut, chased it with red hots, and followed up with a gulp of coffee. After I refilled his cup, he peered at me. "Do you carry your phone when you're working?"

"I hadn't thought about that. My apron pocket would be perfect."

The sheriff tossed down his coffee. "Can I have a sack for my scone and donut and a to-go coffee? I have an early meeting and want to look over my notes. Meetings make me nervous."

I met his gaze. "Grady, you are the bravest man I know, but if you want backup, text me, and I'll arrange for a bad guy to bust into your meeting."

He smiled. "You're the only one I believe could pull that off. Thanks."

After Sheriff left, I topped and glazed another batch of donuts, and Andrew filled the condiment cups with red hots then fried his last batch of donuts.

Shirley bustled into the shop. "Did you hear the news? Gee is much better, and there is hope that Isaiah's burns aren't as extensive as the doctors first thought. Someone said Isaiah and the firefighter rolled in the mud before they entered the burning cars, and the firefighter had his fireman gloves and a spare for Isaiah; neither of them burned their hands. Do you suppose the mud story is true?"

"I don't think so. Why would they take that time to roll around while people are trapped in a burning car?" I poured Shirley's to-go coffee and dropped a scone and a classic into her sack.

"You always make sense, Karen." She peeked into her sack and frowned. "What's red about white?"

"You know that sounds like a riddle. The red is a side of red hots, but I didn't think you'd want any."

"I'll take them to Woody. He's still grounded, but I'll give them to him in the morning with his breakfast. I'll show him who's fun."

I snickered. "Shirley, you are always surprising. If that's not fun, I don't know what fun might be."

Andrew said, "Yes."

Shirley stared at us. "Thank you," she whispered as she rushed out the door.

"You're awesome, Andrew. Ms. Shirley feels much better."

"Yes."

The bell jingled, and Lloyd strolled in. I pulled my pen out of my apron pocket. "Coffee?"

He glanced at Andrew and smiled at me with his mouth but not his eyes as he sat at the counter. "You're Karen, aren't you? I heard you'd moved back to your hometown but thought that was just gossip. I'm Lloyd. Lloyd Ahrens. I guess you didn't recognize me. I barely recognized you." He squinted. "Your hair's gray."

If he says I'm fat, I'll deck him with a tray.

I served him a cup of coffee, picked up a tray for the display case, and filled it with donuts and scones before I slid it into the case.

"Do you care for a donut or scone?" I asked before I closed the case.

"Maybe a donut. The glazed."

I placed a classic on a plate and set it in front of him. "Are you passing through?"

"I'm thinking about buying a business here and settling down."

"Really? What made you think of my hometown?"

"Terry always said you wanted to move back to Georgia. Now that I'm here, I see the charm of a southern small town, and the people are nice. Very refreshing, and I need a change. You wouldn't have a problem with that, would you? It's been almost twenty years. My brother's gone, and I've moved on. I thought you would have too."

I stared at him. *Wonder how long a spider lets her prey strum on her web before she strikes?*

"What do I owe you?" he asked.

I slid the bill face down on the counter and turned away to carry plates to the utility cart for the meeting room. Andrew strolled to the cash register to take Lloyd's money.

After I filled the utility cart, I faced Lloyd and watched as he paid his bill. When he reached the door, he stopped and turned.

"You know a good banker? I need a local account. See you later, Karen." His grin reminded me of Terry's evil grin, but I didn't flinch. *Spiders don't flinch.*

When he left, Andrew said, "I don't like him."

"I don't either, Andrew. He can't be trusted."

"He can't be trusted." Andrew echoed my words.

Jack came in the door. "Who was that? He's not from around here, is he? I hope he's just passing through. There was something about him I didn't like."

I set his cup of coffee on the counter. "He's Lloyd, Terry's brother."

Jack's eyes narrowed. "What was he doing here? Why didn't you text me?"

"He was here to see how much of a reaction he could get out of me."

"We don't like him," Andrew said. "He can't be trusted."

I nodded.

"Did he get any reaction?"

"Dislike. Not much more. You want anything with your coffee?"

Jack stared at the board. "Red Letter Day? I'll take one of each if you'll explain."

"Strawberry lemonade donut and raspberry scone. Our classic glazed donut has a red surprise for the adventuresome."

"I'm adventuresome. If I weren't, I couldn't hang around you."

"Yes," Andrew said.

I raised my eyebrows and glared at Jack.

Jack shook his head. "Not getting into it. I'm ready for my scone, donuts, and surprise."

After I set his donuts and scone in front of him, Andrew gave him the paper condiment cup, and Jack chuckled. "Your idea, right Andrew?"

"Yes." He grinned.

The bell rang, and Henry Worley strolled inside and surveyed the shop before he set his briefcase on the reading table. He was average height and carried the extra middle-aged weight around his waist. His life-long dedication to weightlifting showed in his muscular arms and thick legs. "Good morning, Jack. Haven't seen you in a while."

Jack nodded his greeting as he sipped his coffee, and Judge Worley took a seat at the counter.

The judge read the board. "Coffee and a scone." After I served his coffee and plate, he carried them to the reading table and pulled papers out of his briefcase.

I raised my eyebrows, and Jack winked as my phone rang. *Tammy.*

"Everything okay, Tammy?" I headed to the storeroom to talk to her.

"Yes. No. My friend who said she would take care of Pepper called. She's not allowed to have dogs in her apartment, and she asked me to pick up Pepper this morning. If I left right now, I couldn't make it back until this afternoon, but I don't want to leave Isaiah. I don't know what to do. I couldn't call Tiffany to ask her to find someone to help me, and my cousin is here with me. Do you know anyone who could take care of Pepper until Isaiah is well enough to travel?"

"I'll find someone. Give me your friend's address. Tell her either Jack or I will pick up Pepper in the next half hour."

"Really?" Tammy sobbed. "I'll text you the address. Thank you. I couldn't think straight and hoped you might help me. I can't tell you how much I appreciate this."

After we hung up, I sauntered to the counter and refilled Jack's coffee.

Jack narrowed his eyes. "What scheme do you have up your sleeve now, Donut Lady?"

"Enjoy your coffee and your scone but eat fast. I need you to pick up Pepper. Tammy's friend bailed on her, and Tammy needs someone to care for Pepper until Isaiah can travel."

"What on earth will we do with another dog?" Jack asked.

"I don't know. Feed her?"

Jack grumbled. "My yard isn't fenced."

"I don't understand what you are worried about. My yard is fenced, and I have room for two dogs. When Pepper spent some time at the donut shop earlier, she was a perfect lady. Andrew and I can take turns walking her on the leash during the day, although I won't be surprised if Colonel trains her to stay with him outside. It will work."

After Jack left to rescue Pepper, the judge put away his papers. "How much do I owe you, Karen?"

I smiled and rang up his sale and put his sales receipt on his table. He returned his papers to his briefcase, set his money on the table, and left.

Andrew said, "Judge never sees me."

I glanced at Andrew and the door. *I didn't notice. What else have I missed?*

"I'm glad Mr. Jack is picking up Pepper. Ms. Melinda asked me to take care of Pepper sometimes at the Soup Kitchen. Pepper and I are friends."

"That's great, Andrew. Pepper will be more comfortable at the donut shop with you here, and she loves Colonel."

Alfred, our local banker, sauntered into the shop. He wore a gray suit, white shirt, and a blue and gray striped tie. He had played football in college twenty-five years ago, but unlike most, he retained his muscular build.

Andrew beamed. "Hello, Mr. Alfred. I'm working at the Donut Hole now."

Alfred's face softened. "I heard Ms. Tiffany had to leave and you were taking over for her. That's a huge help for Ms. Karen, I know."

Andrew said, "Yes. Would you like coffee, Mr. Alfred, and a donut or scone?"

"Coffee would be nice. You pick a pastry for me."

Andrew poured the coffee, served Alfred a raspberry scone, and placed a knife and fork on the napkin.

I smiled. *Andrew knows his regulars.*

CHAPTER THREE

Alfred glanced around the shop. "Has Shirley already been here? I was hoping to see her today."

"She stopped in earlier this morning, but why don't you ask her to join you? I'm sure she'd love to see you. I could text her, if you like."

"Would you? Woody is trying to help me learn to text, but I'm all thumbs." Alfred chuckled, and Andrew laughed.

"That's a good joke, Mr. Alfred. All thumbs." Andrew laughed harder.

I turned my back to hide my surprise over a joke from Alfred and sent Shirley a text. "Alfred is at donut shop. He asked if you would join him."

The mayor hurried inside wearing his pink-sprinkled cap and apron. He smiled and nodded at Alfred, and Alfred returned the smile and nod.

"What group do we have today?" the mayor asked.

"All the executive board members of the three radio-controlled vehicle clubs. We have raspberry red scones, strawberry lemonade donuts, and classic vanilla glazed donuts with a side of red hots."

The mayor raised his eyebrows. "Well done, you two. It is certainly a red-letter day."

. "I'm glad I didn't miss it," Alfred said.

Car brakes squealed out front. Andrew pointed to the window, and Alfred swung around and beamed when he saw Shirley's car. Shirley burst into the shop. When she spied Alfred at the counter, she slowed to a casual stroll and brushed her hair away from her face as she peered at Alfred and fluttered her eyelashes.

"Hello, Alfred." Her voice dropped into a throaty southern drawl.

I stared at Shirley. *She's lived here her entire life and always had a southern drawl, but this new one is—*

The mayor turned to his utility cart. "No words," he mumbled, and I nodded.

"What would you like, Shirley?" Alfred asked. "My treat."

"A red-letter day," the mayor mouthed, and I snorted and reached for the tissue in my pocket.

"Why, Alfred. How very sweet of you. I believe I'd like a cup of coffee, please, Andrew, and a classic vanilla glazed with red hots. For Woody."

"Yes, ma'am." Andrew poured her coffee and served the donut. I smiled as Andrew poured red hots into a plastic sandwich sack.

When Andrew placed the sack on the counter next to her, Alfred smiled. "Very thoughtful, Andrew. Thank you."

Andrew ducked his head. "Woody is my friend."

While Alfred ate his scone with his knife and fork, Shirley cooed as she asked him to join her and Woody for dinner.

Andrew returned to cleaning the kitchen, and I joined Mayor in the pink meeting room.

"You missed Judge Worley. I think this is the first time he's been in the shop."

"He's not usually seen except during election time." The mayor shrugged. "I've been wondering about some guy named Lloyd who seems charming enough, and lots of people liked him right away. I can't tell you why, but I was less than impressed. Guess I've known too many politicians just like him; the judge comes to mind. Does this Lloyd really know you from Ohio?"

"Lloyd is Terry's brother."

Mayor nodded. "Terry, the ex-husband who stepped in front of your car. I assume the two of them shared an equally distasteful personality."

I set up the dishes and napkins on the buffet. "When I first met Terry, I thought he was charming. I was young. It wasn't until after we were married that he showed his manipulative side."

"Manipulative." Mayor nodded. "That's exactly the word I would have used. What's Lloyd doing here?"

"I don't know. The only thing that struck me is that he wanted a local bank account and asked if I knew a banker. I didn't understand why he had to meet a banker to open a bank account. It's not the Ahrens' way to say something offhand."

"I'm not worried about Alfred. He's had a lot of experience with unsavory types, but I'll still fill him in with Lloyd's family history."

My phone rang, and the mayor closed the meeting room door on his way out. *Tiffany*.

"Good morning, Miss Lady. I have great news. Aunt Gee told her doctor to bug off. Isn't that wonderful? I gave her a timeout for bad language. She was really mad when the doctor laughed and asked me if I'd go with him on his rounds."

I snickered. "Woody would be very proud of you."

"She's in pain, but she refused to take any medication for it until the doctor told her she couldn't get out of bed until she was pain-free. That's when she got sassy."

"Really good news. I'm not sure I know the extent of her injuries."

"She fractured her right femur and some ribs from the airbag. The airbag busted her nose, and she has bruising and swelling from her seatbelt. The doctor said her left arm is swollen, and they are checking it, but overall, she's very lucky. She knows about Isaiah and is on a tear to get well enough to visit him. She is happy that Tammy is with him."

"That is great news. Is it okay if I share?"

"Of course. It'll save me a dozen phone calls if the gas station has the news."

"Shirley's here with Alfred. I'll tell her."

"Shirley and Alfred? I'm sorry. Where are you?"

"In the pink room. The mayor closed the door when you called. Andrew is gaining confidence. You'd be proud. Thanks for the update."

"I'll tell Aunt Gee today that we're rescheduling the reception. I'll call later to tell you how that went over." Tiffany giggled.

After we hung up, the mayor came into the room. "I was hovering. How's Gee?"

"Broken leg, fractured ribs, and the usual airbag and seat belt injuries but doing fine. Great actually. Tiffany gave her a timeout for bad language."

Mayor laughed. "I would have liked to have seen that."

I smiled. "Tiffany was proud of herself."

"The lovey-doveys are a little hard on the ears, aren't they? Alfred's unusual dining habits never bothered me before, but he puts his fork down and listens while Shirley talks. Don't we have a time limit for occupying a counter seat? Like a buzzer after thirty minutes?" He wiggled his eyebrows.

"I can't believe I'm saying this, but I'm glad they're still around. I'll tell Shirley about Gee, and she'll let everyone know Gee is getting better."

"I'll get the pink room ready for the red-letter day. Let me know when the coast is clear. Oh, wait. I can have a word with our banker." He cleared his throat. "One-on-one."

"I'll pull Shirley away for a minute or two. You'll owe me."

"That I will."

I narrowed my eyes and stepped out of the room. "Shirley, Tiffany just called me. If you'll join me for a second while I finish up some things in the office, we can chat."

"I'd love to. Is that okay, honey bun?" She fluttered her eyelashes.

I can't wait to tell Tiffany about honey bun.

Alfred beamed. "That's fine, sunshine."

Sunshine? That's pretty good, Alfred.

Shirley swished into the storeroom and paused at the doorway as she glanced over her shoulder at Alfred. He winked, and she tittered.

The mayor stood at the pink room door. He shook his head and cleared his throat. "How you been, Alfred?"

Alfred nodded. "Doing well."

"Is Gee okay?" Shirley asked after we were in the storeroom.

"Gee is much better. She has a broken leg and a few fractured ribs, but she's feeling much better. Of course, she's anxious to see Isaiah. Tiffany was very encouraged by how well she's doing."

"That is excellent news. Any idea when she can come home? Darlene is doing an awesome job at the thrift shop. I stopped by to see her yesterday, and I think even Sandy has accepted her. She's in her element, isn't she? She's not Gee and has her own style, but Gee will be pleased about how well she's running the store. I think Darlene enjoys the work. You know the only reason she worked at the donut shop was to help her dad. She told me once that she wasn't meant to be sweetened up. Can you believe I didn't say anything? Probably the one time in my life I had sense enough to keep my mouth shut." Shirley giggled and glanced at Alfred and the mayor who were in an animated conversation at the counter.

"Isn't it great to see what good friends those two are? After all those years. Is that all you wanted to talk to me about? I still haven't told Alfred about Woody being grounded. I'm not sure how he's going to take it."

Shirley rushed to the counter, and the mayor and Alfred shook hands. "Let me know if there is anything I can do," Mayor said.

"Will do." Alfred nodded.

The board members flowed into the meeting room, and Alfred and Shirley drifted out, arm in arm.

"Mr. Alfred likes Ms. Shirley." Andrew grinned.

"Yes, he does, and Ms. Shirley likes him too."

A roar of laughter came from the meeting room. "Your red-letter day is a hit, Andrew."

We had a steady stream of customers, and the remote-control boards kept the mayor busy refilling coffee and shuttling in more donuts and scones.

When the meeting broke up, the mayor retrieved dishes for Andrew, wiped down the table, and swept the room. As he hung up his apron in the storeroom he said, "I don't think the groups will combine, but they discovered their differences weren't as insurmountable as everyone had been thinking. A red-letter day, indeed."

"That's good news. The red-letter day was Andrew's idea."

"Andrew, your red-letter day brought three groups together who haven't spoken to each other in years. Well done."

"Thank you, Mr. Mayor."

Jack hurried into the shop with Pepper trailing him. "Sorry I'm late. Darlene is a hard worker. I've already made three deliveries this morning. Pepper's a good delivery companion. Everything okay?"

Pepper ran to Andrew, and Andrew sat on the floor. She licked his ears, and he snuggled her.

I texted Tammy. "We have Pepper. All is well."

"Tiffany called, and Gee is feeling better. Full details at the gas station."

Jack chuckled. "Tammy's friend gave me all of Pepper's things. Her bed, toys, food and water dishes, and food. I'll bring them in for you. Or shall I put everything in your car?"

"Here's my keys. She'll share Colonel's water dish here. I'll take everything else home."

When Jack returned with my keys, he said, "I loaded your car. Darlene wants to rearrange the thrift shop. We've been pulling out furniture from the back to fill the holes that were left after she sold large items. Darlene wants to organize it like Gee would. After we've rearranged the shop, I'll fill up my truck. Maybe lunch? I'll check in with you later."

Andrew hung up his apron then took Pepper and Colonel out back for a break. When they came back inside, Andrew filled their water bowl and washed his hands. "We have only three donuts and two scones left, Miss Lady. Is it okay if I sweep the shop?"

"That's a great idea, Andrew."

Amber came into the shop. She wore a navy suit and a white and red polka-dot blouse. "Coffee still hot?" she asked. "Doesn't matter. I'll take a cup and a scone."

Amber tasted her scone and sipped her coffee. "This is good. I understand Mr. Lloyd Ahrens dropped in on you. Social visit, I hear. I confirmed that he blocked your appeal. I talked to his lawyer; Lloyd spun a story that wouldn't have fooled a two-year-old. I don't understand why the court gave it any credence. His lawyer has sunk a lot of time into the case and realizes he won't be paid. Lloyd may be looking for a new lawyer. According to your lawyer, Lloyd thinks you have a sizeable stash of Terry's money hidden somewhere, and Lloyd feels entitled. Our Ohio lawyer has already filed a new appeal based on the fact that Lloyd's flimsy claim has nothing to do with your conviction."

"When it comes to Terry's money, I'm pretty sure I found it all, and I gave it to Victoria a long time ago. Although, I happen to know that she's a shrewd investor. Make that allegedly."

Amber snickered. "I told our lawyer if there was any money, it wasn't much, and we turned it all over to the girlfriend for her daughter's education. Our lawyer is familiar with Lloyd. He couldn't understand any reason why he would come here other than to harass you. Let me know if you ever feel threatened."

Amber finished her scone and coffee. "I've got court this afternoon, and my phone will be off. You can call my office anytime, and Leah will get a message to me."

"Thanks. I don't expect any trouble quite yet."

Amber chuckled. "Quite yet. How may donuts and scones do you have left?"

"Three donuts and one scone, right, Andrew?"

"Yes."

"I'll take them all. Leah will enjoy sharing with her afternoon break friends."

When she pulled out her wallet, I waved at her. "Put your money away. We appreciate you taking them off our hands. Right, Andrew?"

"Yes." Andrew placed them into a sack and handed it to Amber. "We appreciate all you do for Miss Lady."

"Thank you, Andrew."

After Amber left, I said, "It was a good day, Andrew. Thank you for all your help."

Andrew locked the front door. "I'll take Pepper and Colonel for a walk while you do your paperwork." He picked up Pepper's leash, and she danced. Colonel stretched before he lumbered to the back door.

I reviewed our sales and prepared my deposit slip. When Jack knocked on the back door, I let him and Roxie inside. Jack's eyes were narrowed, and his face was dark.

"What's wrong?" I asked.

He rubbed his hand over his face. "Sorry. Had a little run-in with Lloyd at the gas station." Jack clenched and unclenched his fists. "He got mouthy, and I told him to stay away from you."

I frowned at his hands. "Shake it off."

He mumbled, "Not easy to do."

After he relaxed his hands, I asked, "Where's Mandy?"

"Mandy is a thrift store dog and takes her job seriously. Darlene was touched that Mandy wanted to stay with her. I saw Andrew and the dogs on their walk. Where do you want to go for lunch? How about a sandwich from Gus's? Is it too hot for the park?" He grinned. "I think I may understand Shirley."

"The park sounds great except I don't know how much time Pepper has spent outside in the heat. She might not be acclimated."

"I could pick up lunch and bring it to your house. We could picnic in your backyard."

"Sounds like a plan to me. We'll meet you there."

"Text me if you need me." Jack narrowed his eyes. "You know that, right?"

"Yes. Go. I'll see you at my house."

Not long after Jack left, Andrew and the dogs returned. He refreshed their water, and both of the dogs lapped up long drinks.

"I will walk you to your car," Andrew said.

After I locked the shop's back door, Andrew led the dogs to my car and opened the door for them. Colonel hopped in, and Andrew set Pepper on the back seat. I glanced at the passing car, and Lloyd waved. I ignored him.

Andrew narrowed his eyes. "We don't trust him."

The dogs and I drove to the bank. After we reached Gus's, I parked next to Jack's truck. When he came out of the sandwich shop, he strode to my car. "Trouble?" he asked.

"Not really. Just chasing you down."

"Wish that was true," Jack muttered as he climbed into his truck.

After we were home, the three dogs drank water, Roxie and Colonel ran around the perimeter of the backyard, and Mia watched from the window. Pepper raced after them as fast as her little Yorkie legs could go. After the fourth time around, Pepper trotted to the water bowl and lapped her fill. She danced in the grass before she flopped on the porch with us.

"Give me the full story on Gee," Jack said. "I know there's more you didn't tell."

I smiled and told him about Tiffany putting Gee in timeout.

"Tiffany is braver than I am." Jack guffawed. "You're right. Gee is getting better. Her injuries don't sound minor, though. "

"I agree. It's amazing that Isaiah was able to get to the other two cars. I don't think one person would have been able to pull out all the occupants. I heard on the news there were four children and their parents in one car and two children, their mother, and their grandmother in the other."

"Ten people." Jack shook his head. "Have you heard from Tammy?"

"No. I've been afraid to call her because she could be sleeping. I might call her later this afternoon if I don't hear from her."

Jack rose. "It's back to the salt mines for me. I'll check in with you later."

After he left, I walked the perimeter of the yard with Colonel to stretch my legs while Pepper chased Roxie.

"Time to go in." The three dogs trotted to the door and waited for me.

Mia was on the refrigerator. When she jumped down to stalk Pepper, Pepper yipped and ran a tight circle. Mia leapt over her and landed on the back of the ugly chair. Pepper jumped onto the chair, and Mia chased her to the bedroom. When Pepper scrambled out of the bedroom, she was covered with dust. Mia pranced into the living room to groom her paws.

As I loaded the dishwasher with our lunch dishes, my phone rang. *Tammy.*

"They let me see Isaiah. It was only for five minutes, but he was awake. He looked terrible because he was covered with burn gauze, but his face wasn't burned that badly. The doctor said he'd have scars on his arms and chest, but not on his face. One of the nurses told me Isaiah's shirt was on fire, but a volunteer firefighter rolled him in the dirt and saved his life. The off-duty firefighter had an old fire jacket in his truck and threw it on. His burns aren't quite as extensive. Isaiah dashed into one car, and the firefighter darted into the other. Isaiah pulled out four children and their parents, Miss Lady. He's a hero." Tammy sobbed, and tears slipped down my cheeks.

Tammy continued, "I know he'll be okay, Miss Lady. After he's healed enough to travel, I'll rent an ambulance, and if I have to drive him home myself, I will. I need a house with no steps."

I grabbed a tissue and wiped my drippy nose. "You tell me when you're headed this way, and I'll put Shirley on it."

"That will work. How's Aunt Gee?" Tammy asked.

Aunt Gee? I smiled.

"She's cranky. Tiffany gave her a timeout for bad language when the doctor insisted that Gee needed medication for her pain."

Tammy laughed. "I'll have to tell Isaiah. He's been worried about her, but if she's got Tiffany sassing her, she'll be out of that hospital in no time. Will Tiffany be mad at me if I marry Isaiah before she and Roger are married? Do you suppose I should tell Isaiah he's engaged?"

I chuckled. "I don't think it will be much of a surprise to him."

"You're right. I'll give him a day or two. I have to take a nap before this evening's visiting hours. My cousin said I need a shower too. Actually, she said, *You stink, Tammy*." Tammy giggled, and I smiled.

"Thank you for the update. What can I share with Tiffany?"

"Isaiah's getting better and talking. He's worried about his mama. Don't tell her the rest. She'll blab to Aunt Gee. I want to tell Aunt Gee myself. Or maybe Isaiah would want to."

I rolled my eyes. "He might."

"Thank you, Miss Lady. You always help."

Tammy hung up.

My phone rang. *Jack.*

"I just have a second. I assume you're not interested in going out tonight. Do you have any potatoes?"

I frowned. "Yes."

"Good. See you later." He hung up.

I picked up my book and sat on the sofa. Roxie sat on one side; Colonel, on the other; Pepper cuddled my feet; Mia jumped onto my lap. I leaned back to read. The shadows billowed in the hallway, and Mia chased them away and trotted back to my lap to resume her spot.

I closed my eyes just for a minute to rest.

I smelled the smoke of burning leaves. Colonel nudged me, Roxie barked, and Pepper yipped and darted to the back door. Colonel jumped down and growled at the front door. Roxie raced from the front to the back and back to front. Mia scampered to the top of the refrigerator. I waved away shadows, but it was smoke. I called nine-one-one as I searched for the source of the fire. I stumbled to the back window and peeked out.

"Odd," I said. "Brush fire in the backyard."

"Fire department on the way. Do you need medical?" Tess asked.

"No."

"Sheriff's on his way too. No surprise, right?"

"I'd better call Jack."

Tess chuckled. "I did that too."

The sound of sirens wailed throughout the neighborhood, and the sound became louder as they approached my block. I peered out the front window and saw Lloyd's car pull away from the curb across the street. *Was I supposed to run out the front door?*

When I checked the fire in the back, the two neighbors behind me had pulled garden hoses to the edge of the fence and doused it. I rushed to the front door at the sound of screeching tires and opened the door as Sheriff and Jack dashed to the porch, and Mandy bounded into the house.

"What happened?" Sheriff asked as Jack smothered me on his chest.

"Can't breathe." I wiggled, and Jack loosened his hold. "I was resting on the sofa when the dogs stirred up a fuss. Pepper was at the back door, Colonel went to the front, and Roxie raced back and forth. I called Tess."

"What else?" Jack asked.

"The neighbors behind me put out the fire with their garden hoses, and when I checked the front, Lloyd pulled away from the curb."

Jack clenched his jaw and his fist, and his face reddened.

"Easy, Jack," Sheriff said. "Let's all sit."

Jack put his arm around me and clutched me as we moved to the sofa. Sheriff rolled his eyes and sat in the ugly chair.

"What do you think, Karen?"

"I'm not sure. It wasn't much of a fire. I wonder if I was expected to panic and run out the front door?"

"I'll have a conversation with Mr. Ahrens," Sheriff said. "I won't be surprised if he claims he drove by and smelled the smoke, but he left when the neighbors put it out."

"Pretty flimsy," Jack growled.

"Right, but if it was a warning—I don't know." I frowned.

"Fire department will be sad. Nothing like a neighbor with a garden hose to ruin their day." Sheriff stepped out front with his radio.

When he came inside, he said, "The fire truck's returning to their station and available for other calls—I put them in service and asked for the fire marshal. You staying, Jack?"

"Darn straight."

Sheriff narrowed his eyes. "Let me know if you think of anything else, Karen."

"I'll check in with Darlene." Jack strolled out with the sheriff.

When Jack didn't return, I peeked out front, and my eyes widened. The sheriff and Jack were in a heated discussion, and both of the men had red faces. Jack paced, and Sheriff put his hand on Jack's shoulder, but Jack shrugged it off. The sheriff crossed his arms and assumed his sheriff stance that I hadn't seen in a while. Sheriff stormed to his car, and Jack stomped to the porch then stopped to make a call.

Colonel stood next to me and leaned against my leg.

"Colonel, what do you think that was all about?" I asked.

After his call, Jack scowled as he came into the house.

He stared at me. "You saw?"

I raised my eyebrows.

"A difference of opinion," he said.

I nodded. *No kidding.*

"That kind of ruined my plans for this evening unless you don't mind putting potatoes in the oven to bake and going to the store with me."

"We can do that. What are we shopping for?"

"A surprise." Jack grinned.

I opened the pantry door and picked out two potatoes. "Not much of a surprise if I go shopping with you."

"Didn't think about that. I need a grill to cook dinner."

"That would be a surprise if you hadn't mentioned a grill every time you talk about cooking." I smiled.

"You're right. Let's go."

"Are we leaving the dogs?"

"Do you think we can?" Jack strolled to the front door and opened it. The four dogs charged out of the house and to the truck.

I locked the door, and the six of us headed to the hardware store.

"I might have to stay in the truck with the dogs," I said.

"You're right. They are well-behaved dogs, but Roxie goes wild in the hardware store where there's always a softie who will give her a treat, and she knows it."

After thirty minutes, Jack returned to the truck. "I got what I wanted. They'll load it for me." He pulled up to the store and dropped the truck's tailgate. Two young men loaded the grill and a canister of LP gas.

"Next, the grocery store to pick out a steak," Jack said. "Do you want me to grab some salad stuff?"

"Maybe romaine lettuce, tomatoes, and cucumber?" I asked.

"Yes, like that. Tell me again, and I'll make a list."

"I'll write the list for you," I said as I pulled out my small notebook. I jotted down the short list and ripped out the page. "Here you go."

While the dogs and I waited in the grocery store parking lot, Lloyd cruised through the lot aisles before he stopped in front of Jack's truck. He opened his car door and stepped out. Jack raced out of the grocery store, grabbed Lloyd by the arm, and whirled him around.

Lloyd laughed, and his face was exactly like Terry's when I hit him with the car. Jack pulled back his fist and slammed Lloyd in the face. Blood spurted from Lloyd's nose, and he swung at Jack, but Jack caught Lloyd's arm, tossed him to the ground, and kicked him.

Four men ran to hold Jack as Lloyd writhed on the ground. The sheriff's car careened into the parking lot, and he walked Jack to his cruiser. When the ambulance crew loaded Lloyd onto the cot, he leered at me.

When I opened my door, Colonel, Mandy, and Roxie leapt out and snarled as they raced to the cot. Lloyd screamed. The paramedic, Carol, snorted as she pointed to the dogs. "Sit."

The dogs dropped into a sit and grinned at Carol.

"Good dogs," she said. "Stay."

Carol and her driver loaded the shaking Lloyd into the ambulance.

"Watch yourself, bud," Carol growled as she climbed into the vehicle. Before the driver closed the door, she glanced at me and winked.

I clapped my hands, and the dogs followed me to the truck. After the dogs jumped in, I adjusted the truck seat for my short legs. When I reached home, I put my head on the steering wheel, and sobbed.

My phone rang. *Monica.*

"Karen, I know what happened. You aren't alone, you know."

"Thank you, Monica."

"Things are not as they seem. Whatever you hear, you aren't alone. Hold the pen."

She hung up, and I removed the pen from my pocket and held it in my palm. The pen warmed, and I was comforted.

The dogs and I went inside. I fed them and Mia before I called Amber. "Jack was in an altercation, and the sheriff drove away with him. I'm afraid he needs help."

"I'll find someone for him. I'm your lawyer, Karen. I look after your interests." Amber hung up.

I stared at the phone, but when I clutched my pen, the warmth surged through me. The dogs had finished eating, so we went outside. I rocked and scratched Colonel's ears while Roxie ran with a ball, and Pepper chased her. Roxie dropped the toy, and Pepper raced Mandy to pick it up. Pepper swooped up the ball and tore around the yard. Mandy flopped down on the grass and grinned.

When I rose, Colonel joined Mandy on the grass, and I smiled. "Nice to have a little outside time to relax, isn't it?"

I stepped into the kitchen, opened the refrigerator, and stared. *What would go with a baked potato?* I pulled out grated cheese and butter. I opened the pantry door and reached for a jar of salsa. *Loaded baked potato.*

After I poured my sweet tea, I pulled the baked potatoes out of the oven and slathered one with butter, cheese, and salsa. I dug into my spicy creation. *Magnifique, if I do say so myself.*

After I rinsed my dishes, I joined the dogs outside. The sun hovered at the horizon, and the orange and red streaks threw brilliant flames through the trees. The sounds of the crickets and katydids filled the evening air as one community after another passed on their raucous call.

I slapped my arm and rose to open the back door. "Time to go in."

The dogs charged into the house, and Mia waved her tail and marched into the pantry. The shadows slid in with her, and the door eased closed.

After I brewed my tea and grabbed my book to read on the sofa, the four dogs sought out their spots to relax. Colonel faced the front door, Roxie lay against the back door, Mandy flopped near me, and Pepper lay on her side next to the pantry door. I placed my empty cup on the end table and closed my eyes as I listened to the sleeping dogs breathe.

Roxie growled at the back door, and I opened my eyes. Mandy joined Roxie at the door, bared her teeth and snarled, and Pepper darted down the hall and through the bedrooms before she backed up Colonel at the front door.

My eyes widened. *We're a pack*

CHAPTER FOUR

I grabbed my phone, and as I headed to the back door, Roxie's bark became incessant and filled the house, and Mandy placed her paws on the windowsill, growled, and barked. Pepper darted down the hallway to bark from the back bedroom.

I changed direction to see what drew her away from the front door and frowned as Lloyd climbed the fence from my yard back to the alley. He dashed to his car that was parked in the alley and stopped at the driver's door. As I turned to leave, the gate caught my eye. *It's open. He's waiting for the dogs to run off to search for an intruder down the alley.*

I clutched my pen and called nine-one-one.

"Hello, Ms. Karen. Are you okay?" Summer asked.

My eyes widened. "How did you all get Tess to take time off?"

Summer snickered. "Sheriff said he'd fire her if she had anymore overtime this week. A deputy is on the way, and I sent the sheriff a text. Do you need medical?"

"No. The dogs raised a fuss, and Lloyd Ahrens was in my backyard." I checked the back window. "He's sitting in his car in the alley. He had opened the back gate. I think he expected the dogs would run away to look for him."

"Oh, no. Are all the dogs okay?"

Summer was a vet tech at the county animal shelter. I had a feeling she was ready to hang up on me and chase down Lloyd herself if he'd hurt a dog.

"Dogs are fine. They wanted to tear him apart, but I didn't open the door."

Summer's sigh of relief mingled with the surge of warmth from my pen, and I relaxed my shoulders. *I'm not alone.*

Lloyd's car lights turned on, and he started the engine. The sound of a far-off siren rose in intensity as it rounded the corner near my house. Lloyd sped down the alley, and a cruiser chased after him.

"Deputy's chasing Lloyd." I hurried to the front of my house at the sound of banging on the front door. "Sheriff's here."

"You be safe, Ms. Karen. Hug those dogs for me, will you?"

I hung up, and when I opened the front door, the sheriff barreled into the house with his gun drawn.

"Anybody in here?" he growled.

"No, your deputy is chasing Lloyd. I'll close the back gate."

"Stay in the house. I'll do that." Sheriff did a fast sweep of the house. When he opened the pantry door, the shadows shrank back, and Mia pranced out. He stood on the back porch before he crossed the yard and closed the gate. When he returned to the house, he said, "Sit where you're comfortable, Karen."

I sat on the sofa, and Colonel jumped up with me. The three other dogs crowded at my feet, and Sheriff sat on the ugly chair.

"Start at the beginning. I'll take the long version." He leaned back.

"It's not all that long." I told him about the dogs guarding me, Roxie alerting at the back door, and Mandy joining her. When I told him about Pepper barking in the back bedroom, he interrupted.

"Did you hear anything? Did you go to the back door?"

"I was on my way, but I switched to the bedroom to see what set off Pepper, and that's when I saw Lloyd. He was in my backyard but was climbing the fence to the alley. That's when I noticed the back gate was open and called nine-one-one."

"You sure it was Lloyd?"

I nodded.

The sheriff's radio crackled, and he stepped to the door to listen.

"Jeff stopped Lloyd. I'll be back." Sheriff slammed the door, and I locked it.

"I need another cup of peach tea." I turned on the burner.

When I sat on the sofa and put up my feet, the dogs resumed their previous guard positions. After an hour, a car door slammed, and Sheriff stepped onto the front porch. He tapped lightly on the door, and Colonel glanced at me as I rose to answer.

I snickered. "Did you just roll your eyes, Colonel?"

Sheriff frowned as he sat down. "Lloyd claimed he wanted to talk to you but wasn't sure you were still awake. He said he drove to the alley to see whether the kitchen light was on when he saw a raccoon in your yard. He said he went into the yard to chase it away, but when he heard the dogs, he decided he better get out of the yard and climbed the fence. He claimed he panicked when he heard the siren but stopped after he realized he should have waited to talk to the deputy. He did pull over less than a half a block away. All very plausible, and Jeff didn't believe a word of it."

"Is he under arrest?"

"No, Jeff said he had the distinct impression that Lloyd hoped to spend the night in jail so he could taunt Jack. Jeff followed Lloyd to his hotel and warned him not to leave the hotel tonight. You told me Terry had tortured you, but I'm not sure I realized how subtle it could be. Not that Lloyd is subtle."

I nodded. "Terry was always smoother than Lloyd around other people. I'm glad you see Lloyd the way I do."

"You've got a houseful of excellent guard dogs, and we're keeping a close eye on Lloyd." He opened the door and paused. "You made Summer's night. She asked me if she and Tess could job share. That'll cause some fireworks." Sheriff chuckled as he left.

I opened the back door, and the dogs dashed outside. I didn't turn on the porch light to avoid drawing mosquitoes, but I was still buzzed and smacked my arms.

"I'm going inside. Anybody going with me?" Mandy and Roxie followed Colonel to the porch, and as they trooped inside, Pepper passed them in the doorway. I gave the four dogs a treat, and Mia meowed for hers.

After I was in bed and turned off the light, Colonel stayed next to my bed, but the other dogs clicked on the hardwood floors as they roamed the house. I listened to their clicking nails on the floors. When they settled down, I rolled over and relaxed.

I woke to a strange odor. When I sat up, dark shadows with lightning shooting to the ceiling billowed out of my closet. My house shadows scattered in their wake as the lightning sizzled and scorched the ceiling. I reached for my blanket to protect myself, and all four dogs jumped onto my bed. When the closet door creaked and flew open, a large snake with glowing red eyes slithered toward the bed and snatched Pepper. I screamed and struggled to reach the howling Yorkie when a second larger snake darted at the bed and grabbed Roxie in its mouth.

When I jumped off the bed and grabbed my lamp to fight the snakes, smaller snakes wrapped around my ankles and pulled me to the floor. Colonel and Mandy attacked the snakes, but more snakes dragged them away. I pulled out the bedside table drawer and smashed it to stab snakes. The first large snake spit Pepper onto the floor, grabbed me, and pulled me under the bed. When it opened its wide mouth and lunged at my face, I retched from the putrid odor. It sank its fangs into my neck, and I screamed. The largest snake wrapped itself around my chest, and I couldn't breathe.

As I felt myself passing out, a dog yipped, and the snake loosened its hold. I blinked and opened my eyes. Pepper licked my face; I was under the bed. My chest ached as I worked to slow my gasping breaths. I struggled and pushed myself out from under the bed. After I crawled to the door and pulled myself up, I flipped on the light and counted dogs. *Four.*

My bedside table was on its side, the smashed drawer lay at the foot of the bed, and the broken ceramic lamp was nestled between the table legs. The clock was upside down on the floor. *Four-thirty.*

I grabbed a piece of the broken wooden drawer and approached the closet. I jerked open the door. *Just clothes. Nothing else.*

After I stumbled into the kitchen and started a pot of coffee, I stepped outside with the dogs. The early birds sang of no rain. *Thank you for the song, birds.*

When we returned to the kitchen, I fed the four dogs and Mia and poured a cup of coffee. "If the message of that nightmare was beware of snakes, I got it." I drained my cup and picked up my broom and dustpan to straighten my bedroom.

I swept my room and carried the broken lamp, table, and drawer to the backyard. The dogs stayed outside for a last romp while I showered. After I dried off and dressed, I combed my hair and stared in the mirror at the two parallel slits on the side of my neck. *I've never had a nightmare more real.* I applied antibiotic ointment to the scratches before I loaded the dogs into my car.

When we reached the Donut Hole, the bright interior lights that streamed through the front window reminded me of a lighthouse. I smiled. *We need a beacon light turning on top of the building.*

When the dogs and I went into the shop, Andrew said, "Good morning, Miss Lady. We have the Liars' Club today."

I smiled. "That's wonderful. The mayor loves to joke with them. We can have imaginary and frosted coffee donuts, but I don't remember what scone we did last time."

"Ms. Tiffany's notes say cinnamon scone with coffee drizzle."

Andrew returned to his fryer, and I hurried to don my apron and mix my scones. We finished our fourth batch before the sheriff strode in.

The dogs danced in greeting, and the sheriff petted each one then approached the counter. "Nothing's on the board," he said. "May I please have coffee and nothing?"

Andrew giggled, and I smiled. "Coming right up, Sheriff." I poured his coffee and placed an empty small bowl in front of him while Andrew served up two donuts and a scone.

"Imaginary donuts." He grinned. "Must be Liars' Club today. I have an idea. Why don't I write *No Special Today* on the board for you?"

Andrew's eyes brightened, and he nodded. Sheriff drank half of his coffee, grabbed the blue chalk, and printed *No Special Today* in large capital letters. We hurried to the front door and admired his handiwork.

I refilled the sheriff's coffee, and he returned to his seat and stared into his empty bowl. "I've run out of imaginary sprinkles, Donut Lady."

Andrew snickered and brought me a large empty container and a cereal bowl. I hefted the container and poured imaginary sprinkles.

When I handed the sheriff his full bowl of imaginary sprinkles, Andrew's shoulders shook with silent laughter, and the sheriff winked at me. I poured myself a cup of coffee and sat next to him at the counter.

The sheriff gazed at me and frowned. "What's up?"

"Rough night." I shuddered. "Nightmare."

He nodded. "Anytime day or night you want to come to our house, load up the dogs, and show up. You can sleep in peace, or Emma will sit up with you and tell you her latest escapades that I know nothing about."

I smiled and sipped my coffee. "I do miss Emma. Maybe after I have fewer dogs, I'll give her a call. When do you sleep, Sheriff?"

"In between your escapades."

Andrew snorted, and I glared at the sheriff and Andrew's back.

The mayor rushed into the shop. He wore his pink sprinkles apron and his ballcap. "Ready for work, Donut Lady."

His eyes widened as he stared at the sign. "I get it." He guffawed. "We've got the Liars' Club today and imaginary donuts."

"Yes, sir, Mr. Mayor." Andrew grinned, and the mayor hurried to load his utility cart and prepare the meeting room.

"When does Jack get out of jail?" I asked the sheriff in a quiet voice.

"Court begins at eight. I'd expect him to be out by ten or eleven. I met his lawyer—fresh out of school, but one of the sharpest I've seen in a long time. Jack grumbled about having a middle-school kid for a lawyer, and I had the distinct pleasure of telling him to grow up." The sheriff chuckled.

I smiled. "I'm sure that went over well."

"I channeled my inner Tiffany for sassy." The sheriff wiggled his eyebrows, and I giggled.

The sheriff rose. "Call me if you need me."

After he left, I cleared the dishes as Andrew filled trays for the mayor.

My phone rang. I didn't recognize the number, but I recognized the Ohio area code and picked up.

"Don't hang up, Karen. It's Lloyd. I've been trying to talk to you, but I've been clumsy, and I'm sorry. Terry said people in small towns know everything, and there are no secrets except from outsiders. He told me about a successful counterfeiter near Conway, Georgia, before he married you. He was pleased he found you at the college in Ohio and said he planned to find out from you who the counterfeiter was. He was good at grooming, Karen. I'm sure you know that now. He had it all planned out. You'd tell him, and he'd leave you to come to Conway or wherever the counterfeiter was, to get a piece of the action."

He cleared his throat. "After he died, I thought I'd pick up where he left off and be your friend, but you went to prison. I got into a little trouble over cars and spent some time away too."

I went into the storeroom and sat at my desk. "You have a point here, Lloyd?"

"If you'll tell me who the counterfeiter is, I can get out of your hair."

"I can't help you. I don't know anything about a counterfeiter."

"You have to tell me, Karen. I know he's here. Someone's been following me since I first got here. If I leave, he'll come after you."

"I doubt it."

Lloyd growled. "I tried to be nice and gave you a second chance, Karen—"

I hung up. My phone rang again, and I silenced it. I held my pen for a few minutes before I left the storeroom.

Mayor squinted at my face and turned away as Alfred and Woody came into the store.

"Mr. Alfred, imaginary donuts." Woody's face brightened as he pointed to the board and grinned.

Alfred nodded. "Go talk to Ms. Karen."

Woody's shoulders slumped, and his brow furrowed. "Yes, sir."

I raised my eyebrows. "Storeroom or back porch, Woody?"

"Back porch. You might need a chair. I'll carry it out for you."

Woody picked up the extra chair in the storeroom and carried it outside, and I followed him. He placed the chair in the shade, leaned against the side of the building, and crossed his arms.

I sat on the chair and waited.

Woody scowled. "I been suspended for fighting."

"Everything making you angry?"

He nodded. "I told Mr. Alfred I needed to talk to you."

"Do you know why you are angry?"

"No." He stared at his shoes. "Mama Shirley will never be my mama."

I frowned to keep from smiling at the irony of his statement. "Why don't I tell you a story?"

Woody relaxed and sat cross-legged on the floor near me.

"When I was young, I didn't have friends except for Mama Shirley. I thought I was okay because I was smart and liked books. I went to college in Ohio because I got a scholarship. I didn't know anybody, but I studied hard. A nice, young man studied with me and told me I was smart and pretty, and I believed he meant what he said. When I graduated, we were married. He wasn't nice anymore. He was mean."

"Like Mr. Dixon?" Woody asked.

My chest ached with the neglect and abuse that Woody suffered as he bounced around the foster care system after his loving grandparents died in the house fire. "Exactly. I made excuses for him. I told myself he'd had a rough day, or he'd be fine if I would be good, but he just got meaner."

"Like Mr. Dixon," Woody mumbled.

"When he died, I was relieved. I went to prison and learned to look out for myself; I had to toughen up to survive."

Woody's eyes widened. "But you're nice, Miss Lady."

I smiled. "When I came back here to live, it was hard for me to be around what I thought of as normal people. Your Mama Shirley was my only friend, but I wasn't always kind to her. I had to learn how to be considerate and think of her feelings."

"It's hard to be nice sometimes." Woody stared at the floor. "I don't want to be too close to Mama Shirley because she might give up on me, and that makes me angry and mean."

"I worked hard on being understanding with everyone, even Mama Shirley. I learned that she will always be herself, and she will never give up."

Woody sighed. "I can prove that. She'll never be anything but Mama Shirley. She's strict about bedtime and school, and she keeps buying me ugly clothes and trying to learn how to cook."

I snickered, and Woody stared at me then snickered too.

"All this tough guy stuff is because you're afraid Mama Shirley will give you back?"

Woody nodded. "I didn't know that's what I was doing, but that's kind of silly, isn't it? She would never give me back. Mama Shirley is fierce."

I smiled. "She is, but it's still important to be nice to fierce people. She tries hard to be a good mama, but sometimes she makes mistakes. Nobody's perfect."

"I hadn't thought of it like that, but you're right, Miss Lady."

"You okay for now? Want to hear the difficult part?"

Woody straightened his back. "Yes."

"You have to learn how to tell her your feelings when you're sad, angry, or tired because it's important that you aren't mean or don't shut her out. Doesn't work to hold it in. I'm still not good at this. It's hard."

Woody peered at my face. "You're talking about you and Mr. Jack, aren't you?"

I nodded. "I think the fierce people are the hardest. Sometimes I have to remind myself that Mr. Jack's heart is soft just like your Mama Shirley."

Woody gazed at the sky. "This stuff is hard."

"Yes."

"I think I could start by telling Mama Shirley that I'm sorry."

"Perfect place to start. Are you suspended just for the day? Can you use the time to catch up on your schoolwork?"

He nodded. "It won't take me long to get caught up if I focus." He rose and headed to the door. "Thank you, Miss Lady."

My eyes misted as I followed him inside. Shirley and Alfred sat at the counter, and Alfred rose when Woody approached Shirley. "I'm sorry, Mama Shirley. Sometimes I mess up."

"So do I, Woody. Care for an imaginary donut and milk before we go home?"

Woody climbed onto the stool next to her and patted her hand, and my eyes overflowed.

Alfred joined me. "Thought it would help for the two of you to talk. Can we grab some coffee to take outside?"

I poured coffee, and we carried our cups to the back porch that had become my new outdoor office.

I sat on my chair, and my eyes widened as Alfred leaned against the wall in the same way that Woody did earlier. *Woody is picking up Alfred's mannerisms.* I bit my lip. *Please Lord, not Alfred's fastidious eating habits.*

"Karen, I've had several run-ins with Lloyd that drove me close to the brink since he showed up in town. If I'd known he had targeted you, I would have smashed in his face yesterday."

He narrowed his eyes. "Any man, even one who has not had past issues like Jack and I had, has a breaking point, and Lloyd's driven for some reason to find that point. He came into my office and said he knew I was the counterfeiter. Karen, I'm a banker and have an impeccable reputation. I can't afford even a whisper of impropriety tainting the bank, and Lloyd crossed the line with that accusation."

Alfred paced. "I reported him to the sheriff and to the Georgia Department of Banking and Finance. Sheriff told me the Georgia Bureau of Investigation will send someone here to investigate Lloyd. We'll see what the Department of Banking and Finance decides to do. Best case, they send someone to interview the staff and me; worse case, we'll undergo a full audit. We will definitely pass an audit, but it's a lot of work for the staff."

"Thank you, Alfred. I don't know how this all fits together, but I'm glad we have the attention of the right people."

"Thank you for helping Shirley and Woody. It's nice to have good friends."

"More coffee?" I asked as we went inside.

"No, it's time for me to get back to the bank."

Alfred stopped by Shirley and Woody. He patted Woody on the shoulder and hugged Shirley.

Wait until I tell Tiffany. That ought to perk up Gee.

The mayor stood at the meeting room door and made a kissy face, and I choked back a laugh with a cough.

"You old stinker," I said as I walked past him, and he grinned.

"We need more imaginary sprinkles in here, Donut Lady. Shall I carry the punch bowl to the door?" He stepped into the meeting room. "Stand by for more sprinkles."

He stood in the doorway and held the bowl with both hands. "Let 'er rip, Donut Lady."

I wound up my arm like a seasoned baseball pitcher and flung imaginary sprinkles at the bowl. Mayor grunted and bent his knees under the imaginary weight, and the roomful of men laughed, applauded, and whistled. Mayor moaned and grunted with each step, until he dropped the bowl with a thud onto the middle of the table and bowed to more applause and whistles.

I turned to leave and bumped into Andrew who had watched behind me.

"That was awesome, Miss Lady." He beamed.

"It was, wasn't it? Only the Liars' Club would have full appreciation of such a corny stunt."

"Corny stunt," Andrew echoed on his way back to the sink and his pans.

I shrugged. *He could be learning worse words.*

I glanced out the front window and was surprised to see the sheriff park his cruiser. When he came into the shop, Andrew said, "Sheriff, you missed the Mayor's corny stunt."

"I'm sorry I did. The Mayor is really good. Can we step out front, Karen?"

I'm glad I'm fond of being outdoors. When we were outside, he said, "I asked for a stipulation with Jack's release, and he won't be happy. He's to stay away from you. I take that back—he'll be irate. I don't want a repeat of yesterday's fight. He'll be harder for Lloyd to find if he isn't with you. It's more for his protection than yours, I'm afraid. I'll take him to your house to pick up his truck and will advise him to stay home except for any necessities. He'll complain about not being able to help Darlene, but I'll talk to her to see if she can postpone the deliveries for a few days. He can call you, but he can't be anywhere close to you, your home, or the shop, and he'll know I'm watching. Will you be okay with that?"

"You're right. I'm Lloyd's target." I told him about Lloyd's phone call and claim that someone was following him.

Sheriff's face softened. "Might have been half the town."

I removed my pen from my collar and held it in my hand. *I'm not alone.*

"Emma sent a formal invitation for you and the dogs to stay at our house."

"Tell her thank you, but I didn't sleep well at all last night and am looking forward to an early night. I'll call her this evening."

"She'd like that, Karen. She's worried about you with both Tiffany and Gee out of town."

"Is Monica out of town?" I asked.

"She went to some librarian or book convention—not sure where." He climbed into his cruiser and left.

I clipped my pen to my shirt and returned to the shop. *Wonder where Monica really is?*

The judge strolled into the shop and stepped to the counter. "Scone and coffee to go."

As I poured his coffee, he asked, "Melinda was a longtime friend of yours, wasn't she?"

I paused before I put the lid on his coffee. "I didn't know her that long, but we were friends. Why?"

"Just curious. She loved her Yorkie, and you have Pepper. I thought you must have been friends for a long time."

"Did you know Melinda well?" I asked as I placed his scone into a sack.

"Only casually." He took his sack and placed money on the counter then picked up his coffee. When I reached into the till for his change, he waved it off and left.

But you knew the name of her dog.

I refilled my cup and sat at the counter as the Liars' Club members streamed out of the shop. Mayor brought his coffee to the counter and joined me. "The Liars' Club members passed around their ten-gallon liars' hat for Gee's and Isaiah's expenses. One of the guys will spearhead a fund drive at the carwash he owns in Conway. Their local Future Farmers of America were looking for a project, and he said they'd do an outstanding job of detailing after a carwash. He'll donate the proceeds from the carwash that day, and the FFA will donate the money they raise. A couple other guys are planning a Liars' Barbeque at the Farmers' Market this weekend to raise money too."

"That's tremendous." I brushed away the stray tears that sneaked onto my cheeks.

"Clean up time." Mayor hustled back into the meeting room with his utility cart and the warm soapy water to wipe down the buffet, table, and chairs. After he finished loading his utility cart, he swept the floor while Andrew loaded the dishwasher.

We had only four donuts left because some of the Liars' Club members bought imaginary donuts and extra sprinkles on the way out. I went into the storeroom for a quick inventory check when I heard the bell jingle and the dogs growl.

"Easy," Mayor said.

"Karen here?" Lloyd asked.

"We have four donuts left. What would you like?" Mayor asked.

"A donut."

"Here you go," Andrew said. "Five dollars."

"Donuts are a little pricey here, aren't they?"

"Five dollars," Andrew said.

"Can I have some coffee?"

"Pot's off. We're cleaning," Mayor said.

I heard the slap of the bill on the counter, and the bell jingled as the door slammed.

I stayed in the storeroom and texted the sheriff.

"Lloyd was here. Asked for me. I was in the storeroom."

I heard a siren a block away.

Mayor came to the door. "Lloyd just peeled out. Did you call nine-one-one?"

"I texted the sheriff."

"What's the scoop on Jack?" Mayor took off his apron.

"I'm not sure I can say."

Mayor nodded. "You text me or Amber if you need either one or both of us. I'll follow you home."

"I'm taking Roxie and Mandy to the thrift shop. Jack can pick them up later."

"I'll follow you to the thrift shop and to your house. I haven't been in Gee's store in ages."

Andrew waited for us near the front door. "I'll lock it behind you and leave by the back, Miss Lady."

"Where did you come up with five dollars for Lloyd's donut?" Mayor asked.

"My favorite number is five." Andrew held up his hand with the fingers spread.

"It was an excellent number." I smiled as the four dogs rushed to the front door.

The mayor took my keys and waited while the dogs took a break before he loaded them into my car. I started my car to let it cool and relaxed my shoulders. When the mayor pulled up behind me, I headed to the thrift shop.

I parked in front of the store and was relieved to see it was open. After Mayor parked, he opened my car's back door, and all four dogs piled out.

When we entered the store, Darlene rose from her chair near the door. "You're a surprise, and you, too, Mr. Mayor. I understand I should reschedule any deliveries for a few days. I have only one sofa scheduled for delivery next week. All the rest of my sales were out the door, or the customer had a friend with a truck."

Mayor wandered off to browse, and Darlene winked at me. "He'll find something. I plan to recommend that Gee look at scheduling deliveries once a week, maybe every Wednesday, to give her young men some relief on being available on such short notice."

"That's really smart. I'm sure Gee would be open to deliveries being more scheduled, especially since Isaiah and his friends have graduated from high school."

Darlene nodded. "Fresh eyes always help. What are you all doing here?"

I flopped onto the chair next to her. "Jack may get out of jail this afternoon. I thought it would be easier for him to pick up Mandy and Roxie here."

Darlene held her pearl necklace with her thumb and fingers and rubbed it gently as she propped up her feet. "I love having those two dogs here. I don't see how Gee ran the shop all these years alone. I've been nervous without Mandy around."

"I understand. I feel safe in the shop and at home with Colonel." I relaxed in the chair and inhaled the light aroma of peach and violet that lingered from the previous owner.

I texted the sheriff. "Mandy and Roxie at Thrift Shop. Can Jack pick them up?"

Sheriff: "Ok."

"Doesn't that chair take you back? Sometimes I wish I could hear the stories the old furniture could tell. I'm always thrilled when I find a note under a cushion or in a drawer."

I rose from the time-steeped chair. "Drawer. Thank you, I'd forgotten. I need a lamp and a bedside table. Mine are broken."

Darlene pulled herself up with her walker. "Let's see what strikes your fancy, and I'll give you the family price. I know you and Gee like to haggle, but I'm no match for either of you." She led the way down an aisle. "I know this isn't exactly a typical bedroom lamp, but this forged iron lamp is one of my favorites."

"I like it. I hadn't thought about an iron lamp, but I love its unique style." I turned it on and stepped back to examine the lamp. "I like the simple shade too. This is perfect."

"Good. You said a bedside table? I've got something toward the back for you."

I followed Darlene, and when she stopped and pointed, I examined the patina of the old, dark-wood table. Under the single drawer, the small table was enclosed on three sides and had a shelf four inches from the floor. *I'll have a place for books.* I opened the drawer.

"That drawer would be perfect for a journal," Darlene said.

I raised my eyebrows, and she snorted. "I don't journal either."

I chuckled. "If I ever get one, I'll know where it goes. The lamp goes great with this table."

"You find something?" Mayor joined us and admired my table. "This is beautiful. Out to your car?"

I nodded and gave him my keys.

"I'll put it in your trunk."

Darlene and I headed to the front; I picked up my lamp on the way.

"If you're ready to go home, and Jack hasn't shown up, call or text me, and I'll pick them up."

"I'll load them up in my car and bring them to your house. I'll let you know," Darlene said.

We settled up, and she placed my check in her bank bag and filled out her bank slip.

"Want me to deposit your day's receipts, Darlene?" Mayor asked.

I followed the mayor to the bank. After he completed the transaction, he followed me home. I unlocked the door, and Pepper pranced inside. The mayor carried in my table and my lamp. I waved, and Colonel and I went inside.

I turned on the burner to heat water for tea and carried my table and lamp to my bedroom. After I made my tea, I claimed my usual seat at the sofa, and Mia rubbed against my legs. I lifted her to my lap and stroked her back. When Mia leapt to pounce on the passing Pepper, I put up my feet and enjoyed the show. Mia chased the dog; Pepper chased the cat. Colonel jumped up on the sofa to get out of the way.

My phone rang. *Darlene.*

"Jack picked up the dogs. It's been a full day. I may go home a little early."

After we hung up, I called Emma. "I'm checking in."

Emma laughed. "It's always a good thing to do. I wanted to offer my cooking, cleaning, and companion services. You know you can call me anytime, and I'll be there in a flash. You were there for me when I needed to talk. I'm itching to return the favor. What's on your mind?"

"Thank you, Emma. I've been so busy with all the extra animals and worry about Gee, Isaiah, and Jack that a normal conversation sounds wonderful. What's new in town that I've missed?"

"The biggest secret in town, which means that everybody knows, is that someone from Atlanta was looking at the downtown buildings to open a new business. Did you already hear about this?"

"No. How exciting if it's really true."

"Oh good. I finally get to tell somebody. Nobody knows what it is, but the rumors are flying, and everyone has an inside scoop. Gus has started up a pool. Is that illegal? Anyway, half the proceeds go to the Animal Shelter if someone wins. If nobody wins, the proceeds will go to the Animal Shelter. According to Gus, the most popular guess is a UFO paint store. Do you know what that is? I don't, but every time someone mentions it, people elbow each other. Do you want to go in with me? I have an idea. I think it's a dog treat bakery shop."

CHAPTER FIVE

I snickered. "I like that. They'd make a mint off me this week, for sure. I'll go in with you."

"Great. I'll drop by the shop maybe tomorrow and pick up your money. I don't think anybody's thought about that. See you tomorrow."

She hung up, and I picked up my book. Mia jumped on top of my book and meowed when I had read only two pages.

"Really?"

She purred but didn't move off my book. I set my book and cat aside and filled food bowls. Mia, Colonel, and Pepper lined up, and I watched them eat to be sure Mia didn't chase away Pepper. After everyone finished their food, I held the refrigerator door open and stared. *I really should get back to planning my meals.*

"I'll run to the grocery store, Colonel, but I won't be long. Don't let Mia corner Pepper while I'm gone."

I parked as close as I could to the entrance and grabbed a cart on my way in. After I picked through tomatoes, Romaine lettuce, and cucumbers, I cruised the aisles to load my shopping cart with my usual pantry and refrigerator items.

As I headed to the checkout, Clarissa waited at the end of the last aisle. "I could have told you Jack has a terrible temper. Would you have listened to me?" she hissed. "No. There's a man following you. I see him all the time. I'm telling you, be careful. Will you listen to me this time? No." She flounced past me and continued to the dairy section in the back.

I rolled to the end of the checkout line to wait and frowned at the anger Clarissa still carried. *I don't know if she's consumed by her sour outlook on life or if this is her version of trying to help me.*

After I was home, I put the groceries away except for the pack of flour tortillas, jar of salsa, and shredded cheese. I pulled out an egg and a slice of bacon to make an evening breakfast taco. My phone rang as I bit into my all-time favorite quick supper.

Tiffany. "Aunt Gee is doing much better, just not as well as she would like. I talked to Tammy. Did I already tell you? Isaiah's burns are not as bad as the doctors thought at first, but he still has a lot of healing and therapy ahead of him. I'm on my way to spend the evening with Aunt Gee. Anything going on there? Anything you want me to tell her?"

Just the usual stalker, and Jack spent the night in jail. "Shirley called Alfred honey bun, and he called her sunshine; they hugged."

"You are kidding me," Tiffany laughed.

"I might have thought I dreamed it, but the mayor witnessed it too." I chuckled.

"I can't wait to tell Aunt Gee. If that doesn't perk up her cranky spirits, nothing will."

"That's what I thought."

After we hung up, I finished my taco and tea and set my dishes in the sink. I checked the gate before I opened the back door.

While Colonel relaxed in the middle of the yard, Pepper grabbed the ball he had dropped for her and tore around the yard. She pitched the ball with a toss of her head, pounced on it, and raced from one end of the yard to the other. I rinsed their outside dish and filled it with fresh water. After Pepper trotted to the water and drank her fill, she flopped next to Colonel.

I rocked on the porch as I gazed at the red and blue streaked horizon. The crickets and katydids chirped, and the buzz of the cicadas filled the air. "Wonder why I haven't heard from Jack?" I pulled my pen from my collar, held it, and Monica's voice resonated in my head. *Things are not as they seem. Whatever you hear, you aren't alone.*

"Sometimes I feel alone," I sighed.

Colonel trotted to the porch, and Pepper followed. I smiled. "Maybe not."

We went inside, and I filled their water dish in the kitchen. I grabbed my book and read the last five pages. I laughed and slammed it shut. "I knew it all along, Colonel."

I started another book but stumbled to bed when my head kept bobbing.

* * *

I awoke at my usual time and yawned. "I can't believe it, but I slept all night, Colonel. No nightmares. No intruders."

I lumbered to the kitchen to start my coffee and flipped on the backyard floodlight. "Gate's closed. Y'all ready to go out?"

Pepper danced, and Colonel nosed the door. I let them out. After my coffee perked, I joined them and gasped when I stepped outside. "That floodlight shines right smack into the neighbor's bedroom window."

I reached inside and turned off the light. "I'll put tape over that switch or maybe Jack could redirect it for me. Sometime."

After I finished my first cup, I went inside to dress for work while Colonel and Pepper explored the yard. I called in the dogs and fed them and Mia. After everyone ate, and the dogs took one last break, I put Mia's carrier by the front door.

"You going, Mia?"

She stuck her nose in the air, sashayed to the carrier, and slipped inside. I opened the back door, and Pepper raced to the front door. Colonel stayed by my side.

When we reached the donut shop, the welcoming lights were on. After we were in the shop, I unzipped Mia's carrier, and Pepper scrambled across the floor to Andrew. He knelt and spoke to her in soft words that I didn't understand, but Pepper must have because her backend went into high gear, and she whimpered dog sounds in the same pitch as Andrew's words. I didn't move because I didn't want to disrupt the magic.

When the sheriff tapped at the window, Andrew rose and hurried to wash his hands.

"It's early, Sheriff. We have coffee, but no donuts or scones."

"Good morning, Andrew," the sheriff said, and Andrew nodded as he started his mixer.

"Wouldn't mind a cup. Make it to go, please?" Sheriff frowned. "Can you spare a minute to talk, Karen? Come out to my cruiser."

I examined his stony face before I filled to-go cups for us. I handed the sheriff his cup and followed him outside. "What's this all about, Sheriff?" I shivered as I held my cup with two hands.

He unlocked his cruiser and opened the passenger's door. "Climb in. There's a chill in the air."

He closed the door behind me. After he slid into the driver's seat, he sipped his coffee. "Thanks. I needed coffee. Lloyd was found dead this morning. Beaten and stabbed."

"It couldn't have been Jack. He's at home." I sipped my coffee.

"Right. According to Jack, Roxie and Mandy found the body on his property this morning, and he called it in."

I sipped my coffee in stunned silence as I tried to process what the sheriff had said. Sheriff leaned back in his seat and drank his coffee. "It was a blow to me too. We've called GBI. I wanted to tell you myself off the record before the news explodes across town."

After we reached the shop door, he stopped and frowned. "I won't be by today. Maybe tomorrow. I'll have a deputy bring the dogs here."

After he left, I went inside and paused at the sight of Andrew's worried face.

"Is the sheriff mad at me, Miss Lady?" he asked.

"No. Why would the sheriff be mad at you?"

"I lost the cell phone he gave me. Mama said I had to tell him, but I couldn't. Mama told him. He's mad at me."

"No, he isn't mad at you at all. Do you remember the man we don't trust, Andrew?"

"Yes. We don't like him and don't trust him."

I sat at the counter. "Somebody killed him last night and left his body on Mr. Jack's property.

Andrew stared at me. "That's not right."

I nodded and hurried to put on my apron and make scones. "I agree. It's not right."

Twenty minutes later, Deputy Jeff opened the shop door, and Mandy and Roxie raced inside. "Hello, Andrew." He headed back to his cruiser and left.

"Deputy Jeff was in a hurry," Andrew said.

I nodded. *I'm feeling a little shunned by the local law enforcement.*

After I filled a second bowl of water for the dogs, I texted the sheriff. "Were Jack's dogs fed?"

Sheriff: "Jeff fed them."

"Andrew, what's our plan for today?" I asked.

"Book club today. Pink sprinkles and maple donuts. I'll make extra donut holes for them. The book club ladies say donut holes are not donuts." Andrew peered at me. "Ms. Amber said we don't tell them they really are. Thursday is cranberry-orange scones."

I nodded and finished my first batch of scones and popped them into the oven. While they baked, I mixed my next batch.

I was drizzling my final batch with orange glaze when the mayor rushed in. "I heard about Jack. Are you all okay?"

I nodded, and Andrew said, "Yes."

"Good." Mayor smiled and hurried to wash his hands and load the utility cart for the pink meeting room.

At eight-thirty, Amber came into the shop in her navy suit and inhaled. "The entire world is falling apart, but the Donut Hole smells like maple and pink sprinkles. Did you know I'd never realized how wonderful pink sprinkles smell?"

Andrew peered at her as he opened the container of sprinkles and sniffed. "I don't smell nothing, Ms. Amber."

She smiled as she strode to the counter. "That's because you're around the sprinkle magic all the time."

Andrew nodded and sniffed again as he replaced the lid. The mayor smiled at his daughter as he stood in the meeting room doorway. I poured her coffee and plated her pre-meeting maple donut. She downed her coffee, and while I refilled her cup, she bit into her maple donut and closed her eyes. "Mmm. So good."

She leaned over the counter and said in a soft voice, "Heard about Jack. His lawyer and I might have a little unplanned, off the record meeting today."

She picked up her plate and coffee and headed to the pink room to help her dad set up while they chatted. The book club members streamed into the shop, and the mayor greeted each one with a smile and closed the door after everyone arrived.

A few minutes later, the mayor stepped out of the room. "More donut holes, please, Andrew."

Andrew was ready with a platter of donut holes and carried it to the meeting room. Mayor encouraged him to come inside the room to set the platter in the middle of the table, and the club members applauded Andrew.

When he came out of the meeting room, his cheeks had bright red spots. "They said thank you, Miss Lady."

He hurried to his sink and scrubbed pots and pans. They gleamed when he rinsed them.

The bell jingled, and my eyes widened at the unshaven man in sweatpants and a paint-stained T-shirt. *I've never seen the county attorney in anything other than a suit.*

"I was at the gas station and heard about Jack," John Padilla said. "Thought I'd stop by for coffee and a scone. According to reliable sources, you might need somebody to take Mandy and Roxie to the thrift shop. I can do that. I don't have any meetings until this afternoon."

I poured John's coffee and plated his scone.

He sat at the counter and gulped his coffee then bit into his scone. "This is great. I'd like to try the donuts too." He smiled. "I don't get out enough."

I texted Darlene. "Ready for Mandy and Roxie?"

Darlene: "Yes."

"I checked to be sure Darlene was at the shop, and she is."

John scarfed down his scone and donuts and drained his cup.

"Want some coffee to go?" I asked.

"I'd love it. How much do I owe you?"

"Exactly the cost of dog delivery to the shop."

John burst out laughing as he rose from his seat. "Okay, Donut Lady. I got the best of that trade."

"I'll help put the dogs in your car, Mr. John," Andrew said. He called the two dogs, and they followed him outside. John opened his car's back door, and after Andrew waved his hand, the dogs jumped in.

When Andrew returned, I said, "Thank you for the help, Andrew."

Andrew nodded and checked the display case before he put away the trays that had dried.

Emma came into the shop. "Mmm. Smells wonderful. I need a donut and coffee." She sat at the counter. She had pushed her short, curly brown hair behind her ears, and her hazel eyes sparkled.

"Pink-sprinkled or maple, Ms. Emma?" Andrew asked.

"Pink-sprinkled sound like magic. That's what I'd like." She smiled as I poured her coffee.

I poured her coffee before I hurried to the storeroom and removed cash from my purse. When I returned to the counter, I gave her the money. "Is this enough?"

"Perfect," she said. "I'll put both our names on our submissions."

"Thanks for letting me in with you. Is your idea a secret? I think Darlene might be interested too."

"Good idea. I'll go by and check with her. If she is, I'll put the three of us in together. Is that okay with you?"

"I like it."

"Good." After Emma ate her donut and drank her second cup, she paid and left.

"It was nice to see Ms. Emma. She doesn't get out much," Andrew said.

I nodded. *Andrew notices everything.*

After the book club members filed out of the meeting room, Amber stayed to help her dad clean.

"Amber," Mayor said, "you'll get your suit dirty. I can take care of this."

"Dad, I'm not four years old. Besides, I already got maple frosting on my skirt." She put her hands on her hips and tossed her hair.

Mayor burst out laughing, and I joined him. Amber flipped her cleaning cloth onto the table and grumbled, "You two need to grow up."

While Amber swept the room, the judge came into the shop. *Three times in one week?*

Mayor crossed his arms and stood at the meeting room door.

The judge sat at the counter. "Coffee and a scone."

"Heard Jack was arrested," he said as I poured his coffee. I plated the scone and wiped down the rest of the counter.

"I also heard he and Edwin Wallace were partners at one time. Did you know that?"

I frowned. "No."

He polished off his coffee and scone and set money on the counter that more than covered his bill. "Heard it at the gas station. I didn't think it was true but thought you might know."

After he left, the mayor called me into the meeting room. Amber's eyes narrowed. "What was that all about?"

"I have no idea. The judge has never been in the shop before this week, and now he's dropped in the last two days and chatted about Melinda and Edwin Wallace."

Mayor sat and tapped his thumb on the table. "It is odd because he's been a recluse for quite a while. He's technically the county chief magistrate. Magistrates aren't required to be a licensed attorney in Georgia. We all call him judge because he handles small claims court and bad checks. No harm in that, I suppose."

I sat next to him. "I didn't know that."

"What exactly has he said?" Amber asked.

I told her about Tuesday when he didn't say anything but left after Jack did.

"I'm sure he got a good sense of the relationship between you and Jack," Amber said. "Was he here yesterday?"

"Yes. He asked if Melinda Wallace and I were good friends. I told him we were friends, but I didn't know her that long before she died."

"Today he asked about Edwin Wallace." Amber frowned as she joined us at the counter. "I can't figure out why. He's not an investigator."

"He's not a novelist," the mayor added. "Who else would research deaths?"

The blank papers. "Could he be investigating counterfeiting for some reason?"

Mayor stared at me. "Why would he do that?"

"Melinda put a stack of blank paper into my basket before her house burned. She said they belonged to Edwin, but she didn't know what they were, and neither did I until later. They were the same size as dollar bills. Sheriff gave them to somebody—the right people, I think he said."

"I'd forgotten all about them," Amber said. "They didn't seem like much at the time because the drug records had the detail for easy convictions. Blank papers weren't as interesting. It's probably nothing, but I'll mention it to the sheriff." Amber rose. "Meanwhile, you two stay out of everything." She stomped out of the shop and slammed the door.

"You have to include me, now, Donut Lady." Mayor beamed as he rose to clear the rest of the meeting room. "We've been accused of getting into trouble and have to stick together."

"I'm not sure that's how it works."

"It's exactly how it works."

I shook my head and covered my mouth to keep back my snicker as I left the meeting room. Mayor made a phone call before he strode out of the meeting room.

"It's all set. My wife says I can't stay at your house. She says that's not proper. She says I can't buy a tent because I'm too old to sleep on the ground. Barbara said we'll sleep in your second bedroom, and you don't have to cook because we'll bring dinner. We'll be there at six."

"Can I uninvite you?"

"Nope." He beamed. "You'll have to make the best of it. Barbara said if I want to talk during quiet time, I can take the dogs out back and talk to them. She said you probably read in the evening to relax. She's bringing our books to relax too. I have a meeting, but I'll be back to follow you home. I can pick up Roxie and Mandy whenever you say."

I glared at him.

After the mayor left, Andrew said, "You are having a sleepover."

"Yes."

"I went to a sleepover once, but I went home at dark. I missed my bed."

"That's a good point, Andrew. I get to sleep in my own bed." *This might work out. I can't remember the last time I had a restful night.*

I called Darlene. "How's it going?"

"Brisk. I'll be ready to call it a day earlier than I usually do. Emma dropped by and told me about the dog treat bakery. I'm in. How are you?"

"We'll be cleaning up soon. The mayor offered to pick up the deposit and the dogs whenever you like. He left for a meeting, but he'll be available any time after that."

"Call me when he returns from his meeting. I might be ready to close for the day. I had a restless night. You ever have them? I wouldn't mind some time to relax this afternoon."

"I will. Gee will be happy that you'll take time to rest."

"I think my smile energy is powering down, and my customer service muscles need a recharge." She chuckled.

"That's awesome, Darlene. Where'd you get that?"

"Two preteen girls came in with their parents and sat across from me while their parents shopped. That's what the sisters said after they asked how I was doing, and I said I was tired. Funniest thing I ever heard, and I told them so. Can you believe they actually asked how I felt? What happened to bratty kids?"

I laughed. "It's taken me awhile to get used to the nice people in Georgia again."

After I hung up, I pitched in to help Andrew with the final touches of straightening up. When we were finished, I said, "Andrew, you can leave whenever you like. The mayor will be back soon."

Andrew went into the storeroom and returned with the recipe book. "Yes." He sat at the counter and read each page by following the words with his finger. I looked over Woody's books on his reading shelf, picked up one of his favorites, and sat in a reading chair. I had five pages left at the end of the book when the mayor tapped on the door. *Story of my life.*

Andrew rose and unlocked the door for the mayor then returned the recipe book to the freezer.

"See you in the morning," Andrew said in a sing-song voice.

"Did you call Darlene?" Mayor asked.

"Sure did. She's as worn out as I am. We can pick up the dogs and deposit her day's receipts. I'll call her to let her know we're on our way. She's closing early today, and I think that's smart."

"I agree."

I called Darlene and checked the back door while Mayor placed Mia's carrier near the front. After Mia sauntered inside, he zippered her carrier and opened the door for the two dogs.

We caravanned to the thrift shop. I opened the door for the dogs, but they stayed inside the vehicle. Before I reached the shop door, the mayor had opened it, and the thrift shop dogs beelined to my open car door. Darlene and the mayor came outside, and she locked the door. Darlene waved and headed to her car.

"Ready?" The mayor closed the car door and headed to his vehicle. We followed him to the bank, and he followed us home.

After we were all inside, and I locked the door, Mayor tapped his horn twice and left.

I opened Mia's carrier and filled the two inside water bowls before I sat at the kitchen table with my lunch of peach yogurt and crackers and hot tea. After I ate, I carried out my cup of tea. I filled the dogs' outside water bowl, closed my eyes, and listened to the birds while the dogs romped.

Colonel nudged my arm. My empty cup was on the porch next to me. When I rose, I was stiff. *Guess it's time to be lazy inside.*

The dogs followed me inside and stretched out on the cool floor. I lingered in a hot shower to ease my aching muscles. Afterwards, I dressed in my favorite pink sweatpants, oversized hot pink T-shirt, and soft, fluffy pink sox. I propped up my feet on the sofa and started the next book in a series that was new to me. I loved the main character and her dog. *They should be here to help me solve this mess.*

I was deep into my book when Mandy and Pepper scrambled to the front door. Roxie sauntered to the back door, and Colonel stayed by my side. *The pack's on duty.*

I glanced at the clock on my way to the door and raised my eyebrows. *Six o'clock. I'm not sure I brushed my hair after my shower.* When I opened the door, the mayor carried in two large picnic baskets. He wore jeans and a Bulldogs T-shirt. Barbara had pulled her shoulder-length, gray hair back with a royal blue ribbon and tied the bow on top of her head, but wisps of fine, curly hair escaped around her face. She held a pie plate with two hot pads.

"Oh good," she said. "You're in sweats too. My evening gown is at the cleaners." Her chortle had musical notes that swirled their magic around the room as she modeled her royal blue sweatpants.

"Come in. Can I carry anything?"

The two of them bustled past me to the kitchen. The mayor set down the baskets on the table and returned to his car. After he brought in a small overnight case and headed to the bedroom, he said, "Don't let its size fool you. We have enough in here for two weeks. Barbara is an efficient packer."

Barbara placed the pie in the oven and turned the dial to a low setting. "Oh look," She pointed to the hallway. "You have shadows. Do they bother you? Shoo." She waved a tea towel at them, and they scurried down the hall away from her.

When the mayor returned from the spare bedroom, he said, "I'll take the dogs out back until you call us in for dinner. Don't wait too long. The dogs might be hungry." He opened the back door, and the dogs trotted outside.

Barbara placed fried chicken in the oven, the ice cream in the freezer, and the rest of the meal in the refrigerator. When she turned, she stared at me and furrowed her brow. "Sorry. Didn't you know you had shadows?"

"No one else has ever seen them," I said.

"Well, that makes sense. They came home with you from prison, didn't they?"

I nodded. "How did you know?"

Her eyes crinkled as she smiled. "I was in an orphanage for eleven years. Sometimes the shadows were my only friends, and sometimes they brought their friends, the nightmares. My parents adopted me when I was twelve. Twelve! Can you believe it? Who adopts a twelve-year-old, gangly, institution-hardened orphan? Only crazy people. Crazy, loving, wacky people that loved me no matter what."

She shook her head. "I learned in the orphanage to hide from people for my own safety."

"What about the shadows?" I asked.

"They helped me hide." She shrugged. "When do you want to eat?"

"Your folks sound awesome. I'm ready to eat any time. What do you need for me to do?"

"Pour sweet tea for the three of us. I told David he could talk to you during dinner; otherwise, he would have hovered until we put it on the table."

I snickered. "I'll call them in and feed the dogs and Mia. Does that give you enough time?"

"Perfect. We're having potato salad, oven fried chicken, white field peas, and dessert."

I opened the back door, and the mayor and the dogs barreled into the house. The mayor rushed to wash his hands while I filled the bowls with food. The dogs sat obediently as they waited for my signal while Mia circled my ankles. I raised my hand then pointed at their bowls. "Okay." The dogs dug in, and Mia scrambled to her food.

I poured the tea, and Barbara set our food on the table. As we passed the food around, the mayor asked, "What's your theory about the identity of the counterfeiter?"

After I helped myself to a generous serving of potato salad, I passed it to the mayor. "It's somebody who's been around for a long time because if Lloyd was right, he was an established counterfeiter before I went to college."

"Why not she?" Barbara asked.

"Lloyd was beaten and stabbed. I'm not sure a woman ten or fifteen years older than me could have done that." I served myself a small piece of chicken and a serving of field peas.

The mayor took the plate of chicken when I handed it to him. "Lloyd was not a frail man. Could an older man have beaten him?"

I finished chewing my last bite of potato salad. "Good point. Our counterfeiter may use a thug for his or her dirty work."

"Would the counterfeiter be married?" Mayor asked.

"Could be, but it's hard to keep a secret in a marriage, and if there were children—children are natural-born snoops," Barbara said.

"We may have stumbled onto a possible scenario for our elderly counterfeiter. What if the original counterfeiter retired and passed his business on to the son?" I asked.

"That narrows the prospects. I can think of a number of men who have retired in the past ten years, but only two have a son still here. Most of that younger generation left home for college and never came back." The mayor waved his fork as he spoke then set it on his plate when Barbara shook her head. "But since we're also talking Conway, I might call on the Conway mayor to talk over old times. Can I leave work early tomorrow, Donut Lady, to go to lunch in Conway?"

"Absolutely, and I'll talk to Darlene after I close the shop."

"Tomorrow night you two can compare notes, and we can decide if we should pursue another path." Barbara glanced around the table. "Anyone care for anything else? If not, discussion closed, and I'll serve dessert."

"I'm ready," the mayor said, and I nodded.

When Barbara placed the peach pie into our dessert bowls and scooped vanilla ice cream on top, a thrill of excitement ran down my back as the ice cream melted into the hot pie. *I should get out more.*

CHAPTER SIX

After we ate, the mayor took the dogs outside, Barbara wrapped and put away the leftovers, and I loaded the dishwasher and started it.

"Hot tea?" I asked. "My hot peach tea slows me down at night."

"I love my wild orange for the same reason. I'll start a pot of coffee for David. He knows he drinks decaf at night, but he likes to think it energizes him."

When the mayor and the dogs came inside, we settled down with our books in the living room and read. I realized I'd nodded off when Barbara said, "Ready to call it a night?" She patted the mayor's shoulder. "Let's go to bed, honey."

As the mayor and I rose, Barbara strolled to the hallway, pointed her finger, and glared. "No shenanigans tonight, you hear? Tell your friends to stay away, or you won't be allowed to remain in the house anymore. Your choice."

I took the dogs out back for one last romp. The tree frogs sang a hopeful song of rain, and the katydids and crickets joined in.

I peered at the clear night sky. "Nothing's forecasted, but if you say so, maybe an overnight shower will drift through." I glimpsed a figure at the end of the alley and stared until I realized a neighbor was walking their dog. When I opened the back door, Pepper led the parade into the house. Colonel was the last. He waited until I stepped inside then joined me.

The door to the second bedroom was closed. After the dogs settled, I turned off the lights, and the shadows slipped to my room ahead of me and slid under the closet door. I set my pen on the bedside table, climbed into bed, and closed my eyes.

* * *

I smiled when I woke. *Another good night.* As I dressed, I inhaled. *My favorite aroma. Coffee.* I stuck my pen into my pants pocket and followed the dogs to the kitchen. Barbara rose from the table, and her eyes twinkled as she smiled and poured me a cup. She wore black jeans, a red and white checked shirt, and sturdy brown oxfords.

I opened the back door, and the dogs trotted outside. I sat with Barbara at the table. "Thanks for the coffee. How did you know I was up?"

She chuckled. "Pepper told me. She nosed open our bedroom door and hopped up onto the bed. David slept right through it. I thought she wanted out, but when I opened the back door, she pranced to the stove."

I chuckled. "Smart girl."

"Don't let me slow you down from your usual routine. If you don't mind, I'll let David sleep in until his usual six o'clock. We'll lock up your house before we leave. He'll want to be at the shop early. Do you eat breakfast before you leave?"

"Not often. I feed the dogs then go to the shop."

"I'll leave lunch for you in the refrigerator and be back this evening. I'm sure you and David will be touching base this afternoon."

After I brought the dogs inside, I fed them and Mia. When I was ready to leave, I unzipped Mia's carrier by the front door, and she darted into the pantry.

"Guess Mia wants a dog break," Barbara said.

When the dogs and I went into the shop, Andrew smiled. "Good morning, Miss Lady. Did you have a nice sleepover?"

"We did. Thank you, Andrew. What's our plan for today?" I put on my pink sprinkles apron.

"The Library Executive Board meets today. Ms. Tiffany said they liked the bookworms, and she showed me how to make them. They can sit inside classic glazed donuts."

"Classic bookworms. We could make banned donuts if we dip one side of the donut in chocolate. We'll let the mayor tell the Board they are only half-clothed."

"Mayor tells funny stories. What about scones?"

"True crime strawberry-filled scones. I'll use strawberry jam for the blood."

Andrew checked his first batch of dough and mixed his second batch. I mixed my scones and rolled out the dough. While my scones baked, Andrew filled the large coffee maker with water, and I measured the coffee and turned on the machine.

I watched Andrew's quiet rhythm of efficiency and smiled. *I never realized how much security is wrapped into a predictable morning routine.*

After the scones had cooled, I drilled a small tunnel into each scone with a corkscrew and squirted strawberry jam inside each one. After I drizzled honey on top of the scones, we filled platters and display trays with donuts and scones.

"These scones are sticky." Andrew hurried to the sink to wash his hands.

"Helps gather fingerprints," I said, and Andrew laughed.

"Helps gather fingerprints," he echoed.

"We'll need tongs to remove scones from the display case."

"Yes, and tongs to put scones on the platters." Andrew hurried to the utensil drawer and removed three pairs of tongs.

When the mayor came in, Roxie and Mandy met him at the door. "I'll take you later," he said. "Darlene's not at the thrift shop yet. Who has the meeting room today?" He tilted his head as I wrote on the specials board—*Banned donuts*, *Classic bookworm donuts*, and *Crime scene scones*—then peered into the display case.

"The Library Executive Board meets at eight thirty," I said.

"I see the classic bookworm donuts. What makes the chocolate donuts banned? Wait, don't tell me." The mayor tapped the case in thought. "Is it because they're only partially covered?"

"Yes," Andrew said.

"But I don't get the crime scene scones. I should taste one."

Andrew said, "but first—"

I put my finger over my lips, and Andrew giggled then continued, "I'll pour coffee for you and Miss Lady. While you pick up one and taste it." Andrew snickered as he poured two cups of coffee.

"I'm being set up, right?" Mayor asked.

"Yes, you are. Taste it," I said.

"Here goes." He reached into the case and pulled out a scone. He examined it then inspected the pads of his fingers. "Why is it sticky?"

"Helps gather fingerprints," Andrew said.

I smiled. "Andrew is right. You're guilty, and we have your fingerprints to prove it. Bite into it. Oh. Just a second." I handed him a napkin. "Hold it under your chin."

The mayor bit into his scone with care. "This is good." He gazed at his scone. "The blood is strawberry jam. It's a crime scene scone. You two are brilliant."

"Yes," Andrew said.

"We have damp handwipes the guilty ones can use to clean their hands. I'll give you a supply you can hand out."

"I'm glad I'm on your side." The mayor washed his hands. "What made you think of honey?"

"Helps gather fingerprints," Andrew said.

The mayor laughed as he set plates and napkins on the utility cart. "Of course."

The bell jingled as the sheriff opened the shop door. He paused to breathe in and exhale. "The Donut Hole smells just like it did when I was a kid, and the floorboards still squeak in the same spot. I should stop more often to soak it in."

He smiled as he strode to the counter. "Rough week. Nice to slow down a second." He read the board while I poured his coffee. "Bookworms, banned, and crime scene. Do you have a readers' group today?"

"Good guess. It's the library board."

"I'll need termite donuts next Tuesday. Suppose I could have a side of worms to go with the termites? I've got six applicants to interview for two deputy positions. Amazing, but the county finally approved the second position. Our applicants will have to get past termites, worms, and Tess. I shudder at the thought." He wiggled his eyebrows, and the mayor snickered.

I served him the two donuts and a scone. "Here are all three."

He ate the classic donut then held his nose as he held the bookworm in the air. He closed his eyes, dropped the bookworm into his mouth, and cringed as he chewed the worm. Andrew laughed, and the mayor and I chuckled.

"That was awesome, Sheriff," Andrew said.

The sheriff rose and bowed, and Andrew applauded.

After the sheriff sat and drained his cup, I refilled his coffee while he stared at the banned donut.

He smiled. "Half of the banned donut is covered, and the other half is bare. Half-naked donut deserves to be banned." He broke his donut into half and put the chocolate on top of the plain. "Now each bite is covered."

After he ate the donut, he stared at the scone. "This one is harder. Crime scene scone—do I lean over my plate while I take a bite?"

"You guessed it. That's exactly right," I said.

Andrew pursed his lips, and his eyes twinkled. The mayor stepped close to the display case to have a better view of the sheriff.

The sheriff glanced at the two men and narrowed his eyes. "There's a catch, isn't there?"

I shrugged. "Don't know why you'd think that."

The sheriff picked up the scone then pulled away a finger. He set his scone on the plate and tapped his finger and thumb together. "This is sticky."

Andrew burst out laughing. "Helps gather fingerprints."

The sheriff shook his head and leaned over his plate as he took a big bite of scone. Strawberry jam dripped onto his fingers and his plate. "This is really good. I'm bleeding." He held up his finger as it dripped jam onto the plate.

"You are awesome, Sheriff," I said as Andrew laughed even harder.

The mayor handed Sheriff a handwipe. "Might want to wait until you finish your crime scene scone before you wipe away the evidence."

Shirley bustled into the shop and grinned as she read the specials board. "I have no idea what any of that means, but I'll take one of each. Woody caught up on his homework last night and was ready for school when I got up. Were we ever that contrary, Karen? I'm sure you weren't, and I'm positive I wasn't."

"Shirley, I can't give you a scone because they are sticky and gooey when you bite into it, but you can have an extra free bookworm donut to make up for it."

Shirley smiled. "Gooey and sticky? Can I have one for Woody for his after-school snack?"

Andrew wrapped a scone with wax paper with care and placed it into a small sack by itself. He placed a bookworm donut with extra bookworms into another sack. "My friend Woody will like the crime scene scone and the bookworm donut."

"Why is the crime scene scone sticky?" Shirley peered into the sack.

"Helps gather fingerprints." Andrew laughed, and Shirley joined in.

The mayor wiggled his eyebrows as he stepped close to me and whispered, "You've created an obsessed crime scene technician."

Andrew placed a circle of wax paper on a second platter, arranged scones on it with care, and added tongs for the mayor. Shirley hummed while she waltzed out of the shop with her sacks and coffee.

I filled a metal mixing bowl with hand wipes and carried the bowl into the meeting room. "Do you think Woody will realize he challenged Shirley to be fun? I never knew Shirley to back away from a challenge. The room looks—" My eyes widened at the sight of the yellow ribbon that weaved around the scone and donut platters on the side table. "Where did you find crime scene tape?"

"Andrew told me that Woody picked up items for the specials. When I looked in the storeroom to see what else might be there besides food, I found a basket on the bottom shelf back in the corner with odd items. I'd never noticed it before."

"The library board will love it. I'm looking forward to seeing Monica. I think she's been out of town."

All the board members were in the room before eight thirty. Mayor winked as he closed the door, and I smiled at the roar of laughter and applause.

The mayor opened the door. "Andrew, the board wants to know why the scones are sticky. Will you come tell them?"

Andrew marched into the room, and the mayor hushed everyone and said, "Remember that Andrew doesn't like loud noises. Maybe you can snap your fingers. Okay, Andrew."

"Helps gather fingerprints." Andrew bowed and left the meeting room as the board members elbowed each other, giggled, and snapped their fingers.

The mayor closed the door, and the noise in the room resumed.

"I like library people," Andrew said. "Ms. Monica isn't here."

"I know. I've missed her."

"Yes."

I smiled at Andrew's sweet affirmation.

My phone buzzed a text. *Amber.*

"Tentative new court date scheduled for next week. No specific day or time yet."

I frowned. *I'm afraid to be hopeful.*

Me: "What about Lloyd?"

Amber: "Dead issue. His lawyer quit."

I snickered. *Amber has a twisted sense of humor. Love it.*

After the board meeting was over and all the members left, I hurried into the pink room. "Mayor, Andrew and I can clean up if you'd like to leave early. Andrew is filling a bucket with warm soapy water, and I'll stack the dirty dishes and platters near the sink. He'll wipe down the sticky surfaces while I wait on customers. We've got it all covered."

The mayor narrowed his eyes. "Are you sure? The Conway mayor can go to lunch at eleven thirty but has a one o'clock meeting. Wouldn't mind not being rushed."

"Go. We've got this."

Mayor smiled. "Barbara said she'd take the dogs to the thrift shop. Do you think Darlene's there?"

"I'll check and let Barbara know. Everything's covered. Go snoop."

Mayor took off his apron and hurried out. I stacked the dishes onto the utility cart and rolled it to the sink. After I tossed the trash and scraped the dishes, I set them in the sink. Andrew placed the soapy solution and rinse water on the utility cart and rolled them into the meeting room.

I texted Darlene. "Ready for dogs?"

Darlene: "Yes, please."

I called Barbara. "Darlene is ready for Roxie and Mandy to come to the store. Andrew will help put them in your car."

"I'll be right there."

When Barbara parked in front of the donut shop, I said, "Andrew, would you put Roxie and Mandy in Ms. Barbara's car?"

Andrew hurried to the door and called the two dogs to go outside with him. He opened Barbara's back door, and the two dogs jumped inside. Barbara waved as she drove away.

While Andrew cleaned the sticky surfaces in the meeting room, I waited on customers.

When Judge Worley came into the shop, he set his briefcase on the reading table and scanned the room then frowned as he took a seat at the counter. "Where's Andrew?"

I poured a cup of coffee. "He's in the meeting room. The table and chairs need an extra scrubbing."

"I'll talk to him. What's a banned donut?"

When I explained it to him, he chuckled. "I'll take a banned donut. Be right back. I'll just take a few minutes of Andrew's time." He carried his cup to the meeting room and closed the door.

Colonel padded to the meeting room door and flopped down. "I don't know whether to mind my own business or rush in there with a broom to save Andrew."

The bell jingled, and a young mother pushed a stroller inside with a baby who wore a pink outfit and a pink ballcap.

"How cute," I said. "Here or to go? We have a few plain donut holes. Could the baby have one? What would you like?"

"I heard about the banned donuts. I'd like two. I'll share a bite or two of one with Missy and pretend like I got it for her, and a coffee to go for me."

I smiled as I poured her coffee and sacked up her donuts. "Nice of Missy to share. I'll get the door for you."

By the time the two of them left, the judge came out of the meeting room. He sat at the counter, and I refilled his cup. "Thank you, Karen. I'm glad I finally talked to Andrew. Long overdue."

He ate his banned donut before he rose to pay. "Has my cousin been here lately?"

"I'm not sure who that might be."

"Sorry. Bradley Sanford. He's the radiologist at the Conway hospital and lives in Conway. My mother and her brother were estranged, but she'd never say why. I guess sometimes families drift apart."

I nodded. "No, I'm not sure I've met him, but I'm sure he hasn't been in. Nobody's been in the door that I didn't know who they were by the time they left. Were you trying to get in touch with him?"

He strolled to his briefcase and pulled out a card. "He's a big guy— blond and his sparse eyebrows are almost invisible. His voice is gravelly. If you don't mind, shoot me a quick text if he comes in. I'd like to run into him casual-like in case there's still hard feelings I don't know about. I've got some family photos he might like to have."

I smiled and accepted his card. "I'll do that. My mother's family scattered. I've never thought about trying to find anybody."

Not long after the judge left, Andrew came out of the meeting room.

I shook my head. "The honey was more of a mess than I expected. We won't do that again. Next time, we'll use powdered sugar to track fingerprints. It will be easier to clean."

Andrew poured the buckets into the sink and wrung out his cloths. "People laughed and had fun, especially Ms. Shirley and the mayor."

"That's true."

After the last donut and scone sold, Andrew loaded Pepper and Colonel into my car while I locked the shop. After we were home, Mia raced to meet us at the door then scampered down the hallway.

I raised my eyebrows when Mia pranced back, and the shadows followed her to the pantry. "Are the shadows your friends now, Mia?"

I poured a glass of sweet tea and carried it to the porch to relax while Pepper chased butterflies and Colonel lay in the grass and soaked up the warm rays of the sun. When Pepper trotted to the door, we went inside, and I opened the refrigerator and reached for my lunch plate. A second plate was on the shelf with it. I read the sticky note, *For Darlene.* My eyes misted. *Barbara has a thoughtful heart.*

My phone rang. *Tiffany.*

"Miss Lady, Aunt Gee's doctor arranged to transfer her to Asbury today for her rehabilitation and physical therapy. She's really excited. Her church ladies will look after her, and I know they'll keep her in line."

"That is great. I can check on her too."

"Aunt Gee said you would. Her doctor said if she behaves, she'll be released from the rehabilitation facility after four days. One more thing. She insisted that I go with Roger to his new job in Savannah. She made a good case, and to top it off, Aunt Gee scheduled her preacher to marry Roger and me tomorrow morning at ten at the rehab center chapel. Roger will talk to the sheriff. Can you juggle your schedule? You don't have to have any matron of honor clothes. Wear jeans and your apron, if you like. We don't care." Tiffany giggled.

"What a wonderful surprise. Andrew and I will figure it out. I wouldn't miss your wedding for anything. What I can do at this end for you? Is this a secret?"

"Not a secret. I'll call you after Aunt Gee, Roger, and I talk. I stepped into the hallway to call you real quick."

I placed our lunch plates in a bag along with silverware, paper cups, two placemats, and a thermos of sweet tea. I carried the sack to the car, and Colonel and Pepper jumped into the back.

When the dogs and I arrived at the thrift store, Mandy and Roxie waited inside near the door. When I opened it, Pepper dashed inside, and Colonel and I followed her.

"You're earlier than I expected, Karen. I haven't ordered our lunch yet." Darlene gave her pearl necklace a slight tug and pointed at the dogs. "I was surprised when Barbara brought Mandy and Roxie."

I shrugged. "Maybe Jack plans to pick her up later today. I'm glad you haven't ordered lunch because I brought leftovers. Barbara made oven-fried chicken for our dinner last night, and she left plates for both of us."

"I love leftovers. Let's eat our lunch in the back. I think Gee has a sign somewhere that says out to lunch and a clock with hands we can set to whatever time we wish. I think the sign is in one of the drawers of the desk I use. I'll find it."

Darlene handed me the sign, and I hung it on the door after I set the time. We headed to the back and selected a table for our lunch. I wiped off the table and set our places.

"What's new?" Darlene asked after she ate her first bite of chicken.

I told her about Gee and rehabilitation in Asbury and Tiffany and Roger's wedding.

"That is absolutely glorious. I'm happy for them."

We ate and chatted about the upcoming wedding until Darlene asked, "What is new on the crime front?"

"Mayor and I have a theory about the counterfeiter." I explained our latest guess of a long-time, local counterfeiter who retired and whose son or daughter had taken over the lucrative business.

"If the original counterfeiter was ten years younger than Dad, the child would be ten years younger than me. Both of them would have the cover of fulltime jobs, probably professionals or business owners. Not mechanics or carpenters because they work long hours, and not anyone who is an hourly employee. Maybe someone who works shifts could be available during the day at times. Just possibilities." Darlene tapped her fingers on the table. "But if I ignore all that, who could have gotten a job anywhere but stayed here because their family is here or in the general area? Actually, I can think of quite a few people. Want me to make a list?"

I raised my eyebrows. "I'd love it."

I gathered our dishes and placed them into my bag. Darlene headed to the front of the store. Before I went outside, I removed our lunch sign then continued to my car and set the sack of dishes on the front seat. When I came inside, Darlene was on her second page.

As she scribbled line after line, I said, "That's more than I expected."

"I'm giving you every possibility I can think of. The mayor can trim it down for you."

I left her alone to work while I dusted and polished furniture in the showroom.

My phone rang. *Mayor.*

"I'm glad I came to Conway. I have a few names, but more than that, the mayor's wife is ill, and he doesn't want to talk about her with anyone in Conway. He said she's improving, and he doesn't need any phony sympathy and people asking him every day how he's doing. We'll get together every month for lunch."

"Sometimes we take a path that turns out differently than we expected," I said.

"You're right. See you later."

I returned to my dusting and glanced at the showroom window. I frowned as a muscular man strode past the shop with a standard poodle-sized dog on a leash. The man wore dress slacks and a shirt and tie. I blinked. *Henry Worley?* By the time I reached the front, he was gone. I glanced at Darlene. She was still heads-down as she wrote furiously on her pad. *Is she listing everyone she's ever known?*

I found furniture oil in the back and rubbed down a small table that had dried out. When I found a loose drawer handle, I went to the back to search for the right sized Phillips screwdriver. My phone rang. *Tiffany.*

"Roger and I are headed home. Did I already tell you that Roger talked to the sheriff? Roger asked Thomas to be his best man to stand in for Isaiah. Aunt Gee cried when Roger told her; I called Tammy, and she cried too. Aunt Gee will be leaving in a half hour in a transport ambulance. I'm shaking from excitement. Can you believe Roger and I will be married tomorrow? Aunt Gee said to tell you she's arranged the important things like a cake, flowers, and a photographer. Roger and I have had our rings since forever."

When she took a breath, I smiled. "Your Aunt Gee is a well-oiled machine. I'm glad she's up to taking charge."

Tiffany continued, "I'm not sure I realized how awesome she was when I was a kid. I certainly didn't appreciate her when I first came back from prison."

"Roger wants Woody at the wedding. Would you ask Shirley for us? Of course, Shirley is welcome. Roger and I are working on our packing list for the clothes we'll need. Roger found an unfurnished apartment in Savannah and signed a lease. I'll have time to get the basics and pull together the apartment before my classes start in three weeks."

After Tiffany hung up, I called Shirley and told her about the wedding. When I said Roger wanted Woody there, she cried and said she'd call me back.

Darlene smiled when I hung up. "What's the latest?"

I told her about the new details.

"Do you suppose Thomas could make a delivery to Savannah? It's a lot to ask," she said.

I raised my eyebrows. "That's an excellent idea."

"I'll call Thomas and see what he thinks before we pick out some furniture and dishes for them."

"Another option would be Jack if he can leave the county. I'll call the sheriff."

"I like that. Thomas won't have to miss any school. I'll pick out a few things for us to consider."

I sent the sheriff a text. "Call when you're available. No emergency. No rush."

My phone rang. *Sheriff.*

"I'm a block away from the thrift store. I'll be right there. Is this about another crime or the wedding?"

"Wedding."

The sheriff hung up, and I snickered. "He'll be right here. He just happened to be a block away."

Darlene snorted.

The sheriff strode into the shop, and the dogs lined up to greet him. After Sheriff petted each one, the four dogs dashed to Darlene and sat for a treat. She pulled a dog treat stash out of her walker side bag and gave one to each dog. *Just as I suspected.*

Sheriff smiled. "Roger called me about the wedding. I think they found a way to speed up Gee's healing."

He leaned against the old-fashioned wooden bar Darlene had found buried in the backroom and rubbed its smooth top then propped up his foot on the brass rail. "This is a nice piece. Emma would never let me have it."

"We thought of something we could do for Roger and Tiffany," I said. "We can pick out a few pieces of furniture for their apartment in Savannah. First we thought Thomas could deliver the furniture, but he's standing in for Isaiah, and we realized he might miss his Monday classes. Another idea we had was that Jack could use his truck to haul the furniture, but I wanted to get your opinion. I'm assuming Jack's available except I don't know if he's restricted to the county or something, and we don't know why he hasn't picked up Roxie."

"I might have another idea. Let me see what I can come up with. I'll get back to you." The sheriff tipped the brim of his ballcap and strode out the door.

"He didn't say anything. Did you notice?" Darlene asked.

"He sure didn't. We could pick out a sofa, lamp, table, and a dining set for basics. We might be limited by towing capacity, but I have no idea how to judge that."

"Let's pick out furniture, and I'll write down our list then we can prioritize."

I scanned the room. "Do we try to pick out contemporary furniture?"

Darlene snickered. "If we stay away from ruffles, we'll call it contemporary."

We started with the sofas. We checked each one for wear. After I handed the cushions to Darlene, she sniffed them for odors. We removed cushion covers and examined the condition of the foam rubber. We found one that was promising, but when I sat, I wasn't comfortable.

"My feet don't touch the floor, and the cushions are too deep," I said.

Darlene snorted. "Both Tiffany and Roger are quite a bit taller than you are. That one might be just right for them." She recorded a description of the sofa and its inventory number.

"What about the matching chairs?" I asked.

"Ugh. Matching. But let's check them anyway."

I pushed down on the seat of one. "I think this chair has springs, but they feel broken." I sat in the other chair. "At least it's comfortable." I flipped the cushion over. "Looks like cigarette burns. We don't even have to check the odor."

We examined and checked furniture until the sheriff parked in front. "That was a successful trip," the sheriff said when he came inside. "I went to the hardware store because they have truck and van rentals to see if there was something I could drive to Savannah. I haven't had any time off in ages, but Jeff was buying new tools and overheard my plan. He wanted to help Roger and Tiffany too. He'll drive the truck, and Andrew will go along. Jeff and Andrew are old buddies. Andrew's dad offered a free rental for the weekend, and I said I'd pay for the gas. Jeff and Andrew will be here in an hour to load the truck. How are you doing?"

"We have living room furniture, lamps, tables, a dining set, bedroom furniture, but no mattress or box springs. We did find a nice bedframe with a headboard, but we couldn't agree on a king or queen-sized bed and decided Roger and Tiffany could get what they want."

"I have some sturdy dishes and silverware I've never used. Everything's already boxed up. Maybe Jeff can drop by this evening or in the morning to pick up the boxes," Darlene said.

"That's a good idea," Sheriff said. "Emma has some new towels that were a gift, but they are tan, and she wants more color in the bathroom. Jorge set up a wedding fund at the gas station."

My phone rang as the sheriff left. *Shirley.*

"I'm in the parents' loop at school. I never thought I'd ever be a parents' loop natural, but I—Hey! No cuts! Get back in line. Can you believe some people? Think they can breeze in twenty minutes late and zip to the front of the line. Uh oh. The principal just sent her around the loop. She's four cars behind where she would have been if she'd followed the rules in the first place. See, that's what you get. I'll call you back, Karen. We're rolling."

Darlene raised her eyebrows after I hung up.

"Shirley. She's picking up Woody at school, and you don't want the details. She'll call back after they are home."

My phone rang. *Mayor.*

Before I answered, Darlene chuckled. "Have you ever had this many calls in one day?"

CHAPTER SEVEN

When I answered, the mayor said, "Just heard about the wedding. Did you plan on closing the donut shop for the day?"

My eyes widened. "My brain is on slow motion. I hadn't thought about it."

He chuckled. "It's a lot to process, isn't it? Amber, Barbara, and I can run the shop for you tomorrow if you and Andrew make the donuts and scones. Would that work?"

"That's wonderful, Mayor. I really appreciate it."

After we hung up, I shook my head. "The mayor and his family offered to run the donut shop while I'm at the wedding. People are amazing, aren't they?"

Darlene smiled. "It's why we live here."

When Alfred parked in front of the shop, I said, "I wonder if Shirley was supposed to tell me Alfred was on his way?"

Alfred smiled as he entered the shop. "I'm here to pick up Roxie. Did Shirley have a chance to call you?"

"She called, but she was in the parents' loop and had to hang up."

Alfred nodded. "She's passionate about the parents' loop. Here, Roxie."

Roxie trotted to Alfred, and he scratched her ears. "Hello, pretty girl. Ready to go?"

"Where are you going?" I asked.

He stopped at the door and furrowed his brow. "To Jack's."

He headed out the door, and Roxie followed him. Mandy stared as Roxie left before she flopped next to Darlene who reached down and stroked her back. "We're thrift store kind of gals, aren't we?"

"One surprise after another today, and not all were pleasant." I frowned.

"I've known Alfred a long time," Darlene said. "I've never known him to be a dognapper."

"I don't know what's going on, but I'll text Jack. What do you think?"

"I've always been a fan of the direct method."

I picked up the phone and sent the text. "What's up?"

When I showed my phone to Darlene, she nodded.

A customer came into the shop. Darlene smiled and greeted her as she patted her pearls. I filled out bright yellow sold tags and put them on the furniture we'd selected for Roger and Tiffany.

My phone rang, and I stepped out front to answer. *Tammy.*

"Hello, Miss Lady. I wanted to check up on Pepper. How's she doing?"

I told her stories about Pepper and Mia and how much Pepper loved running the yard with the ball that Colonel threw for her. "You were right, Tammy. She fits right in with the big dogs. Sometimes she acts like she's Colonel's sister."

Tammy giggled. "I'm glad she's with you. I always took her to work with me. She loves the company of other dogs. I talked to Tiffany. Isaiah and I are excited that Aunt Gee is on her way to Asbury. She'll be much happier surrounded by her friends. I talked to Isaiah's doctor and asked when Isaiah will be well enough for rehabilitation too. He said he'd have a better idea next week, but he's encouraged by how well Isaiah is doing."

"That's exciting news. I know you're relieved."

"I sure am. My cousin left yesterday afternoon after we moved me to a hotel that has an around the clock shuttle and is cheaper and closer to the hospital. I was glad she agreed to leave. She was getting anxious about her job."

"It will be easy to find someone to pick you up and bring you home. Let me know when, and I'll take care of it."

"Thank you. I told Isaiah's nurse I planned to pester Isaiah's doctor until he kicked Isaiah out of his hospital. She said she had every confidence in me. She's a hoot." Tammy giggled.

"Thanks for calling, Tammy. It was great to hear your news." After we hung up, I headed into the shop. *I'd expected Jack to call or at least send a grumpy text.*

After the customer left, I said, "Tammy called. She was checking up on Pepper. She's pestering Isaiah's doctor."

Darlene nodded. "Tammy's a sweet girl, but I'm not surprised she's ferocious when it comes to Isaiah. Any response from Jack?"

"No. I don't know if he's being stubborn or a jerk."

Darlene glanced out the window. "There goes Henry Worley and his dog. We were all worried about him until he got his new dog."

"I thought I saw him a few times near my house." I furrowed my brow, and Darlene stared at me.

"I forget sometimes you haven't always been here and may not know about Henry."

I sat in a soft chair near Darlene. "I don't remember him."

"Henry and his wife had a special needs son almost twenty years ago. In those days, all the special needs children were in one class at school. Henry's son was small and a target for bullies until Andrew befriended him. Somehow, Andrew taught him to have confidence in himself, and the bullies moved on. Henry and his son found a dog at the animal shelter twelve years ago and would walk their dog together every morning and evening. Andrew would often join them on their walks. The boy's health improved, and he became stronger."

"You're right. I didn't know about any of this."

Darlene furrowed her brow. "Henry's wife and son were on their way home from the grocery store when a drunk driver slammed into their car. They were killed instantly. Henry took an extended leave from work, and no one saw him except when he walked the dog. We were all worried last year when the dog died, but he adopted an older dog, Maisie—boxer and pit bull mix—from the animal shelter. The dog had been there for quite a while. Turns out the unadoptable canine just needed the right person, but isn't that how it goes? The two of them have followed the same route that Henry and his son walked together every day."

"He came to the shop and talked to Andrew this morning."

"Did he? We had the theory that being around Andrew reminded him of his son."

"You might be right. Maybe Judge Worley is healing."

Shirley and Woody parked in front of the shop. When they came inside, the three dogs swarmed Woody, and he laughed as he took them outside.

"When I told Woody I planned to call you back, he asked why we didn't come to the thrift shop. I think he misses the dogs, don't you? When he comes back inside, I'll let you tell him about the wedding." Shirley peered at the furniture. "I haven't been here in a while. Gee has a great eye for style, doesn't she? What a perfect—"

"Darlene and I have picked out furniture for Tiffany and Roger's apartment, and the sheriff arranged for a truck to transport their furniture, but we don't know what to do about a bed."

"I can take care of that. What size bed were you thinking? It needs to be a king-sized bed. They'll need a bedframe too. Does Gee have a king-sized headboard? I don't see any. Why don't you check the back? Is it okay if Woody stays here for a bit? I don't think I can drag him away." Shirley stepped to the door. "I'm going shopping, Woody. You can stay here if you like, or you can go with me. Your choice."

"I'll stay with Miss Lady and the dogs." Woody and the dogs came inside, and Shirley bustled to her car.

"That was easy," Darlene said. "A bit hard on the ears, though."

I smiled. "Woody, Aunt Gee will come to Asbury today to finish healing before she can go home, and Tiffany and Roger are getting married tomorrow. The wedding will be at the rehabilitation center where Aunt Gee is staying, and they want you there."

He peered at my face. "I'm not the flower girl, am I?"

I swallowed my laugh, and Darlene fake-sneezed.

"Bless you," I said automatically then cleared my throat. "No, they just want you there."

He grinned. "In that case, I'll be there. Does Mama Shirley know? She may come back from shopping with a suit for me, if she does."

I chuckled. "I hadn't thought about that. I'll bet you're right."

Forty-five minutes later, Shirley parked in front of the thrift shop, and Woody peered out the window and giggled. "We win. I see a suit on a hanger."

When Shirley came inside, she said, "I found a mattress, box springs, and frame at the new furniture store. Do you think the sheriff could have the truck swing by to pick it up? I'm not sure they could deliver it here today. The salesclerk told me their truck was out making deliveries. Alfred wanted to pay for the new bed. He's a wonderful man."

"That is awesome, Shirley. I'll call the sheriff."

I stepped outside to make my call. As I hung up, Shirley and Woody came out of the shop.

"We can't stay. Woody needs to try on his new suit. I want to be sure it fits. Alfred said he'll teach Woody how to tie a full Windsor knot. I don't even know what that is. Woody is good at finding videos for us to watch to learn things. Did you know you can learn how to do almost anything from videos? What will you wear, Karen? Do you want us to shop for a dress for you? We have plenty of time and don't mind a bit."

"Thanks for the offer, but I already have my dress."

Woody glared at me, and I stared at the ground. *Busted.*

The two of them climbed into Shirley's car and left. When I returned to the shop, Darlene asked, "What's wrong?"

"Woody caught me in a tiny lie. I said I already have a dress to wear tomorrow."

"Of course, you don't. What's your plan?"

"I don't know."

"Why don't you give Emma a call to go shopping with you? Or Barbara? The dogs and I will nap."

I called Barbara, and she suggested we meet at the downtown boutique. When I entered the shop, Whitney, the shop owner, and Barbara were waiting.

"We've selected five dresses for you to try on," Barbara said. "They are in the first dressing room."

I trudged to the dressing room. *Maybe this was a mistake.* I stared at the dresses. *I don't like any of them.*

Barbara stood outside the dressing room door. "Pick one and put it on for a better perspective. Dresses always look different when you try them on."

I sat on the small chair in the dressing room and glared at the ugly dresses as I felt the material of each one. I selected the royal blue A-line with cap sleeves because it didn't grate between my fingers when I touched it. *Cotton. I like the color.* I slipped it on and peered at myself in the mirror. *This is nice.*

When I walked out, Whitney and Barbara giggled.

"I said you'd pick the blue one. It looks good on you. How does it feel?" Barbara asked.

"More comfortable than I expected."

"You can try on the rest if you like," Whitney said.

I glanced at my feet. "It's perfect, but I need shoes."

"I have a few styles of dress shoes. Navy would work. Pick out a style, and I'll see if I have your size," Whitney said.

"I like this one." I pointed to a simple pair of flats.

Whitney returned with two pairs. The first one was too tight, but the second pair was a good fit.

"This was easy," Whitney said as we headed to the register. "Do you want a small purse or a scarf?"

"No. I'm shopped out."

"I'll bring your dress and shoes when we come this evening. You'll have the dogs with you when you leave the thrift shop," Barbara said.

Whitney handed Barbara the dress on a hanger with the boutique logo and a paper sack with the shoes inside. Barbara left while I was paying.

When I returned to the thrift shop, Darlene raised her eyebrows. "I didn't expect you back this fast. Did you find something?"

I rolled my eyes. "I was ambushed. Whitney and Barbara had already selected dresses for me to try on, and I had the feeling I couldn't leave until I picked one. Barbara will bring the dress to my house this evening to save it from the dog hair."

Darlene chuckled. "Glad you survived."

A truck rumbled to the front of the store and parked. Jeff and Andrew hopped out, and Jeff threw open the rolling door in the back of the truck. Andrew pulled out a dolly, and Jeff slid out a ramp. Andrew wore a hardware store ballcap.

"We picked up the bed. We'd like to balance our load. Can you give us a tour of what else goes into the truck?" Jeff said.

"I have some boxes at my house for Tiffany," Darlene said. "Will you have time to pick them up after you load?"

"Sure will, Ms. Darlene," Jeff said.

As I showed Jeff each piece, Andrew carried the smaller items to the front. Jeff and Andrew conferred before Jeff marked a number on each sold tag to indicate the order to be loaded. When passersby gathered outside the shop to watch them load, Darlene pointed to a blue vase with painted white roses.

Andrew carried a small table out for me, and I placed the vase on the table. "If you'd like to pitch in for Tiffany and Roger's wedding, here's a tip jar."

When the folks laughed and applauded, Andrew bowed, and we went inside.

Darlene filled out the day's deposit slip. "I'll go home and pull the boxes for Tiffany if you'll do the banking and close up."

"We'll handle it, Darlene."

She put the bank bag on the desk and the list she'd made on top. I folded the list and stuck it into my purse.

Andrew loaded the next item, the heavy dresser, on his dolly. When he reached the ramp, two of the bystanders helped push the dresser into the truck. With the extra help, all the items were soon loaded. Andrew set his dolly in the back, and Jeff pulled down the door and slid the ramp into its slot. Jeff honked as they drove away, and the crowd cheered.

I locked the door and loaded up the dogs, and we headed to the bank. Mandy curled up on the floorboard, Pepper pranced from one window to the other, and Colonel leaned his chin on the back of the passenger's seat and peered at the windshield. While I was in line, my phone buzzed with a text. *Monica.*

"What are your dinner plans?"

I called Barbara. "Would you mind if I invited Monica to dinner tonight?"

"That sounds like fun. Hasn't she been out of town? It will be nice to hear where she went."

The line inched up one more car. *Nothing moves fast in Georgia.*

I texted Monica. "Come to my house at six. Mayor & Barbara are guarding me."

Monica: "Formidable. See you at six."

I chuckled. "Would you call the mayor and Barbara formidable, Colonel? Maybe Barbara."

When we reached the drive-up window, Mandy joined Colonel and put her head on the front seat; Colonel shifted to the window on my side and placed his head on my shoulder. Mandy scooted closer to Colonel, and Pepper yipped when she realized she'd been blocked by the big dogs. She stood close to Mandy and jumped to see out of the side window.

"You got yourself a regular circus of green-eyed monsters there, don't you, Ms. Donut Lady?" The bank teller chuckled as he pulled in the bank bag. He sent out treats for the three dogs. He included three more treats with the deposit receipt. The big dogs barked their appreciation, and Pepper yip-yapped.

After I pulled away from the drive-in window, the dogs settled down, and I gave each one a treat before I pulled out of the bank exit and onto the road. After I opened the back door for the dogs, we trooped inside the house. Before I closed the door, I frowned at the figure with a dog on a leash at the end of my block. Judge Worley scanned the area as he strode with his dog.

"The judge looks more like a sentry than a man taking a leisurely walk with his dog."

I headed to the sofa to relax but remembered the dirty dishes I'd left in my trunk. I popped my trunk, carried the dishes inside, and placed them in the dishwasher. "I could do laundry, vacuum and mop, or read."

I grabbed my book and settled on the sofa to dive into the story. When Mandy whined, I glanced at the clock. "It's five thirty. Let's go out back. We could use a stretch and some fresh air."

Colonel and Mandy explored, Pepper romped, and I rocked. When I heard the faint tap at the front door, I hurried inside and opened the door for the mayor and Barbara.

"Jeff has our boxes for Tiffany and Roger. We caught him before he parked the truck for the night in the sheriff's compound," the mayor said.

"I'm trying out a new recipe." Barbara put a foil-covered casserole into the oven. "It's actually an adaptation of an old recipe. David wanted lasagna and salad tonight, but I made it with chicken because I can't eat beef anymore. We're having cheesecake with blueberries. I haven't made a cheesecake in ages, and this was a perfect excuse to dust off my recipe. Almost forgot—I'll get your dress and shoes out of the car."

When Barbara returned, she carried my boutique dress and shoes to my room. "I hung your dress in your closet and left the sack on your dresser. Where's Roxie?"

"Thank you. Alfred picked up Roxie at the thrift shop for Jack."

"Oh, really?" Barbara raised her eyebrows.

I shrugged and handed the mayor Darlene's list, and he flipped through the papers.

"Comprehensive list," he mumbled.

"She didn't try to trim it at all," I said.

He glanced at Barbara. "I'll give it a first pass later."

The mayor set the table for four, and I fed the dogs and Mia while Barbara tossed and dressed the salad.

At six o'clock, Monica tapped on the door and came inside.

"Something smells good. Lasagna?" she asked.

"Good nose. I'm ready to hear where you've been."

Barbara set the salad on the table and placed the casserole dish on a hot pad. "Let's eat while we listen."

After we all sat at the table, Barbara served each plate with lasagna, and we passed around the salad.

"Six months ago, I applied for a grant for our county for a reading specialist to work with children and adults at the library," Monica said. "I was inspired by your experience teaching in the prison and teaching Woody to read, Karen. I used you as a model."

"Now you're a model, Karen. What an illustrious resume." Mayor smiled.

Monica took a bite of lasagna. "Mmm. This is delicious, Barbara." She stabbed her salad. "I got a call from the foundation that sponsored the grant to present my proposal. I don't know how many were submitted, but there were three of us who were finalists. The top three were funded at one hundred, seventy-five, and fifty percent, depending on the order of award. The first day, we explained our proposals, although we weren't allowed to listen to each other's presentations. I would have enjoyed hearing their ideas. The second day, we went through a round of questions, and I must say, they were thorough almost to the point of being brutal. This morning, the awards were presented, and our county received the highest award. Not only were we first, but we're also invited to submit our findings for a follow up award next year."

Monica beamed and stabbed her salad.

Barbara's eyes filled. "That's the best news I've ever heard."

The mayor nodded. "We need a parade or fireworks."

"Let's eat. We can share all our news after dessert," Barbara said.

After the meal was over, I cleared our dishes while Barbara served our cheesecake with blueberries.

"Your cheesecake is wonderful," Monica said.

"Mmm. Sure is." I licked blueberries off my top lip.

After we finished our dessert, I told Monica about Gee, Isaiah, Tiffany, and Roger. Mayor joined in with details as I told her about Lloyd and our latest theory about the two-generation counterfeiting business.

"Are you thinking that counterfeiter junior murdered Lloyd and thinks you know something, Karen?"

"That's our latest theory. Darlene gave me a long list of fathers and offspring for the mayor to trim down."

Monica nodded. "I brought you copies of my proposal. Would it be okay if I work with you, Mayor?"

"Absolutely."

Barbara loaded the dishwasher and started it before she and I read the proposal while the mayor and Monica pored over the lists. Mayor used a pencil to mark off the second generation that had left the area.

"Ready for a second pass?" he asked. "Might be a judgement call, but let's mark off the families with jobs that aren't flexible enough for them to be away at odd times. I don't think I'm saying that very well."

"I think I understand. Let's give it a try," Monica said.

I opened the door for the dogs. Barbara and I moved to the sofa to continue reading the proposal while Monica and the mayor argued.

"This is really good. What do you think, Karen? Is it workable?" Barbara asked.

"Absolutely. Monica's developed different approaches for each subgroup she defined. For example, she doesn't have a generic plan for adults, but instead, she starts with identifying reading deficits, and her approach fits the person's needs. She has a similar approach for children, except it is age-appropriate."

Barbara narrowed her eyes. "What were Woody's deficits?"

"Woody actually had three. First, he was hungry. Nobody can learn when the tummy rumbles. Second, he was ADHD; third, he was dyslexic. There's a fourth one I'd forgotten about—he was exhausted. All correctable except dyslexia which takes a little longer the older the child is."

"Monica's proposal states she plans to use experts to mentor her reading specialist. Did you see your name flashing in lights like I did?" Barbara giggled.

I grumbled. "I don't have time for anything like that."

"If you say so." Barbara rolled her eyes, and I opened the back door and called the dogs inside.

My phone buzzed a text. *Tiffany.* "We're in Asbury at the nursing and rehabilitation center. Aunt Gee will be here soon. We're exhausted. See you tomorrow."

Me: "Thanks."

"I just heard from Tiffany. They are in Asbury at the center and expect Gee soon."

"Good news." Barbara yawned as she rose.

"How are you two doing?" Mayor asked. "Monica and I have been through the list twice, and we're calling it quits for the night. Monica had a long drive today, and we've got an early day tomorrow."

"Thanks for letting us read your proposal, Monica. We have some questions, but maybe we can get back together Sunday or Monday for dinner?" I asked, and Barbara nodded.

Monica rose and stretched. "Sounds good. Let me know. I am tired."

After Monica left, Barbara said, "Monica is really dedicated to reading. I love her proposal. I see why it came in first. Do you care for any hot tea?"

"I think I'd like to go straight to bed. I'll take my book, but I have a feeling I won't last long. I have to leave the door open for the dogs, but don't worry about disturbing me."

I snuggled in my bed and read. An hour later, I turned off my light and realized the rest of the house was dark. *They slipped off to bed.* I rolled over and snuggled with my soft pillow and fluffy blanket.

* * *

A low growl woke me. *Dream?* I peered at the clock. *It's only two.* Colonel growled again. When I tiptoed down the hallway and peered into the living room, Colonel and Mandy nosed the front door. I glanced at the back door, and Pepper was poised with her teeth bared. I padded back to my bedroom and peeked out of my window.

A large man strolled away from my driveway and headed to the end of the block. I narrowed my eyes a few minutes later when a car rounded the corner where the man had disappeared and crept toward my house.

The car stopped at my driveway, and I stepped away from the window. The car continued on, and the dogs trotted to my bedroom and flopped down.

If they're okay, I'm okay. I climbed into bed. *I'll talk to the sheriff tomorrow.*

The aroma of perking coffee woke me at four. I hurried to the kitchen for a cup. *No dogs?*

When I reached the kitchen, Barbara set a cup of hot coffee on the kitchen table and smiled. "The dogs came out of your room when I started the coffee. I let them out, but the three of them are sitting on the porch and didn't want to come in."

I yawned. "The dogs woke me at two. I saw a man in the driveway, but he was leaving. I don't know if he heard the dogs growl—Colonel and Mandy weren't very loud. Pepper was ready for battle at the back door. After he left, the dogs settled down."

"I thought I heard something too." Barbara frowned. "I still have nightmares, but they aren't quiet."

I sipped my coffee. "Now that you mention it, I've never had a quiet nightmare either." After I finished my coffee, I hurried to dress.

When I returned to the kitchen, Barbara asked, "What time do you want to leave the shop? Are you taking the dogs when you leave for the shop?"

"I'll leave at nine thirty. The wedding's at ten. I'll take the dogs with me this morning."

I raised my eyebrows at the sweet, familiar aroma of donuts as they sizzled in the fryer when I opened the shop door.

"Did you get here extra early?" I asked as the dogs rushed inside, and I locked the door behind us.

"Yes," Andrew said.

I hurried to the storeroom for my apron. "What's our plan?"

"Mama and I found small sugar wedding bells yesterday. Wedding bell donuts. Mama said we need something blue. Blueberry scones?"

"I love the idea. Our wedding bell donuts can be something new. Pink-sprinkled donuts were one of Mr. Otto's original signature donuts. That can be something old. What can we do for something borrowed?"

"Mama said sometimes Ida's Diner makes tiny tarts. We could borrow her recipe."

I called Ida's Diner, and Mary Rose, my favorite waitress, answered. "What's up, Donut Lady? You got a Tiffany and Roger wedding emergency?"

I smiled. "I actually do. Andrew and I are planning our pastries for the day and ran into a snag for something borrowed. We were looking for something we could borrow; Andrew suggested the small tart recipe, or maybe we could borrow the tart pans."

"That's a good idea. I'll call you right back."

I mixed the dough for the blueberry scones and decorated the pink-sprinkled donuts.

When my phone rang, it was Mary Rose. "We'll have eight dozen miniature cherry tarts to you before seven. Will that be enough? What else are you doing?"

"That's great. We'll have wedding bell donuts with tiny sugar bells for new, pink-sprinkled donuts for old, and blueberry scones for something blue."

"We'll settle up later for the loan of tarts." Mary Rose giggled as she hung up.

It'll be worth it.

I scooted my stepladder to the specials board and took it down. After I wrote *Something Old, Something New, Something Borrowed, Something Blue* on the board, I hung it back in its place. "I forgot to check the calendar. Do we have a meeting this morning?"

"Yes. The quilting team."

"Good. It's a small group." I smiled. *And only a bit rowdy.*

By six-thirty, Andrew and I had all the donuts and scones ready for the day. Mary Rose parked in front then tapped on the door, and I hurried to unlock it. Andrew and the three dogs followed me.

Mary Rose crouched to snuggle Colonel and pet Mandy and Pepper, and her black hair that she had twisted on top of her head and held in place with a hair clip escaped and tumbled into her face. She pulled her hair away as she stood and reclipped it at the back of her neck. "Happens all the time." She laughed. "I keep threatening to cut it. The tarts are on the back seat."

Andrew strode to her car and lifted out the flat boxes, and I closed the door.

"You might want to refrigerate them," Mary Rose said. "They have a tiny dollop of whipped cream on top." She hugged Colonel. "Sorry. I have to go back to work. Ms. Karen, we've missed you and Colonel. Come have breakfast with us. How about tomorrow?" She grinned and climbed into her car.

After I was inside, Andrew said, "Look, Miss Lady. There's a tiny leaf on each one. I think it's mint."

We admired the tarts. "These are beautiful. Set one aside for your break, Andrew."

Andrew grinned. "Two."

The bell jingled as the sheriff came inside, and he raised his eyebrows as he read the board. "You two have outdone yourselves. I thought you might do something for the upcoming nuptials, but this is genius. I'll take one of each."

I poured two cups of coffee while Andrew plated the sheriff's pastries. After he served the sheriff, Andrew said in a loud, official voice, "Break." He marched to the refrigerator and pulled out the tarts. He set two plates on the counter and grinned.

I chuckled, and the sheriff laughed. "I see two new things on my plate—the wedding bell on the glazed donut and the cherry tart; something blue—the scone. Is the pink-sprinkled something old?"

"The tart isn't ours. We borrowed it from Ida's Diner," I said. "Andrew's idea."

I joined the sheriff at the counter. Andrew pulled off his mint leaf and popped the tart into his mouth. "We need tart tins. I could make tarts if you teach me, Miss Lady, or maybe you could find me a recipe, and I can read it." He hurried to scrub the pots and pans.

When the sheriff was on his second cup of coffee, the mayor and Barbara came into the shop. Barbara carried two white sparkly bells, and the mayor carried a box with white streamers that spilled out of one side.

"We thought we might decorate a little," Barbara said. "Amber will be here soon. She said we're not allowed to climb up on things. Did you know she's really bossy sometimes? Gets that from her father."

The mayor rolled his eyes, and the sheriff snorted.

I glared at them. "I'll get you an apron and a ballcap, Barbara. Today's group is the quilting club."

CHAPTER EIGHT

When Barbara shuddered, the mayor said, "I'll take care of the group, and Amber will manage the cash register and taking orders. I'll need donuts and scones—wait." He read the specials board. "There are four things listed. Do we have an extra donut or scone?"

"Neither." Sheriff explained each one. "You'll tell the story better."

"He surely will." Barbara smiled.

I hurried to the storeroom for Barbara's apron and cap and handed them to her. "I'll show you where the platters are for the meeting room and the trays for the display case."

"Thank you." Barbara popped on her hat at a rakish angle and tied her apron. "If you show me how you record the day's receipts and fill out the bank deposit, I can take care of that too."

"I assumed the wedding wouldn't take more than thirty or forty minutes, but it never hurts to have backup."

"We'll be here," Barbara said.

My phone buzzed a text, and Barbara headed to the storeroom as I picked it up.

"Whoa," I said, and Barbara returned to my side. "What? Did I forget something?"

She peered at my phone and gazed at my face. "Want some privacy?"

"No," I said. "I might need moral support."

We read the text together.

Jack: "Is anyone accompanying you to the wedding?"

"What will you say? Want me to send David home to put on a suit?" Barbara asked.

"The last time I heard anything from Jack was Tuesday." I raised my phone to slam it on the counter, but Barbara caught my arm and nodded toward Andrew.

"You're right. I don't want to startle anyone. Can we step outside? I need some fresh air."

Barbara joined me out front, and I crossed my arms while I paced and clutched my phone. "I know the Sheriff told him to stay away from me because Lloyd was targeting him, but after Lloyd was killed on Thursday morning, there was no reason for him to avoid me. I even sent him a text yesterday, and he never answered. I haven't heard squat, and now he suddenly asks who is accompanying me to the wedding? Like it's any of his business."

I continued to pace and fume until I inhaled a big breath and blew it out through my pursed lips. "Okay, I'm better. Let's go inside. I'll send him a text."

As we went inside, Barbara asked, "Do I get veto power?"

I chuckled. "Sure." After I tapped in my response, I showed it to Barbara.

She snickered. "I can't explain why, but I like it."

Me: "No." I tapped send.

"That's done. Now I'll show you how I record the day's business. The deposit slip is easy."

Barbara picked up the simple bookkeeping in less than two minutes. "Easy. Time for you to leave. It's important for you to look really classy when you snub a certain someone."

I snorted. "You're right."

I waved to Andrew and the mayor and hugged the dogs as I left.

When I got home, I showered and flipped strands of wet hair off my face. *Suppose I should do something about my hair.* I towel-dried my hair and ran a brush through it.

I brushed a little pink blush on my cheeks, penciled in the few bare spots in my eyebrows, and applied a rose-colored lipstick. I narrowed my eyes to examine my handiwork in the mirror. *Not bad.*

I slipped on my new dress and shoes and dropped a change of clothes into my pink-sprinkled donut tote. When I arrived at the nursing center, the visitors' parking lot was packed. I cruised the lot until someone pulled out.

On my way to the door, Jeff strode up behind me.

"Where'd you park?" I scanned the parking lot for the truck.

He chuckled. "At the gas station across the street. I wasn't about to try to weave my way through these tight aisles with that truck. I'm here to pick up the keys to Gee's house and the new apartment from Roger. Roger and Tiffany packed last night when they got home, and all their boxes and luggage are at Gee's. I'll pick up Andrew, and we'll finish loading the truck and head to Savannah. Andrew and I are looking forward to our road trip."

When we went inside, we signed in.

Jeff pointed. "Down the right hall."

When we reached Gee's room, her dark brown eyes sparkled when she saw me. "Donut Lady, you look gorgeous. Did you bring the law to spring me?"

The head of her hospital bed was raised, her right leg was splinted, and her left arm was casted. Her skin was paler than her usual chocolate brown, but the light touch of blush suited her. Someone had pulled her hair away from her face with a green silk ribbon.

I chuckled. "How are you feeling? You look great yourself. Not near as delicate as I expected."

Gee snorted. "I've been called a lot of things but never delicate."

"I can believe it," Roger mumbled as he handed the keys to Jeff.

"See you in Savannah, Roger. Glad you're feisty, Ms. Gee." Jeff strode out of the room.

"Wait up, Jeff. I'm right behind you. I have to pick up Tiffany." Roger hurried out.

"I have a way with men, don't I?" Gee snickered.

I sat in the visitor's chair next to Gee and chuckled. "Special skill."

"How's Isaiah? When I ask Tiffany, she says he's improving. Is that right?" Gee asked.

"That's what Tammy said the last time I talked to her. You want to talk to Tammy yourself? I'll send her a text. I know she hasn't wanted to bother you."

Gee brushed away a tear. "I'd like that. I've been worried about Tammy being all by herself as much as I've worried about Isaiah."

"Nothing could pry her away from Isaiah."

I sent Tammy a text. "Call me when convenient. I'm with Gee."

"What do you plan to wear for the wedding?" I asked.

"I have a green shirt I'll wear over my hospital gown. One of the volunteers at the hospital gave me a heritage wedding ring patchwork quilt before I left when she heard about the wedding. I'll use it as a lap quilt over my legs, and my wheelchair will get me to the wedding. I'll be very stylish."

"Where will the wedding be held?"

"We finally decided the chapel would be appropriate for a quiet wedding, but we'll have punch and wedding cake in the dining room. We've invited the other patients to the reception. Some are long-term residents and may not have many visitors, and we thought they would especially enjoy a party."

"How do I get to the chapel and dining room? I'd like to snoop. I'll leave you my phone in case Tammy calls back."

"Down my hallway to the end and turn left. The chapel is on the right. Go past the chapel and turn left again, and the main dining room is on the right. We considered having an outdoor wedding in the center courtyard, but our weather is too unpredictable."

When I reached the chapel, I peeked in. Tess held a long garland of pink and yellow flowers as a muscular young man with dark hair placed the garland along a white trellis that was at the front of the chapel. Tess wore high heels and a pale green midi-length dress that suited her slender figure. She had braided her long, red hair into a single braid, and it was tied with a green ribbon. "That's beautiful, Tess." I strode down the soft red carpet that covered the center aisle inside the chapel.

"It is, isn't it? Have you met Perry, Karen? He teaches at the middle school."

The young man strode to me, and we shook hands. "Nice to meet you, Ms. Karen. Woody talks about his Miss Lady all the time."

"It's nice to meet you too, Perry. Woody says you're an awesome teacher, and I know how challenging middle-schoolers can be."

"Have you seen the dining room, Karen?" Tess asked. "Emma and Tammy's friends have gone all out."

"I stopped here first. This looks wonderful."

"Can you imagine how much more we could have done if we'd had one day's additional notice?" Tess snickered.

I hurried down the hall to check the dining room. Emma and two young women placed small floral centerpieces on each dining table while a pregnant woman sat at one of the tables and filled small glass bowls with soft, pastel mints. All the tables were covered with white tablecloths. A clear vase wrapped with a green, silky ribbon and filled with pink and white roses decorated a long table with a pale-yellow table runner.

"This is beautiful," I said.

Emma grinned. "Good to see you. We have no idea what Tiffany might have wanted for colors, but we pooled what we had, and this is what she'll get."

The young woman who poured the candy into the bowls folded the empty candy sack and struggled to her feet. "I have black and orange tablecloths and plenty of Halloween decorations, but I was outvoted even though I claimed two votes." She giggled and patted her pregnant belly.

"We promise we'll use those for your baby shower if you get the approval from both of the new grandmas," one of the other women said.

"We know that won't happen," another woman said.

Emma laughed. "Karen, it's a wonder we've gotten anything done. We have argued over everything, and it's been wonderful. We have the wedding cakes in the refrigerator. Want to see?"

She led the way to the kitchen. "We made four cakes. Tiffany and Roger will cut one, but we thought we could serve the guests and patients faster if we're cutting and serving four cakes at the same time. The kitchen crew will cut and help us serve cake and drinks. We were worried about the stamina of some of the patients, especially Gee, but don't tell her I said that. The staff will help deliver slices of cake to the patients who aren't able to make it to the dining room."

After she opened the refrigerator, I admired the cakes. "Each one of them looks like a professionally decorated wedding cake. How were you able to get them made so quickly?"

Emma chuckled. "They are all homemade. I made one; Barbara made one; Alana, the animal control officer, made one; and the fourth was made by Jorge's wife."

"You may just have started a trend. What a brilliant idea."

"We have a punch bowl that we'll put on the table and fill with lemonade, but we made up pitchers of lemonade for quick pouring and serving."

"It will be a wonderful reception."

Emma walked with me to the door. "See you later."

As I strolled back to Gee's room the way I came, I smiled when I reached the chapel.

Tess and Perry stood at the doorway. "Gee's pastor should be here soon. We're waiting for any last-minute instructions."

"The chapel is beautiful. You've created a wonderful setting for a wedding," I said.

When I reached Gee's room, Thomas stood at the window. He wore a charcoal gray suit, white shirt, and a blue tie. "I'm watching for Roger. He texted me that they are on their way. He's supposed to pretend he can't see Tiffany because they are riding together. Weddings make people weird, don't they?"

I laughed. "They actually do."

"Glad you're back, Donut Lady." Gee was in her wheelchair, and her new quilt covered her legs. "I talked to Tammy. She's hoping Isaiah can be transported to Asbury next week. She'll call me tomorrow. She thinks Isaiah will be well enough to talk on the phone for a bit. She sure is crazy about him, isn't she? I know he feels the same because all he ever talked about lately was Tammy."

Shirley and Woody came into the room. "Is this where the wedding party is gathering? Where are Tiffany and Roger? Am I supposed to go to the chapel, or do I stay here?" Shirley asked.

"Woody stays with us, and yes, you can go on to the chapel. Tiffany and Roger are on their way," Gee said.

After Shirley left, Woody said, "You look pretty, Miss Lady."

"Thank you, Woody. I like your new suit. You look very distinguished."

The sheriff stopped by. "Everybody ready? Tiffany and Roger are on their way inside. Tiffany's wrapped in a blanket, and Roger's shading his eyes so he can't see her. I'm telling you because I laughed, and Tiffany growled at me." He chuckled as he strode away.

"This is the plan, Thomas," Gee said. "When Roger and Tiffany are here, you and Woody go with Roger to the chapel. The three of us will be along directly."

Thomas and Woody waited outside the door. "They're coming down the hallway. Are we supposed to cover our eyes too?" Woody asked.

"No," Gee said. "Just don't stare."

When they were close, Thomas took the suitcase Roger carried and set it in Gee's room. "Roger, come with us."

Blanket-covered Tiffany slipped into the room, closed the door then threw her blanket to the floor. "That was the dumbest idea I've ever had. I thought I would die of heatstroke."

Gee and I gasped at Tiffany's silky, white ankle-length dress and the wreath of white flowers and beads nestled in her hair.

"You are beautiful, Tiffany," I said.

She grinned. "When I called the boutique and told Whitney I'd need a wedding dress, she told me she'd ordered the perfect one for me three weeks ago and got it in last week. I guess everybody except me knew we'd be getting married."

I rushed to answer the tap at the door, and Tiffany scurried to hide in Gee's bathroom. When I opened the door, Emma handed me a bouquet of white flowers with green and blue streamers. "Forgot to give you this."

After she left, I glanced at the clock. *Two minutes until ten.*

"Are you ready, Tiffany?" I asked.

She came out of the bathroom. "I'm ready."

I pushed Gee's wheelchair, and Tiffany followed us. When we reached the chapel, the sheriff waited at the door. "After we go inside and Gee is parked, I'll come back to the door."

He pushed Gee's wheelchair into the chapel then returned.

"Karen, when you reach the pastor, go to the left. After I bring Tiffany down the aisle, she'll hand you her bouquet, and I'll sit next to Gee."

"I didn't know the sheriff was giving you away," I whispered.

"It was either him or the warden." Tiffany snickered, and I snorted.

I strolled down the aisle and didn't fall or even trip. I turned to the left and faced Tiffany. Her face beamed as Sheriff took her arm, and they strolled down the aisle together. She handed me her bouquet, and I stood next to her and faced the pastor.

Tears welled in my eyes during the ceremony, and I heard Gee sniffing behind me. Woody managed the wedding rings like a pro. When Roger and Tiffany kissed, we all applauded. They hurried down the aisle, and I followed with Thomas on one side and Woody on the other. We gathered in the dining room, and when everyone was there, the pastor said a wedding blessing, and Sheriff and Thomas toasted the newlywed couple. Gee, Emma, Shirley, and I were teary. Tiffany and Roger cut a slice of cake together, and everyone ate cake and chatted. Tiffany threw her bouquet, and while Tammy's friends fought over it, Shirley picked up the bouquet. Everyone laughed and applauded, except the disappointed young women who pouted. Tiffany and Roger slipped out, and the party continued until Emma rang a cowbell and thanked everyone for coming. After she handed me two white sacks with wedding stickers on them, she said, "I've wrapped slices of cake for the Lehmans since they're taking care of the donut shop for you, and the second sack has a piece for Darlene."

"Thank you, Emma. I know they'll appreciate it."

Emma spotted a small group that had lingered in a corner and hurried to herd them out. "Take it outside," she said. "I've always wanted to say that, now, shoo." She waved her apron at them and winked at me as they rushed to the door.

A man came up behind me and spoke quietly in my ear.

"Am I still on the team?"

I whirled around and glared at Jack. "Of course, you are. How else can I get even with you for ignoring me all week?"

Sheriff strolled by. "You're in trouble, Jack. Not sure you noticed." The sheriff whistled as he continued to the kitchen.

Jack followed me as I hurried to rescue Gee. Gee raised her eyebrows and smirked as I shrugged.

"I'll take you to your room, Gee," I said. I pushed Gee's wheelchair, and Jack followed us. When we reached her room, Gee said, "I'll buzz for help to get back into bed. Wasn't this a beautiful wedding?"

"It certainly was," I said. "One of Tammy's friends slipped into the chapel and recorded the service for Tammy and Isaiah."

"I didn't know that," Gee said. "Could you believe that Shirley got the bouquet? I think Tammy's friends were fighting to get it for her."

"Not how it looked to me." I chuckled.

Gee's nurse and two assistants came into her room. "See you later, Gee."

"Exciting day," I said as Jack and I strolled to the parking lot.

"What's next on your agenda?" he asked.

"I'll relieve Barbara and help the mayor and Amber clean up."

"Can we have lunch somewhere?" he asked.

"Sure. You want to pick up lunch and bring it to the thrift shop?"

"That's a good idea. I've let Darlene down this week too."

I nodded. "I'll see you at the thrift shop."

I narrowed my eyes as his shoulders slumped as he headed to his truck. *Straighten up. I was nice.*

When I reached the donut shop, I parked in front.

"How was the wedding?" Mayor asked when I opened the door. He finished sweeping then put away the broom.

"It was wonderful. Emma sent cake for you three." I held up their sack as I placed it in the refrigerator.

Amber came out of the meeting room and closed the door behind her, and Barbara hurried out of the storeroom,

"Did I hear you say wedding news?" Barbara asked.

I gave my detailed report and concluded with Jack showing up.

"He has a lot of nerve," Barbara grumbled. "You're speaking to him, aren't you? Otherwise, how could you torture him?"

The mayor's eyes widened, and Amber and I laughed.

"Seems like the best course to me," I said, and Barbara nodded.

The mayor cleared his throat. "We don't have any donuts or scones left, and I have the dishwasher running with the last of the dishes."

"The meeting room is clean," Amber said. "I'm taking off unless there's anything else."

"The deposit's done," Barbara said. "We'll drop it off for you."

"Let's go. I'll lock up," I said.

The three dogs jumped into the car, and we headed to the thrift shop. When we arrived, the dogs hopped out of my car, and I grabbed my pink-sprinkled tote, and the four of us went into the shop.

"I brought you a piece of wedding cake." I pulled out the small sack with Darlene's slice and set it on her desk.

"I'll want details," Darlene said.

"After I change clothes? Be right back."

Darlene nodded, and I hurried to change. When I returned to the front, I sat on the comfortable chair next to her and told her the details about the wedding. When I'd covered the wedding and the reception, I told her about Jack and lunch.

"We're still mad at him, but we're happy for him to bring us lunch, aren't we?" She asked. "I have four deliveries for today. I'm glad we can snub him in person. No reason for us to suffer too."

"You're right. How are you doing? Are you worn out? If you'd like to go home, I can manage the shop."

"Heavens, no. I love being here, and I can't miss the opportunity to stick Jack with a dig or two. I might have to find myself a job after Gee is well enough to take over here."

"Emma sounds serious about her idea for the dog treat business," I said.

"If the elusive Atlanta buyer falls through, do you suppose Emma is interested in baking dog treats? I wouldn't mind waiting on four-legged customers who come in with their owners. I might talk to Emma about a joint venture, or would that be too forward?"

"Not at all. I suspect she's already considered something along those lines herself."

"That's what I think too." Darlene glanced out the front window. "There goes Maisie."

"Do you know the names of all the dogs in town?" I peered out the window and saw Judge Worley and his dog on their lunchtime walk.

"I don't know about that, but I do know the name of every dog that lives within two blocks of my house, or maybe it's two miles. Now ask me if I know their humans' names." She smiled. "No, I don't."

"I never thought about that before. I was never around dogs very much and didn't even know I liked dogs and cats until I came here. I'm learning how much I missed."

Darlene reached into her side pouch and pulled out her wallet. She handed me two folded bills. "Put us in for more guesses in Gus's scheme to raise awareness and money for the animal shelter. I don't believe for a minute that a big city person from Atlanta would be interested in starting up a business in small town Asbury, but I love Gus's creativity, the old con artist."

I laughed. "I've had thoughts along that line, but I kept them to myself."

"As you should." Darlene rose as a customer came into the shop. "Good morning. Feel free to look around. Do you have anything special in mind?"

"Just browsing." The customer patted a sofa and sat on each cushion.

Darlene winked at me as she settled at her desk. "Enjoy."

I picked up a lamp and carried it toward the back room.

"That's a cute lamp," the customer said. "Is something wrong with it?"

"Not at all," Darlene said. "We had a call from someone who asked us to put it back for her."

The customer smiled. "That's nice. Let me know if she changes her mind."

Darlene nodded, and I continued to the back with the lamp.

The customer browsed, and Darlene pulled out her notebook and doodled.

After ten minutes, the woman returned to the first sofa she'd tried when she came in. "I'd like this sofa, the two matching chairs, and the coffee table. I need a small lamp too. I'll look around."

Darlene smiled.

After a few more minutes, the woman returned to the front. "I found a nice table to go with the side chairs. Will you call me if the woman changes her mind about the lamp?"

"I certainly will." Darlene turned the page in her notebook. "Write your name and number here. Did you want your furniture delivered on Monday or Tuesday?"

"I'll send my son to pick it up. He'll be here in an hour or so," she said. "How much?"

Darlene helped the woman haggle a bit before they agreed on a price for everything the customer had picked out. The woman wrote a check and smiled as she left with her receipt for her son to bring back when he returned.

When I brought the lamp to the front, Darlene said, "Another customer has learned the thrill of bargaining, and she's happy with her purchases. I love working here."

"Why didn't you sell her the lamp?"

"If it's not paid for on Monday, I'll call her Tuesday morning." Darlene peered at me over her glasses. "Why do you think you picked up that particular lamp?"

I raised my eyebrows. "I thought I wanted to look like I was doing something."

"Right, and you picked it up because it was in the wrong place. I brought it up here to remind me not to sell it."

I rolled my eyes. "You totally bamboozled me."

"I know." Darlene tittered. "That was a bonus."

"That's exactly the type of thing that Gee does to me all the time," I grumbled, and Darlene laughed harder.

Jack came into the shop with our lunch. "What's so funny?"

Darlene wiped her eyes. "Just having fun with Karen."

"Her fun. Not mine." I wrinkled my nose.

He glanced at my face and cleared his throat. "Where do I put lunch?"

Darlene pointed to her desk. "I'll take mine here where I can keep an eye out for customers. You two can eat in the back."

Jack set Darlene's tea, sandwich, and chips on her desk then carried the rest of the lunch to the back.

I put my hands on my hips. "You got me good earlier, Darlene, but just now you were as subtle as an elephant with tummy troubles."

She chuckled, and I flounced to the back. Jack had set the sack with our lunch on a table.

He pulled out our sandwiches and unwrapped his. "I'm glad I forced myself to go to the wedding, but I'm not ready to be around people to face the judging faces and whispers quite yet."

"I understand. That's how I felt after I ran over Terry, and large groups are still a problem for me." I unwrapped my sandwich and bit into it. "Yum. Ham, swiss, mustard, mayonnaise, and pickle. This is delicious."

Jack bit into his sandwich and closed his eyes as he chewed. "Mmm. My pastrami's great."

I peered at his sandwich. "Is that horseradish sauce and sauerkraut?"

"Sure is," he grinned.

After he'd eaten half his sandwich, Jack sipped his iced tea. "When do they stop? The stares and whispers."

My pen buzzed. I reached into my pocket and clipped it onto my shirt pocket, and it warmed my heart. I gazed at his downcast face. "I don't know. They've lessened but have never completely gone away for me. I thought I'd left them behind in Ohio after I was released from prison, but the looks and hateful comments here still give me knots in my stomach if I let them. It's hard to remember I can't fix other people and their prejudices, but I do know that friends make a difference. You don't live in a vacuum, Jack. When you shut out your friends, you're hurting them."

Jack shuddered and met my gaze. "I was too immersed in my self-pity to think of that."

I nodded.

Jack finished off his sandwich. "Saying I'm sorry is too trite, isn't it? Alfred's stuck by me. You and Darlene haven't booted me to the curb yet."

"You brought lunch. What can I say?" I sipped my tea and peered over my cup with my most wicked smile.

His mouth quivered. "Lunch. I'll have to remember that."

"Ms. Darlene?" A young man came into the shop. "I have Mama's receipt. I'm here to pick up her sofa."

Jack hurried to the front. "I'll help you load."

The two men carried out the sofa, and Jack helped ratchet it down.

After I finished my sandwich, I collected our trash and met Jack and Darlene up front. "How's Roxie doing?" I asked.

"She's glued to my side," Jack said. "I think she knows I've been feeling down. When we go outside, she runs to the truck. She's always ready to go." Jack frowned as he read over Darlene's delivery list. "None of these are on the way to my house. They're all on the other side of town. I carry work overalls and a change of clothes in the truck, but I planned to pick up Roxie before I make any deliveries."

"There's not enough time," I said. "If you change before you load the truck and deliver the furniture, I'll pick up Roxie. Is the house locked? Can you give me a key?"

"She can get out the dog door. She'll be on the porch when you drive up."

CHAPTER NINE

"Sounds like a plan," Darlene said. "If you leave now, Karen, you might be back before Jack's changed and loaded anyway."

I grabbed my purse and paused at the front door. "Who's going with me to pick up Roxie?"

Colonel and Pepper trotted to the front door, and Mandy flopped down next to Darlene.

"We won't be long." I loaded Colonel and Pepper into my car, and we headed to Jack's house. When I stopped, Roxie dashed out the dog door and to the car. I opened the back door for her, and she leapt in.

"Pretty smooth." I headed down the dirt road to the highway. When we came to the unmarked railroad crossing, I stopped as usual and looked both ways before I headed over the tracks. The car hit a hard bump then wouldn't move. I accelerated but the wheels seemed stuck on the tracks. I glanced at the dash and raised my eyebrows at the low tire indicator. *I didn't notice that earlier.*

I reached to open my door when I heard a train horn blast. I glanced out the passenger's window, and a train was on the tracks, but it was far enough away that I had plenty of time to move the car. I stepped out and examined the tires on my side. *Flat rear tire.* The train horn blared even louder, and my eyes widened as I stared at the monster engine that barreled toward us.

My pen glowed in my pocket. *People misjudge trains.* I grabbed my purse, opened the back door for the dogs, and the three dogs followed me as I ran away from the tracks. When I heard the screech of the engine brake, the long wail of the horn, and an ear-splitting crash, I closed my eyes and covered my ears as I jumped into the ditch by instinct, and the dogs joined me. I cringed in terror at the crunch of metal and the piercing scream of brakes and pulled the dogs closer as I tightened my body into a fetal position.

When the screeching stopped, I raised my head and pulled my phone out of my purse and tapped nine-one-one.

When Tess answered, I couldn't speak.

"Karen. Karen. Are you there? Karen?"

"Wreck. Train." I sobbed.

"Train wreck. Is that what you said? Where are you?"

I shivered. "Ditch."

"You're in a ditch? Are you close to the tracks near Jack's house?"

My breathing was ragged. "Yes."

"I'll stay on the line with you. I'm sending everybody. We'll find you. Can you slow down your breathing? I'll breathe with you. Breathe in through your nose."

I shook even harder but breathed in with Tess and was comforted by the warmth and easy breathing of the dogs.

"Good. Now out. Rest. Breathe in."

While Tess and I breathed together, a car drove past me toward the tracks. I raised my head, and a large blond man parked near the freight cars. When he stepped out of his vehicle, he peered down the track toward the engine. He strode closer to the tracks and walked a few yards as he held onto the freight cars. He returned to his car, turned around, and drove away.

I sat up. "Tess, I had a flat tire and couldn't get off the tracks at the unprotected crossing. The train came up so suddenly. It hit my car, but I don't think the train derailed. I don't see my car, but I haven't checked yet. I ran away from the tracks, and so did the dogs. We're all fine. I'm really shook up."

"Yes, you are, but so am I. You're not hurt?"

The sound of approaching sirens was a comforting violin symphony, and I relaxed.

"No. I hear sirens. I'm in a ditch. I don't think I can be seen from the road because a car stopped at the tracks but left."

"Really? That's strange. Your call came in, and we got a call from the railroad. That's why I thought you were near Jack's. We didn't get any other calls."

The sirens sounded like they were overhead, and I craned my neck to see the road. When I tried to get up, my legs failed me. The siren stopped, and Tess asked, "Can you see them?"

"I tried to get up, but my legs are still shaken up."

"Karen!" I heard the sheriff's voice.

Colonel barked, and the sheriff rushed down the ditch to us.

"Thanks, Tess," I said. Colonel and Roxie ran to the sheriff and back to me, and Pepper wiggled away from my arm where I'd held her.

"Are you okay, Karen?" The sheriff knelt next to me, and Pepper danced around us.

"Yes. Not hurt at all. Just really scared."

"That makes sense. What happened?"

"I picked up Roxie at Jack's house, but on our way back to town, I had a flat tire on the tracks and couldn't get the car to move. When I realized the train couldn't stop, I ran away from the tracks with the dogs and jumped into the ditch, but I don't know why I did that."

The sheriff shook his head. "Didn't your low tire light come on?"

"It was on, but I didn't notice it until I couldn't move off the tracks."

"The national transportation safety board will have a team here soon for a thorough investigation. They'll talk to you later. You sure you're okay? The ambulance will be here in just a minute."

"I am fine. The dogs and I wouldn't mind a ride home, though."

"I'll have Tess call somebody." Sheriff stepped away and spoke into his radio.

"Do you think you could stand if I help you?" he asked.

"Thank you." I rubbed my hands on my pants, and the sheriff lifted me to my feet and kept his arm around my shoulder as he helped me out of the shallow ditch onto the roadside. The road was crowded with fire engines and patrol cars, and firefighters in full gear swarmed the side of the track. The ambulance was blocked by all the other vehicles. Paramedic Carol waved at me as she and her driver rolled the cot to us.

"Hey, Ms. Karen. You don't look so bad for someone involved in a train wreck," Carol said.

"I'm not hurt. I dived into the ditch. Seemed like the thing to do." I brushed my shirt with my hands, but I just smeared the dirt.

I gazed at my shirt and pants and pushed the hair away from my face. My scalp was gritty. "Is my face as dirty as my clothes?"

"Sure is," Carol said. "If I gave you a face wipe to clean up, it would just make mud. You'll need an honest-to-goodness shower. Maybe two. If you're sure you don't want to ride with us, we'll get out of your hair. Want me to take your blood pressure before we go?"

"Oh no. I can't be responsible for getting anything else dirty." I smiled.

"Call me if you need me." Carol followed her driver who had returned the cot to the ambulance.

The sheriff's radio crackled. "The mayor will be here soon to take you and the dogs home. He'll pick up Mandy from the thrift store because Darlene is ready to go home too. She wants you to call her."

"Would someone walk with me to meet the mayor?" I asked.

"My job," Sheriff said, and he held onto me as we made our way to the end of the vehicles that crowded the roadway.

The mayor's car crept down the road toward us. After the mayor turned around and stopped, Roxie and Pepper dashed to his car to see Mandy. The mayor opened the back door for them while the sheriff, Colonel, and I made our way to the passenger's side.

The sheriff opened the back door for Colonel who crowded in with the rest of the dogs. After the sheriff opened my door and helped me inside, he reached over to buckle my seatbelt.

"Thank you."

"Just don't go anywhere the rest of the day," he growled as he closed the door.

When the mayor climbed into the driver's seat, I said, "I'm so sorry. I'm getting the seat dirty."

"Don't worry about it." He peered at me. "Tess said you're not hurt. Is that right?"

"I'm not hurt, but I am dirty from jumping into a ditch." I glanced at his back seat. "Dogs are dirty too."

"I am really sorry about your wreck," the mayor said. "I dropped Barbara off at your house. She'll have dinner in the oven when we get there. Darlene wants you to call her. You'll want to call Jack. As far as I know, no one has called him. Barbara said if you want to, you can invite him for dinner because she'll have plenty."

I sent Jack a text. "Call when you can talk."

My phone rang.

"I have one more delivery. I was worried about the second one, but the neighbors pitched in. I've pulled into a gas station so we can talk. What's up?"

"I wrecked my car. I'm okay, and all the dogs are okay."

"You what?" Jack yelled, and I pulled my phone away from my ear.

I cleared my throat and narrowed my eyes. "You done?"

"Yes. How did you wreck your car?"

"My tire went flat—"

"That doesn't make sense. We got your new tires—when was it? Last month?"

"That's right. I'd forgotten. There's a little more."

Jack breathed in a deep breath then whooshed it out. "Okay."

"I was on the train track when the tire went flat." I waited a few seconds, but he didn't explode or interrupt. "The dogs and I ran away from the car before the freight train hit it. None of us were hurt."

"Where are you now?"

"Are you clenching your teeth? Sounds like you are. The sheriff called the mayor, and we're on the way to my house. Barbara's cooking dinner, and you're invited."

"I'd like to take a shower first."

I frowned. "The tracks to your house might still be blocked. Didn't you wear your overalls? You could shower at my house."

"I don't know. I'm used to my shower. I could take the long way and go home first, but it would take too long to get back at a reasonable time for supper."

"Whatever you think. If you make your last delivery then come to my house, you can have dinner, and Roxie can go home with you."

"I guess."

After we hung up, I said, "Jack has one more delivery. He'll come to the house for dinner and maybe shower here. After dinner he and Roxie will go home the long way. I'll call Darlene."

When Darlene answered, she said, "I usually enjoy your adventures, but this one was over the top."

"I agree completely. I just talked to Jack, and he has one delivery left. How are you doing?"

"Few more sales but no urgent deliveries. I'll visit Gee this evening to talk to her about a weekly delivery schedule and charging for deliveries too. That will give us something to argue about."

I chuckled. "You can tell her about the wreck, if you want to. If I'm not too achy tomorrow from running and jumping into a ditch, I'll visit her."

After we hung up, my phone buzzed a text.

Emma: "I called Shirley. I knew Woody would want to know you are ok."

Me: "Thank you so much."

The mayor raised his eyebrows.

"Emma called Shirley," I said.

"I think you've got your important bases covered. Oh, one more. What about Monica?"

I glanced at the pen that was still clipped inside my shirt pocket, and it glowed.

"I think she knows, but I'll call her after my shower."

"Aren't you glad tomorrow's Sunday? How late do you sleep in on your alleged day off?"

I snickered. "Sometimes I wake up at my regular time because I forget it's Sunday. Otherwise, I get up when the dogs get me up."

"Want to go car shopping tomorrow afternoon?"

"That's a good idea. Maybe I should think about a minivan for all the animals I haul around."

When he parked in my driveway, the mayor chuckled. "Alfred told me one time that when the boys have a great day at camp, the counselors send them to an outside shower before they're allowed to take a regular shower to keep from clogging the drain with sand and dirt. Do you have an outside shower?"

I laughed as he let the dogs out of the car and came around to help me out. I held onto his arm as we went into the house.

"Oh my goodness," Barbara said. "Go into the bathroom and strip, Karen. I'll shake out the dirt before they go into the washer. I'll bring you some clean clothes."

I turned on the shower to warm up and removed my dirty clothing. My eyes widened at the small pile of sand and dirt. I stepped into the shower and rinsed my hair before I shampooed. After I rinsed again, I scrubbed with my girly-smelling soap and let the hot water soothe my muscles as I rinsed. When I peeked out of the shower, Barbara had swept the floor and left me clean clothes. I towel-dried my hair and dressed. After I combed out the tangles, I put on my soft slippers and padded into the kitchen.

"I feel a thousand percent better. Mayor outside with the dogs?"

"He is, and I didn't even banish him." Barbara chuckled. "I brewed a cup of hot tea. Sit where you're comfortable, and I'll put your tea next to you and grill you for details."

I laughed and told Barbara about picking up Roxie, my flat on the train tracks, and how shocking the perception of the train speed was.

Barbara rose. "I have a theory that the human eye is mesmerized by the sheer size of the train, and when you throw in the lack of any reference points, the speed becomes difficult if not impossible to judge."

I widened my eyes. "That sounds plausible to me."

Barbara cleared her throat. "I've been worried about you. I don't know how you might feel about this, but Amber insisted I have pepper spray because I stay at home alone most of the time while David works or goes to meetings in the evenings. I bought you a small canister. It's pocket-sized, and it streams, not sprays. It's not long-range, but it doesn't spray droplets that would have an impact on the dogs. I know they'd try to get between you and an attacker. The purpose is to give you an element of surprise and a few seconds to run away. Drop it in your pocket and keep it with you. I'll feel better."

She pulled a container out of her pocket and handed it to me.

I frowned and dropped it into my pocket. "They'd have to be pretty close for the stream to hit them and not the dogs."

"Right, but don't wait around and don't tell David. If he knew Amber wanted me to have pepper spray, he'd never go anywhere."

Her face was so serious, I couldn't help but smile. "I won't."

When the mayor and the dogs came inside, the dogs and Mia lined up for me to feed them. I set their dishes in front of them, and as they ate, Jack knocked at the door.

"Would you get that, Mayor? I have to watch Mia, or she'll chase Pepper away from her food."

The mayor opened the door and waved his hand in front of his face.

Jack grinned. "If I laugh at your corny joke, may I borrow your manly soap? I realized I could change into my clothes I wore to the wedding earlier."

The mayor snickered. "Good trade. It's on the bathroom counter. Help yourself."

"Leave your dirty clothes and towel in the bathroom. I'll start a load of laundry before we eat," Barbara said.

When Jack came out of the bathroom, Barbara hurried to pick up the dirty laundry and pitched it into the washer.

"Felt good, didn't it?" I said.

"Sure did." Jack called the dogs to the back door. I picked up the food bowls and joined them outside.

"You have a limp," Jack said as the dogs investigated the yard.

"I found a scratch on my shin. It's a little tender. I must have scraped it when I jumped into the ditch."

Jack shook his head. "Start from the beginning for me."

I told Jack about Roxie, the flat tire, the ditch, the dogs, and the wreck.

"I'll be interested in hearing if the investigators discover what caused your tire to go flat."

I nodded.

The mayor opened the door. "Barbara says to come to the table."

Jack offered his arm, and I held on to it as we went inside.

"Is your leg okay?" Barbara asked.

"It's tender. I have a scrape on my shin."

Barbara had placed pork chops on our plates. After we were all seated, we passed around the wild rice casserole and tossed salad family style.

After we ate, Barbara pulled a cobbler out of the oven. "Blackberry," she said. "Who wants ice cream?"

The three of us raised our hands, and she chuckled as she dished up our cobbler then added a generous scoop of ice cream on top.

"This is delicious," I said.

After we finished our dessert, Jack helped Barbara clear the table while the mayor helped me to the sofa.

Barbara loaded the dishwasher. "Do you have anything you can take for pain? You might want to take something before bedtime to help you sleep."

"Yes. That's a good idea. I can't remember the last time I ran or jumped into a ditch." I snickered.

"Dryer stopped. I'll get your things, Jack," Barbara said.

"I'll do that. I think Roxie and I will head out. Sorry to leave so early, but it will take us close to an hour to get home," Jack said.

The mayor opened the back door, and the dogs ran inside.

After Jack and Roxie left, Barbara asked, "Where do you keep your medicine?"

"In the pantry," I said.

Barbara came out of the pantry with a bottle. "This it?"

"Yes, thank you. I'll take one now. I may try to read for a bit, but this has been a truly eventful day."

Barbara brought me the bottle of medicine and a small glass of water, and I took a pill.

"Care for anything else? Tea?" Barbara asked.

"No. Do you mind taking the dogs out for their last walk and locking up?"

"I'll take care of it," Mayor said.

As I read, my phone buzzed a text.

Monica: "Glad you're okay. Keep your pen close."

I left my pen in the bathroom.

"Barbara, do you mind getting my silver pen for me? I left it in the bathroom."

"I saw your pen when I picked up the laundry and put it on your dresser. Shall I get it for you? Do you need your notebook too? Where is it?"

I don't have a notebook. What would I write in? I frowned as I scanned the room but smiled when I glanced at the bookcase. "Yes, please, and my journal is on the bottom shelf of my bookcase."

After Barbara handed me my pen and the new journal Shirley had given me, I opened to the first page and jotted down a list of random words that popped into my head. After I closed the journal, I clipped my pen onto my shirt's neckband. I opened my novel and relaxed.

"Karen." I felt a soft tap on my shoulder and opened my eyes.

"Sorry to wake you, but would you be more comfortable in bed?" Barbara asked.

"I think I would. Help me up? I'm stiff."

The mayor gave me a hand up, and I limped to my bedroom while I hung onto Barbara's arm for balance.

"I'll open your door after you're in bed so the dogs can guard you." Barbara closed the door.

I changed to my pajamas, put my silver pen on my table next to me, and turned off the light after I climbed into bed. I heard Barbara open the door as I closed my eyes.

* * *

I opened my eyes. *It's light outside.* I rolled to check the clock. *Seven o'clock.* I listened, but the house was quiet, and I shuddered. I furrowed my brow and sniffed. *Coffee. Not a nightmare after all.*

I swung my feet to the floor and stood. *Not too bad.* I clipped my pen to my pajama pocket and slid my feet into my bedroom slippers and slogged to the kitchen. I heard Barbara and Mayor on the back porch. I poured myself a cup of coffee and opened the back door. Colonel trotted to greet me, and Barbara smiled. "Good morning. I'm excited you got a full night's rest."

"Would you like to sit, Karen?" Mayor rose and offered me the rocker.

"No, thanks. I'll dress after I finish this cup."

"I know you don't usually eat breakfast, Karen, but today's a special treat. I made fresh biscuits." Barbara wiggled her eyebrows. "We can have eggs, bacon, and biscuits. What do you think?"

"Sounds great. It's practically lunchtime for me anyway." I drained my cup and followed Barbara to the kitchen.

"You're not limping," Barbara opened the refrigerator. "How are you feeling?"

"Much better. Do I have time to take a quick shower before breakfast?"

"Of course. You'll probably be out about the same time as I finish frying the bacon."

When I stepped out of the shower, I caught a whiff of bacon, and my stomach rumbled. *Guess I've missed bacon in the morning.* I hurried to dress then joined Barbara in the kitchen and refilled my cup.

The mayor and dogs came inside, and the dogs crowded me for attention.

"They're kidding you, Donut Lady," Mayor said. "I fed them this morning. Mia told me I did it all wrong, by the way."

"That's Mia." I petted and scratched each dog. Mia stepped out of the pantry with her nose in the air. She flicked her tail and hissed at the mayor before she leapt on top of the refrigerator. She posed on her perch as she tracked Pepper. Pepper paraded just out of Mia's potential pounce reach.

"These animals are a hoot," Barbara said. "I felt sorry for Pepper at first because I thought Mia bullied her, but Pepper antagonizes Mia, doesn't she?"

My phone rang. *Jack.*

"Roxie and I checked the railroad crossing earlier and watched them clear the freight cars away. We hiked along the tracks and found the engine and your car. The car's definitely totaled. The train engine looked fine. Have you thought about another car?"

"I haven't had enough coffee yet to plan. Is it okay if I call you later?"

Barbara waved her hand and pointed to the table.

"Have you had breakfast?" I asked. "Barbara's cooking, and you're invited."

"On our way." He hung up.

I smiled. "He'll be here soon. The tracks are cleared at the crossing."

Five minutes later, I raised my eyebrows when I heard a vehicle pull into the driveway.

"Was he cruising the block?" Barbara asked.

I opened the front door, and Roxie bounded in. When the mayor opened the back door, the girl dogs raced outside, and Colonel ambled out behind them.

As Jack strolled into the house, I asked, "How'd you get here so fast?"

Jack shrugged. "Roxie and I were kind of at the thrift shop to feed Sandy."

I nodded. "You're busted."

"I have an important egg question—fried, omelet, or scrambled?" Barbara asked.

"If you make all the eggs the same, I'll bet nobody will complain," I said.

"I know we won't." The mayor poured a cup of coffee and handed it to Jack.

"That's easy. Mess of scrambled eggs coming up." Barbara waved her spatula.

She waved that like a wand. Barbara does cooking magic.

While the eggs underwent their transformation from raw to scrambled, Barbara stirred butter and flour together for a roux, added a touch of bacon grease for flavor, and whipped in chicken broth. After Barbara was satisfied with the scrambled eggs, she tipped them into a bowl and poured the gravy into a gravy boat. After she pulled the bacon and biscuits out of the oven and placed them on serving plates, she set the coffee pot on a hot pad on the table. "Let's eat."

We passed the bowl of eggs, the gravy boat, and the platters of bacon and biscuits around the table. Mayor drowned his eggs and biscuits in gravy, and Jack copied him. I poured a little gravy on my eggs, buttered my biscuit, and topped it with Barbara's homemade cherry preserves. I served myself a piece of bacon before I passed the plate to Barbara, and she served herself two.

She winked and placed the plate between the two men. "Help yourselves. Karen and I have what we want."

While we ate, the mayor told his fanciful version of my train incident.

"I never knew you could fly, Karen. You'll have to teach me after I lose a few pounds. Do you have a cape? I can make us capes," Barbara said, and Mayor and Jack stared at us while we giggled.

After we ate, Barbara said, "We've got the dishes. David scrubs pans like a champ while I load the dishwasher. Karen, find yourself somewhere to relax and read your book."

"What's my assignment?" Jack asked.

"The dogs haven't been to a park in ages," I said. "Do you think you could manage all four of them?"

His eyes widened, and Barbara snickered.

"May I be released to go to the park, Barbara?" I asked.

"If you'll be okay until I make your cape." She wiggled her eyebrows.

On our way, we passed Judge Worley and Maisie on their morning walk. Jack waved, and the judge smiled and nodded.

"Do you know the judge very well?" I asked.

"Known him for a long time. He stood by me when Ava—" He cleared his throat, and we continued to the park in silence.

When Jack opened the door for the dogs, I laughed as they poured out and fanned the park to search for any unaware squirrels.

"We looked like a clown car with dogs spilling out." I giggled.

Jack pointed to a bench. "It's in the shade. Shall we sit there?"

After we sat, Jack asked, "Aren't you worried Pepper will wander off?"

"She idolizes Roxie. If you call Roxie, Pepper will chase after her."

Jack shook his head. "You sure know your regulars."

Pepper chased a squirrel, and Roxie darted to the squirrel's target tree. When the squirrel spied Roxie, it doubled back and almost ran over Pepper. In desperation, it made a mad leap over Pepper's head to the tree behind the dog.

"I thought that squirrel was a goner," Jack said.

"So did I. Sometimes the best plan is the desperate one. Do you suppose I could find a coffee cup that says that? It's somehow comforting." I chuckled as I scooted to the edge of the bench. "I'd like to stretch my legs. Shall we see if the dogs are interested in some water?"

Jack rose and offered me a hand. I smiled as he helped me up then let go of my hand.

"Thanks. I get enough hovering from Barbara."

"I noticed. It's a wonder she let you come to the park without handing you bubble wrap."

"She wouldn't have done that. She'd have wrapped me herself." I headed to the water spigot.

While Jack rinsed and filled the water bowl for the dogs, I scanned the park. *No squirrels on the ground.* I frowned as a car pulled into the far parking lot. The driver rolled down his window then scanned the treetops with a pair of binoculars. I narrowed my eyes. *I see blond men everywhere.* He swung his binoculars toward us, and I reached down to pet Colonel who waited for all the other dogs to drink first. When I checked the car, it was pulling out of the parking lot.

So much for the blond guy thinking I was killed in the crash.

The dogs drank and investigated the park one more time before they trotted to the truck.

"Guess they're ready to go," Jack said.

On the way back to the house to drop off the dogs, Barbara called.

"We're leaving. David said to call him when you go car shopping today. He loves to look at cars. If you and Jack go after you see Gee, call him."

When we reached my house, Jack asked, "Do you want to wait in the truck while I take the dogs inside? Save your energy for Gee?"

"It will be a lot faster. Thanks."

Jack dropped me off at the entrance to the center. I went inside while he cruised for an empty parking space.

When I entered Gee's room, she said, "I have all the news from the gas station. Now I want the real facts. Sit."

"You want my version or the mayor's version?"

"That's tempting. Let's start with yours."

I told her about Lloyd, the unknown blond guy, Jack, Mayor, Barbara, Darlene, the judge, and the crash.

"There aren't many men that would meet the description of the blond guy. Did you say the judge mentioned his cousin?"

"He did. Bradley Sanford."

"When are y'all getting together to go over Darlene's list?"

My eyes widened. "That meeting kind of got lost in this week's events. Do you know something?"

"It will be interesting to see who comes up on the mayor's list. Also, I'd be interested in hearing what Jack found in those documents. Get them together tonight, and come see me tomorrow. I don't have anything to do now that Tiffany's married, and Isaiah and Tammy are still in Florida. We'll still have to pull off a wedding with less than twenty-four hours' notice. Emma and Tammy's friends are doing some advance work. I plan to be out of here before the wedding, but it's a race."

Jack strolled into Gee's room. "I may get reported as a potential kidnapper. I couldn't find anywhere to park. I offered to give a woman a ride to her car when she was leaving the center, but she turned back around and went inside. Another bad judgement lesson learned. I parked across the street."

Gee laughed. "You should have had all the dogs with you. She'd have jumped right in."

"I'd like to step out into the courtyard to make some calls. Don't talk about me while I'm gone."

"You go ahead, Donut Lady. We promise nothing." Gee smirked.

I called Barbara. "The mayor, Jack, Monica, and I were supposed to get back together to go over what we'd found about a potential counterfeiter. If I picked up dinner for all of us, would you be offended?"

"Of course, I would. Now if you let me cook tonight, I'll let you ask Monica if her personal chef will cater tomorrow."

"Deal. You've already cooked for the crowd, haven't you?"

Barbara chuckled. "Certainly. David reminded me about the overdue meeting on our way home. I'm glad you thought of it. David wanted me to call Monica. He said he'd tell you and Jack I had something to ask you all."

"I'll call Monica. I'm sure Jack won't mind an invitation to dinner."

"Excellent. See you later."

I called Monica and was surprised when she answered.

"I'll be there tonight for dinner. That's why you called, isn't it?"

I touched my pen, and it glowed. "Did my pen tell you?"

She giggled. "Mayor did. He caught me at the gas station and said our meeting was overdue. I've expected you to call. See you at six."

"I must still have brain fog from the crash. Everybody's ahead of me on this one."

"Different, isn't it?" She cackled as she hung up.

When I returned to Gee's room, she raised her eyebrows, and I nodded.

"When does the doctor say you can be released?" I asked.

"He's changed his approach a couple of times. He claimed he would tack on an extra day every time I nag him. I trained the staff to ask him on his way in. He switched and said I could go home when the physical therapist released me. My next target."

She rubbed her hands together, and I laughed. "Deflection. Good plan in theory on the doc's part."

"What's your plan for today, Donut Lady?" Gee winked.

"I need a car. At Barbara's request, I'll call the mayor to meet us at the car lot. If you don't mind, we'll head out. I'll check back soon."

As we walked to the lobby, Jack said, "I'll meet you at the front." He strode away, and I enjoyed the artwork on the walls as I sauntered along.

When I arrived at the lobby, the blond man was signing in at the reception counter. I stepped into a corner of the alcove as he turned and headed toward Gee's corridor.

CHAPTER TEN

I pulled out my phone to send Gee a text as the desk clerk called out, "Sir. It's the other way."

Blonde man strode past her to the other hallway, and I exhaled as I dropped my phone into my pocket.

Jack pulled to the entrance, and I hopped into the truck. As he headed to the exit, I said, "I'm seriously thinking about a minivan. What do you think?"

"It might not meet the gas mileage of your car, but it will make transporting a dog or four easier. One thing I regret about my truck is the thought of Roxie having trouble getting in as she gets older. A minivan is a simple step in and out."

"I'd thought the extra room would be nice, but I hadn't thought about the longer term. Do you think the automatic side and back doors are worth the money?"

"Might be. I hadn't thought about that. It will be interesting to hear what the mayor has in mind."

I sent the mayor a text: "On our way to dealership."

When we arrived at the car dealership, Jack dropped me off at the office door on his way to park. When I stepped inside, I smiled as a tall twenty-year-old girl with red hair and tattoos on her arms hurried to greet me.

"Nice to see you, Peyton. How are you doing?"

"I was promoted to assistant manager. Can you believe that? Dustin takes weekends off to spend time with his family. He's an awesome manager. Are you here to replace your car?" She snickered. "Gas station news. I've been watching for you."

"I've got helpers on the way. I thought about a minivan, mostly for the room for the animals. What do you think?"

"You'll like the extra room. Let's look at several that have different options, so you can get a feel for what you might like. I'm going with the larger engine for you because the extra engine power may come in handy because you are you." She smiled and led me to a corner of the car lot.

"These are last year's models, but you'd be the first owner. Our new models arrived two months ago. We'll look at them if you don't find anything here that you like."

After we looked at the first car with the dark-tinted automated windows, doors, and rear power for the air conditioner, we looked at a similar model with fewer extras. We discussed a third car that was a good basic vehicle with few extra options.

"The price on this car is significantly lower than the first one. I'm not sure who would be a good fit for it, though. I'd never show it to a young family who had a tight budget. I'd find them a two- or three-year-old car with the features they need for the same price as this one. Automatic doors are a must for a family, in my mind. Can you imagine corralling children and loading groceries while unlocking and opening the door? Brutal."

As we strolled back to the office, Peyton pointed. Jack and the mayor hurried from their cars toward the building.

"They must have stopped to talk," I said. "It'll be interesting to hear what they came up with."

Peyton put two fingers in her mouth and whistled. The two men turned our way, and she waved.

"Impressive, Peyton."

"I had brothers. I was the only one that could whistle loud, but they're proud of me now." Peyton chuckled.

When Jack and Mayor reached us, I asked, "What did you decide?"

The mayor cleared his throat. "We decided we agree with the vehicle you have picked out, especially if it's an old pink army tank."

Peyton laughed. "Fine. Now we have to start over, right, Donut Lady?"

I smiled. "You're right. The one we picked as all the features on my list except I forgot about pink."

"I'll grab the keys, and we'll take it for a test drive."

"Perfect."

"We'll wait here," The mayor said. "You don't need us leaning over the seat pretending that we're not backseat drivers."

Peyton brought the minivan to the office, and I took over the driver's seat.

"You have this set for your long legs." I adjusted the seat before I ran through my mental list of what Peyton taught me to check before I drove a vehicle for the first time.

I drove to the end of the parking lot and made a U-turn. "I'm surprised. It has a better turning radius than my small car had."

"One of the things I like about this model."

I headed to the highway and used the cruise control then returned to the office. "I need you to show me where the spare tire is."

Peyton showed me where it was, pulled out the owner's manual, and pointed out the pages that were most relevant for me. We went inside and completed my paperwork.

She hugged me. "Congratulations. Good choice for you. Come back in a month, and we'll do another tour of your car. It's too hard to digest everything at once."

"I'll see you later. Love your minivan, Karen," the mayor said.

"I'll follow you home," Jack said.

When we arrived at my house, I lowered my window. "Want to get the dogs, and we'll go for a ride?"

Jack unlocked the front door, and the dogs spilled out to the lawn. After they had a brief break, I pushed a button and opened the passenger's side back door. Pepper dashed into the van and jumped to the row of seats at the back, and Roxie joined her. Colonel sat on the seat behind me, and Mandy stretched out on the floor.

Jack climbed in. "Do you mind riding out to my house?" He glanced at the back of the van. "We might want to put a rug on the floor for Mandy. It would be more comfortable."

I closed the side door. "Start my list for me. I need a water bowl too."

I backed out of the driveway and headed to Jack's house. "I wanted to see how it does with tracks, anyway. Is my old car there? I wouldn't mind seeing how far the train went before it could stop."

"Your car is gone, and I think the tracks are cleared, but I'll bet we can see how far it was from the crossing."

When we reached the train tracks, I pulled off the road. I let the dogs out on the passenger's side, and we all picked our way through the rough trail that was bulldozed for the tow truck to pull out my car.

I paused and leaned against a pecan tree for a break as I inhaled the earthy scent of freshly turned soil and gazed at the blue sky with puffs of white clouds. The treetops of the surrounding white oak trees swayed in the high breeze. The downed pine trees were piled on the side away from the tracks in the style of a giant pickup sticks game, and the sharp conifer odor hinted of Christmas.

"I didn't expect it to be this far down the tracks. This is shocking," I said as I continued on the uneven path.

"I think it's about a mile away. Are you sure you want to make the entire trip? That makes it two miles round trip."

"Wow. No, this is far enough." I glanced back at the crossing. "I'm glad I got the dogs out." We turned back. "Thanks for coming with me. I had to see for myself. For some reason, I expected my car to be a dozen or so yards from the crossing."

After we loaded up, I drove across the tracks and continued to Jack's house. When we reached the driveway, it was blocked by downed tree limbs halfway to the house.

"Forgot about that. I've been going around them in the truck. Not a good idea for your new minivan. Stop here. I'll run inside to pick up the contracts and my notes for tonight's meeting."

While he was gone, I surveyed the yard. Ava's flower beds were overcome with weeds, and the azalea Jack had bought was in the shade and wilting at the side of the house and was still in the pot from the store. My eyes welled up. *Wonder if Ava's leprechauns are gone?*

When he jumped back into the minivan, I backed out and headed to my house. I parked in my driveway, and Jack said, "I didn't think you'd want to ever go across those tracks again."

"I was nervous, but I didn't want to deal with a lingering fear of crossing train tracks." I opened the van's back door, and the dogs jumped out. While Jack headed to the house to let the dogs inside, I noticed a car parked at the vacant house down the street, but no one was in the car. I scanned the area but didn't see anyone on foot until the judge and Maisie approached from the other direction. The seemingly empty car pulled out of the driveway and sped away in the opposite direction. The judge nodded as he and Maisie continued on their way past my house. *Is the judge guarding or stalking me? Could he be a partner to the unknown driver? A lookout?*

I rubbed my forehead as I went inside the house.

Jack frowned. "Did you overdo?"

"Maybe. I think I'm worn out." I stumbled as I headed to the sofa.

"What would you like? Water? Cold or hot tea?"

"Water and hot tea sound good."

Jack turned on the burner under the tea pot and filled a glass of water for me and dropped in three ice cubes.

"How's my Barbara impression?" he asked as he handed me my glass.

"Just what I was thinking. You're doing fine." I glanced at the clock. "Barbara and the mayor will be here soon. I forgot to invite you to dinner."

"The mayor did. That's why I grabbed my notes while we were at my house."

I shook my head. "I'm glad Mayor suggested I buy a car today. I can't imagine walking to the donut shop in the dark with my pack of dogs."

Jack poured the hot water into the cup with my tea bag. "Four minutes?"

I raised my eyebrows. "That's right."

"Glad you're impressed, but I cheated. Barbara told me."

When he set my hot tea on the table next to me, I asked, "Were you bragging or confessing?"

He shrugged. "Confessing to bragging?"

The mayor tapped on the door, and Jack opened it.

"More out in the car." The mayor hurried to place the hot casserole dish on top of the stove then turned the oven on low and placed the casserole on the bottom rack.

Jack carried in two trays of rolls and placed them on the counter. He left and returned with a large bowl that he put it into the refrigerator. Barbara handed Mayor a casserole in a carrier, and he placed the casserole on the top shelf of the oven. Barbara returned to the car then brought in a covered dessert pan and placed it in the oven.

"I'll make our sweet tea here." Barbara filled two small pots with water and put them on the stove to boil. She mixed her simple syrup and set it on the third burner.

My pen glowed. "Monica's here."

Jack stared at me but sauntered to the front door and opened it. Monica glided into the room, and Jack raised his eyebrows. "How did you know?"

I shrugged, and Monica giggled.

"I'm glad you're here. We need this meeting," I said.

"Eat first." Barbara pulled out the casserole and put the first tray of rolls in the oven. "Fifteen minutes."

Mayor opened the back door and followed the dogs to the backyard.

"Fresh air sounds good." I joined the mayor. "I'm conflicted about Judge Worley. He's a complex man. I've never seen him before this week, but now I see him all the time. Sometimes twice a day."

"I've known him a long time. He's never been random. He's walked Maisie for two years at least twice a day. What's it called when you don't see something until suddenly you always see it'"

"Baader-Meinhof phenomenon or frequency illusion," I mumbled.

The mayor stared at me. "Did you make that up?"

"What? No. You asked me what it was called. You aren't the first one to ask me that. I taught fourth grade science one year, and those rascals came up with the darnedest questions. It was the longest year of my life."

"Wow. Please don't fire me from the donut shop. I have new respect for Mr. Collins."

"So do I. Woody's entire class is at the obnoxious stage in their development, but Mr. Collins sticks with them."

Jack opened the door, and the aroma of hot, fresh rolls wafted from the kitchen. "Barbara said to come inside for dinner." The dogs rushed to the door and trotted inside.

When I stepped in, Darlene was seated at the table. "Barbara invited me. She said I might hear something that jogs my memory. I think she was worried I don't eat right on the weekends."

"Welcome. I'm glad to see you." I furrowed my brow. "I can't think that you've ever been here before. Shame on me. I guess we all get too busy sometimes."

Darlene smiled as she surveyed the kitchen and living room. "I love your home. It has a happy, loving atmosphere. I never knew how drab and lonely my house was until your bright, cheerful colors pulled me in. The instant I rolled inside, I felt at home. Did you know your house overflows with the presence of dogs?"

I giggled. "There's no spray that can cover up the eau de parfum canine."

"That's it. That's what I like. You need a sign: *Don't love the smell of dogs? There's the door.*" Darlene guffawed.

Jack fed the dogs. When he opened the back door, they trotted to the backyard.

Barbara and Monica placed casseroles and two platters of chicken wings on the table. The hot casserole was scalloped potatoes, and the cold bowl held a tossed mixed greens salad with strawberries, toasted pecans, and crumbly feta cheese.

We passed our plates to Barbara who served the potatoes. We passed the chicken, salad, and rolls around to serve ourselves.

I shook my head at my plate. "I'm glad we have salad bowls; otherwise, I'd have to buy larger dinner plates."

Barbara didn't have to repeat her rule of no talking business during dinner. The room was silent except for munching and requests for seconds.

After we ate dinner, Barbara asked, "Dessert now, or during a break?"

"Break for me," Darlene said. The rest of us nodded.

Monica and Barbara cleared the table, Mayor scrubbed the pots and the wings pan, and I sat in my place on the sofa next to my table. Darlene sat at the other end of the sofa. "I'm saving the middle seat for Monica unless she'd rather sit on one of the chairs. Did you see Gee today?"

I caught up Darlene on Gee's progress and the team that was on standby for Tammy and Isaiah's wedding. She chortled. "Can you imagine someone in Asbury trying to plan a wedding months in advance? The entire town would call them amateurs."

When Jack opened the door and invited the dogs back into the house, they ignored him. "Don't blame them." Jack shrugged. "Fresh air, low humidity for a change, and the temperature is in the seventies." He moved a kitchen chair to the living room and sat on the periphery of the room.

Monica joined Darlene and me on the sofa, and the mayor and Barbara sat in the chairs.

"I have my notebook if anybody wants me to take notes," Barbara said.

"I'll start," the mayor said. "I went through Darlene's extensive list. First off, there were no mothers or daughters who met any of our criteria. Next, I narrowed our list down to twenty fathers and sons who trained as professionals or had positions that gave them flexibility to set their own hours."

"Could I see the list of people who didn't make the cut?" Darlene asked. "I can tell you if there are any sleepers. You know, those who could have made your list in spite of their stated positions."

Mayor nodded. "Good idea. Here's the original list. I've marked the twenty-three that I identified. From there, I eliminated ten because the son left the state. I've marked them too. A second pair of eyes never hurts."

Mayor gave us his list of thirteen.

"I have Lloyd's work history," Monica said. "I found it interesting that he trained and worked as a vet tech for years, but he never stayed at any one position more than two years. He worked in vets' offices, animal shelters, and animal hospitals. From what I learned from my conversations with different employers, he was good with animals and terrible with their human owners. I guess that's not terribly rare for vet techs because the employer was happy to have someone who provided excellent care for the more difficult animals behind the scenes and hated to see Lloyd leave."

"That's an interesting side of Lloyd I never knew," I said.

Monica nodded. "I understand. Too bad he wasn't satisfied with the stability of noncriminal work. His employment history had multiple gaps where he was in prison for one reason or another—robbery, fraud, blackmail, illegal drugs, home invasion, fights—he had a distinct pattern of violence. If I'd read his criminal record or knew his history, and someone told me he was involved in a beating death, I would have assumed he was the killer, not the victim."

"I don't see where he fits with any of the thirteen, other than loosely with some who are in the medical field," Jack said.

"Unless it's the pattern of violence," Mayor said. "Darlene, you may have some insights as we go through our list. Our counterfeiter may be stronger than Lloyd. For example, may have a hobby of weightlifting, boxing, or martial arts. Just a thought."

"I'm next," Jack said. "I reviewed the wills and some of his notes. There was a stack of other documents that compared the prices of real estate and large ticket items like boats, but as far as I could tell from flipping through his receipts, he didn't purchase any of them. Terry's original will left everything to his parents. No mention of Lloyd. After Terry and Karen were married, he changed his will to Karen as the sole beneficiary and took out a second high-value policy with Karen as the sole beneficiary. One theory might be that he planned to stage his death and have the money go to Karen then manipulate her into giving him the money. That doesn't explain his pattern of abuse though unless torturing Karen became an obsession. His additional documents point to a counterfeit scheme but not much more." Jack snorted. "However, he did have a nickname for the unknown counterfeiter. He called him *Pear.*"

"That's strange," Darlene said. "Usually when someone is called a pear it refers to a body shape."

"Here's our list of thirteen. Darlene, would you go through these first?" Mayor asked.

While Darlene pored over the list, Monica and I went outside for fresh air and to check on the dogs. I meandered as I mulled over the evening's discussion and stopped at the back fence.

When Monica joined me, I said, "I wonder what I'm missing. I never saw the judge walking Maisie until this last week. Now I see him all the time. The mayor asked me what was the word for not seeing something that's always been there, but after you see it once, you see it all the time; I came up with the word right away."

"Baader-Meinhof phenomenon," she muttered.

"Right. So what am I missing?"

"What if I asked what do you think you're missing?" Monica raised her eyebrows.

"I would look again because you hinted there was something I wasn't seeing."

I scanned the evening sky and smiled. *Looking for answers?*

"I get it. You were telling me to look at things differently, so I can see what is there."

Monica smiled. "It's amazing how that works, but there's more."

I gazed at her face. "Taking it a step farther, and hurting my head—this doesn't apply only to just seeing, does it? I may know something but haven't realized that I do." I smacked my forehead. "Like the name for frequency illusion."

"Know and don't know that you know. I'd label it unconscious competence. Now my head hurts." Monica tittered, and I giggled.

On our way back to the house, Monica said, "The good news is that you have the talent to put unlikely pieces together."

I opened the back door, and we followed the dogs into the house.

Darlene smiled. "I trimmed the list of thirteen to seven but found two on the original list for consideration because of a history of violence. I've marked my list if you'd like to see why. Barbara said I earned dessert. Care to join me?"

Barbara dished up dessert into bowls. "Tonight's dessert is Apple Betty."

After his first bite, Jack said, "Barbara, you are an amazing cook. I can't remember the last time I had Apple Betty. Thank you."

Barbara's cheeks reddened. "You're welcome."

After we ate, Darlene rose from the table. "Marvelous meal. Thank you."

Barbara smiled. "I love to cook, and cooking for more than two people is exciting for me."

"What's our next step?" Mayor asked.

"I suggest we analyze what we have individually and get back together to touch base," Jack said.

"Does Tuesday give everyone enough time?" I asked.

"Barbara, would you be offended if my personal chef caters on Tuesday?" Monica asked.

"Heavens, no. Let me know if I can bring dessert."

"Tuesday works for me. Does anyone mind if I eat and run?" Darlene asked. "I've been gone all day and have a few chores to catch up."

"I'll head out too," Monica said.

"We'll walk you to your car." Mayor helped Darlene to the door, and Barbara and Monica joined them as they made their way to Darlene's car.

"Sounds like a good idea. Roxie, you ready? Mandy, are you coming with us?" Jack held the door open, and Roxie trotted outside. Mandy flopped down next to Colonel.

"Okay, girl. We'll see you later. Goodnight, Karen."

"Goodnight, Jack."

After he closed the door, I frowned. *Things aren't the same.*

I propped up my feet, and Mia jumped onto my lap. I stroked her back. "Maybe we'll get back to normal soon."

The shadows danced in the hallway, and I smiled. I read over my list of nine names.

I recognize some of these, but I don't know any of them. I'll share my list with Gee tomorrow.

When Barbara and the mayor came inside, Barbara said, "Are you tired? I'll brew you a cup of tea."

"I am exhausted. Hot tea sounds good." I held my pen and relaxed. Barbara set my cup on the table next to me, and I sipped my tea.

"Karen, would you be comfortable if David and I go home tonight? We'll bring supper tomorrow, but I thought you could use some private time," Barbara said.

My eyes welled from the kindness in her face. "I do feel strong enough to take care of myself, thanks to you. You don't have to bring a meal tomorrow. I'll visit Gee and stop at the grocery store."

Mayor headed to their bedroom, and Barbara nodded. "You know you can call us anytime. We'll be here on Tuesday a little before six, as usual, unless you'd rather we host the crowd at our house."

"I think it works out best to have everyone here because of the dogs, unless you would like the opportunity to host. I hadn't thought about that."

"I agree that the dogs are more comfortable here. I get nervous even thinking about people coming to my house. I love to cook, but I can't entertain. Living with anxiety is hard sometimes." She shook her head. "False pride is a terrible thing."

The mayor came out of the second bedroom with their suitcase. "I've stripped the bed and put on clean sheets. I'll set the laundry on the washer and take care of it on Tuesday. You'll leave it for me, right?"

"Yes, I can do that. Thanks for making the bed."

"It's what I do." Mayor chuckled. "I'll see you in the morning."

After they left, I relaxed and read. Mandy startled me when she nosed my book, and it fell to the floor. I stretched, padded to the back door, and joined the dogs outside.

When we came inside, Mia dashed to her pantry, and the shadows billowed and danced in the hall as I headed to bed.

"You missed me?" I turned off the light and closed my eyes. *Exhausted.*

* * *

A blast of icy wind and the sound of waves lapping against my bed woke me. A pale light drifted out of the closet, and Mandy swam through the rough water as she pulled a rope tied to a skiff. Darlene held a lantern with one hand and clutched the side of the boat with the other. "Don't leave me out here alone, Mandy." She sobbed and shivered in the cold.

I dove in, and the frigid water took my breath away. Colonel grabbed my collar in his mouth and tugged me back to my bed. Mandy and Darlene drifted away into a mist, and I screamed.

Colonel barked, and I opened my eyes. *Nightmare. Thought they were gone.*

I peered over the side of my bed, and the floor was dry. I padded to the kitchen, and my hands shook as I turned on the burner for the tea kettle.

I leaned against the kitchen counter. "Why am I worried about Darlene?" Mandy leaned against my leg.

"You're a good girl, Mandy." I rubbed her face and glanced at the clock. *Three.*

"Not sure I can go back to bed."

Pepper danced at the back door, and I went outside with the three dogs and shivered. *Chillier than I expected.*

"I'll talk to Darlene tomorrow. I mean, today. She knows something." I sat on the sofa with my tea and book. Mia meowed at four, and my tea was cold.

After I dressed, I opened Mia's carrier, but she darted to my bedroom.

"I can take a hint."

The dogs and I headed through a light fog to the donut shop. When we arrived, I smiled at the beacon of light from the shop.

"Good morning, Miss Lady." Andrew grinned as we entered the shop.

"Good morning, Andrew. What's our plan for today?"

"We have the Write Now Authors and the Methodist men today." He turned out his dough to rise. "I thought chocolate glazed and pink-sprinkled donuts. We haven't done anything special with our donut holes in a while."

"It was chilly this morning. Why don't I make cranberry-orange scones with orange drizzle. If we feel ambitious, we can drizzle the donut holes and have tiny, early pumpkins."

"We have orange sprinkles."

"For the chocolate glazed? Perfect."

"Yes."

After I put on my apron, I mixed my dough then rolled and cut my scones. While the first batch baked, I made orange drizzle.

I removed my first batch of scones from the oven and popped in the second batch. *Darlene.*

I drizzled chocolate on Andrew's first batch of donuts while the second batch of scones baked. "I'll be in my office, Andrew. I won't be long."

I hurried to the storeroom that doubled as my office and called the nonemergency number for the sheriff's office.

Summer answered. "Why didn't you call nine-one-one, Ms. Karen?"

I smiled. *Her finger must be hovering over the key to alert the sheriff.* "I called for a wellness check. Do you suppose someone could check on Darlene Rothenberger?"

"Sure can. Any special reason? Never mind, doesn't matter. You had a feeling, right?"

"You're right. I just thought of something. Did Lloyd Ahrens apply for a job with the animal shelter?"

"I think he did. I was taking care of a sick beagle when he came in. Any special reason? You might want to talk to Alana."

"Just curious, but that's a good idea. Thanks. How's the beagle?"

"She's doing great. Her forever home family will pick her up later today."

After we hung up, I drizzled orange, chocolate, and strawberry on the appropriate pastries while Andrew fried the donut holes and filled the coffee machines with water. I measured coffee and started the machines as Andrew sprinkled and drizzled the rest of the donuts and donut holes.

The bell jingled as I wrote on the special's board, and the sheriff strode into the shop. "Early fall? Makes sense to me. The wind's come up, and it's nippy out there." He rubbed his hands together; Andrew poured his coffee and put away my stepladder.

Sheriff sat at the counter and sipped his coffee. "I'll have one of each. Are the early pumpkins ripe enough to eat?"

Andrew snickered as he served the sheriff the pastries.

"We'll let you judge," I said.

"These are good." He drained his cup.

I refilled his coffee and joined him at the counter after I poured a cup for me.

"We checked on Darlene, Karen. Summer said you had a feeling." He cleared his throat. "Can we sit at the reading table?"

I sat on one of the soft chairs, and the sheriff knelt next to me. "Jeff found her unconscious on the ground in her backyard, and there was a trash sack next to her. Our best guess is she was taking out her trash for today's pickup, but we don't know if it was late last night or early this morning. She was admitted with hypothermia. The doctors are trying to determine if she fell because she slipped or if there was a medical reason. She wouldn't have lasted much longer."

My head swirled, and I reached for the table.

"Let's put up your feet. I know it's a shock."

Andrew brought a box from the storeroom for my feet. "Are you okay, Miss Lady?"

"I'll sit a minute. I'll be fine." An icy chill ran down my spine, and I shivered. My pen glowed, and when I held it for the warmth, I frowned. *I know something.*

Andrew refilled our coffee cups, and after I drank mine, I narrowed my eyes. "Jeff found a trash sack next to her? What about her walker? Or cane?"

The sheriff's eyes widened. "He didn't say. Be right back." The sheriff strode outside and stood near the door as he used his radio.

"More coffee, Miss Lady?" Andrew hovered with a carafe in his hand.

"Thank you, Andrew. It's helped clear my head."

He refilled my cup and set the carafe on the table next to me.

CHAPTER ELEVEN

When the sheriff returned, he refilled his cup. "Jeff didn't remember seeing anything except the trash sack. He'll check. How are you doing? Should I call Emma to work with Andrew today, Karen?" Sheriff asked.

"No, the mayor will be here soon. Thank you for telling me about Darlene. You're right. It was a shock."

"Thanks to you, she's got a chance to get well." After the sheriff drank his coffee, his phone buzzed with a text.

"Jeff found her walker in the yard near the back door and no cane. He'll go to the hospital to ask the ambulance crew if they moved her walker or took her cane to the hospital." He shook his head and patted my shoulder.

He paused at the door. "You're amazing, you know?"

"That's scary about Ms. Darlene," Andrew said after the sheriff left.

I rose to my feet and made sure I was stable before I stepped away from the chair. "It is, but the doctors and nurses will take good care of her."

By the time I reached the counter, I was ready for the day.

Good thing. I smiled as the bell jingled, and Shirley burst into the shop. "I saw the sheriff leave. Did he talk to you? Can I do something?"

Andrew poured Shirley's coffee and put a scone, two donuts, and four donut holes into a sack. "Donuts and donut holes for Woody, Ms. Shirley."

Thank you for the donut holes for Woody, Andrew. Those are the early pumpkins, right?"

"Yes."

"The sheriff told me about Darlene, Shirley. I don't know quite yet what we'll do to cover the thrift store. I'll let you know if we plan to take turns keeping it open."

"Thank you. I have an appointment this morning at nine, but after that, I'm available all day until school lets out. Woody didn't have a chance to do your shopping on Saturday because of the wedding. He wants to take inventory, so we can shop. We'll check with you first."

Shirley dashed out the door. The mayor sidestepped to keep from being run over before he came inside.

"You know, right?" he asked.

"Yes. The sheriff came by earlier."

"Good. Barbara will go to the thrift shop later this morning. She said she'll cover the shop until Gee is better."

"That is awesome, Mayor."

"We have two groups today," Andrew said. "We made extra coffee."

The mayor peered at the specials board, and I said, "We're celebrating Early Fall with fall colors and early pumpkins, and our groups are the Methodist men and the Write Now Authors. The men's group is scheduled for nine, and the authors at ten."

"I better get busy." The mayor hustled as he put on his apron and ballcap and loaded the utility cart.

When the Methodist men filed into the meeting room, the mayor greeted them, and Andrew hovered near the utility cart.

I snickered. *Andrew wants to hear the mayor's stories.*

The mayor opened the meeting room door. "Would you mind coming in, Andrew? I might need extra help."

Andrew stared at me.

"It's fine, Andrew. Go ahead."

Andrew grinned as he strode into the meeting room, and the mayor winked and closed the door.

A few minutes later, I was smiling at the laughter and applause as Amber came into the shop. She wore her navy suit and white shirt. *Court day.*

I poured her coffee and put a scone, two donuts, and two donut holes into a sack. The meeting room rocked with more laughter and applause.

"Methodist men?" Amber smiled as she sipped her coffee and peeked into her sack. "Ooo. Vegetables."

I giggled. "You're right. I didn't think about that."

Amber sat at the counter. "I was sorry to hear about Darlene." She pulled out her scone and bit into it. "Mmm. Good. I have unexpected news for us."

The bell jingled, and a woman came into the shop and read the board and studied the display case. She wore sweatpants with sage-green paint stains and a stretched-out T-shirt. She had pulled her unbrushed hair back into a low ponytail.

The woman glowered. "I need donuts for a group that will be at my house in fifteen minutes."

"Are you the surprise host?" I asked.

"You guessed it, except I'd call it bushwhacked. I'm being passive-aggressive in retaliation. I missed the last meeting where they decided I'd host the next one, and Clarissa didn't call me until this morning to mention it. I was in the middle of cleaning my oven, and my messy house stinks."

She collapsed onto the stool near the register and grinned. "I plan to arrive at my house ten minutes after the meeting time. They can stew on the front porch until I show up. No, they'll sit in their cars. What do you recommend for a group of five, sneaky women?"

"You might consider five scones and five donuts. You could cut them in half or quarters to give your guests a chance to decide which they like best."

She nodded and decided on six scones and six donuts.

"Do you want me to cut them for you?" I asked before I boxed them up.

"No. I think I'll enjoy making them wait while I take my time. All the pieces have to be the same size, right?" She cackled.

When I handed her the box of pastry, she asked. "Am I carrying this too far?"

"Not at all," Amber said.

After the customer left, I refilled Amber's coffee. "You have news?"

She sipped her coffee. "Remember the judge who was ready to sign your appeal? He didn't sign it, but he didn't deny it. He left it open and asked Lloyd's lawyer for his evidence to support Lloyd's allegations. We didn't have that information until this morning, and I'll admit, I was shocked. The judge is meeting with your lawyer and Lloyd's lawyer tomorrow afternoon. I don't think Lloyd's lawyer will show, but we'll see."

My eyes widened. "That's remarkable."

"Yes, it is. I have court in—oops, gotta go—but I had to tell you as soon as I heard. And pick up my vegetables."

I refilled her coffee, she dashed out, and I stared at the door. *Wow.*

My phone buzzed. *Jack.*

Jack: "Heard about Darlene. What's the plan?"

Can't call?

Me: "Barbara will open the shop."

Jack: "Thanks."

Andrew carried a platter as he came out of the meeting room. "The mayor is funny. We laughed." He filled another platter with scones, donut holes, and donuts and returned to the meeting room.

A steady stream of customers kept me busy until the Methodist men filed out. Mayor and Andrew scrambled to clean the room, replace napkins, plates, sugar, and sweeteners, and refill the coffee carafes and pastry platters.

As the Write Now Authors filed into the meeting room, the mayor asked, "Ready for your writing prompt?"

The authors giggled and pulled out notebooks and pens. The mayor closed the meeting room door.

"What's a writing prompt?" Andrew asked.

"It's a word. The author writes a story or poem about the word."

"I like stories." Andrew ran hot, soapy water into the sink for his pots and pans while I loaded the dishwasher.

Andrew scrubbed pans and set them in the drainer to dry. As he wiped out the sinks, he said, "I like to walk."

Andrew's not random. "I know you do." I waited.

"I don't like that man." Andrew wrung out his wet cloth.

"What man is that?"

"That man that follows you all the time."

I nodded. "Does he walk too?"

"No. He drives his car. I always see him when I see you."

"What color is his hair?"

"Yellow."

The mayor opened the meeting room door. "Andrew, would you bring in more early pumpkins?"

As Andrew filled the platter, the mayor said, "Donut Lady, can we borrow Andrew? We need someone to listen to the stories and poems."

Andrew's face brightened.

"Good idea, Mayor. Of course, he can."

Andrew marched into the room with the platter, and the mayor closed the door.

A few more customers came into the shop and left with the remaining scones, donuts, and donut holes while Andrew listened to stories. Andrew grinned as he came out of the meeting room. "The stories were good, Miss Lady."

The authors chatted and tittered as they left the shop. The mayor loaded the utility cart with dirty dishes and picked up trash, and Andrew unloaded the dishwasher. While the mayor swept the meeting room and the shop, Andrew placed the final load into the dishwasher, and I flipped the sign on the door from *Open! Come on in!* to *Closed! See You in the Morning!*

After the shop was in order, Andrew left, and I recorded our sales. "I'll drop off the bank deposit on my way to see Gee, Mayor, if you want to go to the thrift shop."

He nodded. "I'll take the dogs with me, and we'll see you later. Take your time."

I slid into a parking spot near the entrance to the rehabilitation center. *About time I got a break.* I signed in and sauntered down the hall to Gee's room.

When I tapped on the door, Gee said, "I heard about Darlene. Are you here to bust me outta this joint?"

"You'd make too much noise clacking down the hall with that brace, Gee. We'd never get away with it." I sat in the visitor's chair next to her bed and shook her empty water pitcher. "You need water. I'll fill it. How are you feeling?"

"Cooped up. Thanks for asking." Gee pouted and scooted up in her bed. "Tammy called me. She's hoping Isaiah will be released for rehabilitation in two weeks. She said the doctors are treating him for possible infection. Minor setback, according to the doctors. I'm not convinced. Have you heard how Darlene's doing?"

"Not a peep. I may drop by the hospital to snoop."

"If you find out anything, let me know." She waved her cell. "I have my phone now. Did you close the thrift shop? It's okay if you did, by the way."

"Barbara's taken over, and the mayor's there now."

"You know what a big deal that is for Barbara. She gets anxious when she leaves her house for even a few minutes. Please tell her how much I appreciate her time." Gee shook her head. "We're getting spread a little thin. Did you rent a car?"

I told her about my new minivan, and she laughed. "Just like you to buy a vehicle specifically for all the animals. How are Mandy and Sandy doing? What about Pepper?"

"Sandy is king of the thrift shop. You know at first, I didn't understand why a black cat with a white face would be named Sandy until I read about Sandy King, an Arizona outlaw in the eighteen hundreds, and it fits. Plus, a king would wear a tuxedo, right?"

Gee snorted. "Definitely fits. Leave it to you."

"Mandy adores Darlene and the thrift shop. She stays with us at night then we all go to the donut shop in the morning and the thrift shop in the afternoon. Mayor took all the dogs with him to the thrift shop today when he left. I always thought Pepper was a lightweight—an inside dog, but she thinks she's a big, outdoor dog like the rest of the canines. She and Mia have an antagonistic relationship and torment each other."

"I'm glad to hear that Pepper has come out of her shell. What about Jack?"

I frowned. "I don't really know. He's been standoffish. Maybe he needs some time to forgive himself."

Gee shrugged. "I thought he had more backbone than that. How's Woody doing?"

I rolled my eyes. "He's acted too big for his britches a time or two, but Shirley's right on top of him."

"Good for Shirley," Gee said. "I had serious doubts about her when she signed up to foster Woody, but she's doing great."

"What about you? Do you need anything?"

"I need a couple of books to read. They have magazines, but they're fluff. I need something I can't read in two minutes."

"I'll bring you some next time I visit."

Gee's physical therapist tapped on the door. "You ready, Ms. Gee?"

"I suppose." Gee wrinkled her nose.

I rose and headed to the door. "Work hard, Gee, and get out of here."

The car was hot when I climbed into the driver's seat. *So much for our early fall.* I turned on the air conditioner. I pulled in at the hospital entrance and circled the parking lot a few times. When a car pulled out, I zipped into its spot.

The volunteer at the Information Desk smiled as I approached. "I loved the early pumpkins and the orange scone, Ms. Donut Lady." She glanced over her shoulder and scanned the room before she whispered, "You're here about Ms. Darlene? I can't—"

She scrolled through her screen then grinned. "Never mind. You're listed as her contact. She's on floor two. That's the regular medical floor. She didn't go to ICU. That's good, and it says no visitors until this afternoon. That's you."

"Thank you." I smiled and returned to my car.

Grocery store next.

After I parked, I jotted down a quick list and hurried inside. The cool blast of air felt good on my damp neck. I dropped off the groceries at my house and continued to the thrift shop.

"There you are," Barbara said when the dogs mobbed me at the door. "I made sandwiches for us. Ready for lunch?"

"Sounds great. Shall we eat up front and watch for customers?"

"You two can eat in peace in the back," the mayor said. "I'll watch the front."

"I have news." I wiggled my eyebrows, and Barbara giggled.

"Or we can all enjoy lunch together." Mayor beamed.

Barbara opened a cooler and handed us home-made pimento cheese sandwiches and sweet tea. "I'll even relax my rules about no business during meals."

I chuckled. "You fell for my bribe."

I told them about Gee, Isaiah, and Darlene. "Of course, the news about Darlene is totally unofficial—"

"And probably the most reliable source we have," the mayor continued.

"You're right." I ate the rest of my sandwich. "This is really good, Barbara."

A customer came into the shop, and Mayor greeted her.

"He takes care of sales, and I take care of finance and scheduling," Barbara whispered.

"Any deliveries?" I asked.

"None, and I haven't heard from or seen Jack. I'll call him if we have any deliveries before I schedule anything. Is he trying to usurp me as town recluse?"

"He's an amateur. You have nothing to worry about." We snickered.

"How did you sleep last night?" Barbara narrowed her eyes.

I bit my lip. "A nightmare woke me up at three, and I couldn't shake it off."

"Darlene?" she asked.

I nodded.

"Makes sense," Barbara said. "When I have nightmares, I pay attention to them too." She rose and brushed off her pants and gathered our trash. "I know you're exhausted, and I also know you won't leave. Why don't you find a comfy chair or sofa in the back and prop up your feet. Maybe you can nap a bit. David has a meeting in an hour and will be leaving for most of the afternoon. I'll wake you if you're sleeping."

"I am tired. Good idea, and you'll wake me, right?"

"You know I will. Somebody has to do the people stuff."

When I went to the back, I found an overstuffed chair and a footstool. I propped up my feet and closed my eyes.

"Karen? Sorry to wake you, but David just left."

I yawned. "Thank you. I may have fallen asleep the second I put my feet up."

"You can relax back here if you like, and I'll come get you if a customer comes in."

I shook my head. "I'm ready to move around a bit. Why don't we see if we can rearrange some furniture?"

"I have just the area that needs attention. I'll show you."

When we reached the front of the store, Barbara pointed to a grouping near the left wall. "I know we can't move the heavy furniture like the sofa very far, but can we make it more conversation-friendly? It looks like a waiting room."

"Darlene planned to tackle that cluster too. She said she'd never complain—of course, I laughed—but Jack and Thomas brought the pieces from the back to the front and dumped them willy-nilly. She planned to rearrange all the front groupings. I'll bet this was number one on her list."

Barbara snorted. "I can hear Darlene saying willy-nilly in her most disgusted tone."

After we shifted the angle of the sofa, Barbara carried one of the small tables to a different group.

"What about this lamp?" I asked. "The shade seems frilly for the rest of the furniture."

Barbara glanced toward the front. "Might have to wait. A car turned from the road to the parking lot."

I shivered when I saw the blond man's car and felt the blood drain from my face. When I grabbed onto the back of the sofa to steady myself, Barbara rushed to the front door, locked it, flipped the sign to closed, and turned off the bright interior lights. She grabbed my arm, and we hurried to the back room as I called nine-one-one.

"Sheriff's on the way, Ms. Karen. Where are you?" Summer asked.

"At the thrift shop. The man who has been stalking me pulled into the parking lot. The mayor's wife and I locked ourselves in the shop."

"Is he still there?"

I headed toward the front, but Barbara pulled me back.

"His car is," I said.

"Stay on the line. Sheriff is rolling in quiet-like."

I glared at Barbara and hissed. "You cheated. I wasn't ready."

She stuck her tongue out, and I giggled.

"You okay?" Summer asked.

"I'm a little nervous," I said.

"You are not. Tell me later. Sheriff's almost there," Summer said.

I darted to the front. "Oh no. He's leaving."

Barbara appeared next to me and snapped a photo of the rear of the car before it pulled onto the road. She smirked. "You're a bad influence."

"That's the truth," Summer said. "Sheriff's there."

I hung up, and Barbara turned on the lights and unlocked the front door as the sheriff parked then came into the shop. He crossed his arms. "Give me the long version."

I told him about the man at the railroad tracks, Andrew's description, and all the times I thought I saw someone following me, and Barbara told him about locking the door and turning off the lights.

"We went to the back of the store where he couldn't see us, and Karen called nine-one-one.," she said.

"We didn't see if he got out of his car," I said, "but when he started to leave, we ran up front—"

"And I snapped a picture of the back of his car." Barbara showed the sheriff her phone. He zoomed in on the license number and shook his head as he transferred a copy to his phone. "Out of date. We'll still check."

Barbara and I sat on the closest sofa, and he leaned against Darlene's desk. "What else?"

"There are a couple of things. Analysts are studying Terry's documents, right? What kind of analysis are they doing? Financial? Tracking the dispersion of the counterfeit money?"

Sheriff nodded. "They're focused on the documents that describe the amount of counterfeit dollars put into circulation by date and location."

"That's surface stuff Terry would have fabricated to divert any analysis of his records. Most of it is probably phony. What about Terry's personal notes?"

He frowned. "What do you mean?"

"Terry kept meticulous records. He documented his observations about people for future reference. I would have been surprised if he'd left out the counterfeiter."

"Nobody's mentioned anything like that. Can you show me?"

"I can, but it won't make any sense to you. He thrived on being devious and playing word and mind games to prove he was superior to everyone else."

The sheriff narrowed his eyes. "You're saying that a casual reader wouldn't catch the depth of what Terry wrote, but a trained analyst would? You're smart and observant, and you have remarkable instincts, but you aren't a trained analyst."

I smiled. "You're right, but a victim knows her tormentor. I know exactly how Terry thought."

Barbara nodded.

"So, what about the counterfeiter?" Sheriff asked.

"It's complex. Lloyd came here to find the second-generation counterfeiter to blackmail him by threatening to uncover his identity. Lloyd's downfall was that he didn't have Terry's cunning."

The sheriff paced and returned to the desk. "You said a couple of things. What else?"

"I think the counterfeiter is an angry, violent man, but he also has a heartless predator streak like Terry. He likes to watch his victim suffer."

"Lloyd's manner of death certainly bears that out."

"If there was someone like that who grew up in our area, who would know?"

"Easy answer. Alfred." Sheriff frowned. "Too easy?"

"Yes. Even as a kid, his instincts would have kept him off Alfred's radar screen. I'll give you a hint. Terry had nothing but contempt for me."

"A woman." Barbara's hand covered her mouth. "Did I give away the answer? Sorry. I got pulled in."

I smiled. "Yes. Our counterfeiter wouldn't have considered a woman smart enough to figure him out. You know who he fears, don't you, Barbara?"

"Yes."

Sheriff slammed his hand down on the desk. "Well, I don't!"

Barbara raised her eyebrows. "Darlene, of course.".

"We'll look deeper into Darlene's fall," Sheriff growled.

Barbara nodded. "It was set up to look like an accident. Maybe there was something stinky in her garbage, but why she would take her walker outside but not use it? As far as her fall, I can think of a hundred ways to do that." Barbara winced. "But I didn't do it."

"You two are—"

"Spooky?" I asked.

"I was thinking unbelievable or even scary, but spooky works." Sheriff shook his head. "Wish I could write this up before tomorrow. This would be a perfect test case for the applicants to analyze."

"We could do it, if you're serious," I said.

Barbara nodded. "We could write half a page. You can give them whatever hints you like."

The sheriff rose. "Appreciate it. If nothing else, it will provide a great group discussion to see how they interact with their peers."

As Barbara and I prepared to close the shop, she asked, "What did you plan for your dinner?"

"I have a chicken pot pie to throw into the oven."

"We'll be there at six. I'll bring homemade chicken pot pie. David can watch the dogs if you want to visit Darlene this afternoon."

"Good plan." I stuck the deposit into my purse, and the dogs and I headed to the bank.

After the mayor arrived at the house, I grabbed books for Gee and dropped them off then headed to the hospital to visit Darlene. The volunteer at the Information Desk smiled. "I am so glad you're here, Ms. Donut Lady. I saw you walk up and already signed you in. Ms. Darlene's been asking about you. She's in room 211."

I smacked on my paper badge and headed to the second floor. Darlene's bed was next to the window, and she smiled when I entered her room. "Saw you park, Karen. Glad you're here. Make yourself comfortable."

I scooted the visitor's chair close to her.

"I've been thinking about our counterfeiter and Lloyd. Pretty violent, right? Beyond what was necessary to kill the incompetent blackmailer. I looked over our list to see if I recognized any of the kids I've known over the years that were bullies and came up with three from the mayor's list of thirteen. Haven't seen any of them in ages."

A family strolled past her room. "Close the door, would you?" she asked.

After I returned to my chair, she continued. "Last week, and I don't remember what day, but it was in the middle of the week, I saw one of them who had been especially vicious to younger, weaker children, particularly girls, but always managed to charm his way out of trouble. I hadn't seen him in thirty-five or more years, but he still had the same mean eyes of a viper. When he stared at me, I knew." She cleared her throat. "My mouth's dry. Nerves."

I poured out her pitcher of water than gave her a fresh cup of water from the faucet. "I like how you think, Donut Lady." Darlene drank half her glass. "He knew I recognized him, and he didn't like it one bit. It was Bradley Sanford."

My eyes widened. "He's the judge's cousin from Conway."

She nodded. "I take my trash out every night after supper. It's usually dark this time of year, but I've lived in that house since forever, and I know every inch of the yard. It was overcast, just like it's been for the past week, but I was surprised that the bulb in my porch light was burned out. It was even darker than usual."

She drank the rest of her water, and I refilled her cup. "I had my walker, but on the way to the garbage can, something slammed me in the back, and I fell forward. I think I was startled for a few minutes because I just lay there. Maybe I cursed a little bit. My glasses fell off, but I found them. When I reached for my walker, I couldn't find it. I tried to crawl but the pain in my shoulder stopped me, and my arm couldn't support my weight."

She frowned. "At first, I thought someone was there, but my head was fuzzy, and I shook it off. I tried to call out, but my voice was too weak. I was sure somebody would come by the alley, and I'd catch their attention. I was miserable—worn out and cold. I closed my eyes to rest and wait. Must have been hypothermic. I had thrown on my fall jacket for my arms but didn't zip it up before I hurried outside."

She sipped her water and winced as she placed her cup on the tray. "Look at my left shoulder in the back."

I untied her gown at the neck and slid it to the side to expose the back of her shoulder. My eyes widened at the sight of the reddish-purple bruise that was the size of a baseball in the middle of her scapula. The angry red abrasion at the center of the spreading bruise added to the illusion of a horrifying target on her shoulder.

"This is ugly. Did they take a photo?"

"No. I didn't realize how sore it was until they moved me to this room, and the poor nurse's aide tried to help me sit up higher in the bed. When the doctor came in later, he told me he didn't find any medical reason for my fall. I told him about the pain in my back, and he said I must have hit my back on my walker as I went down, or a car sped by and threw a rock that hit me. I'm not sure anybody really looked at it. Go ahead. Take a picture."

I snapped a photo then retied her gown and snorted. "Did the rock bounce off you and knock your walker all the way back to the house? Jeff found it next to the back door."

I showed her the snapshot of her shoulder, and she gasped. "That's awful. You giving this to the sheriff?"

"Sure am. I don't have any idea what could have caused a bruise that bad, but the sheriff probably will. No wonder you fell so hard face down with a blow like this. Where will you stay after you're released from the hospital?"

"Barbara called. I'm staying with her and the mayor. I was worried about encroaching on her privacy, but she said if I'd talk to the people at the thrift shop, she'd take care of the bookkeeping and cook. You're okay if Mandy stays with you at night, right?"

"Absolutely."

"How's Jack doing?"

"I have no idea. He's either avoiding me for some reason or licking his wounds. He's gone into a shell."

Darlene shook her head. "Hope he gets help. Meanwhile, he's missing out. We're a fun crowd."

I snickered. "We are, aren't we?" I rose. "Take care of yourself. Do you want me to check your house? Make sure it's locked?"

"Jeff took care of that for me, and Barbara will pick up my mail. I'll let you know if I come up with anything else."

Before I left the hospital, I sent a text to the sheriff.

"I talked to Darlene. Meet me at my house?"

The sheriff was parked in front of my house when I pulled into my driveway. He rushed to my car door and opened it.

"Is Darlene okay?"

"She's doing well." I climbed out of the minivan. "I have a photo—"

"Why am I not surprised?" Sheriff growled.

CHAPTER TWELVE

On our way to the front porch, I showed Sheriff the photo of Darlene's back. After we were inside, he asked, "What's your theory?"

I shrugged. "A projectile of sorts?"

He examined the photo then transferred a copy to his phone. "Not a bullet or a BB. I'll have Jeff look too."

"Darlene said something else. She said the bulb in her porch light was burned out when she went out with the trash."

"Oh really? I'll have Jeff check that."

"Barbara and I will have the write up for you in the morning. We'll use Darlene as the case study."

He smiled. "That's perfect. I've got some sharp applicants. I'd like to hear their theories. Anything else? Please don't tell me there is."

I bit my lip and frowned. "I think that's it."

After the sheriff left, I grabbed a pad of paper and a glass of iced tea, and the dogs and I went out back. I jotted down notes for Barbara and me while I sipped my tea, and the dogs romped. When I rose, the dogs rushed to the door, and we went inside. The dogs lined up, and I fed them, but Mia refused to come out of the pantry. I placed her dish in the pantry, and she flicked her tail and ate. Pepper stood outside the door and stared at Mia's bowl. Mia turned her back on Pepper and continued eating while Pepper whined.

"I don't think she plans to share, Pepper, and you don't need cat food. It would upset your stomach."

At quarter till six, I answered the knock at the door.

The dark look on the sheriff's face startled me as I opened the door. "I expected the mayor and Barbara."

"I won't be long. This is an unofficial visit. I need you to be extra careful. Andrew was walking along the river and found Maisie running alone along the bank. He managed to grab her leash, and Maisie led him to a culvert near the road. Andrew found Henry Worley inside the culvert. He had been badly beaten but had crawled into the culvert." He narrowed his eyes. "Don't go anywhere alone. Andrew took Maisie home with him. Maisie will stay at the hardware store during the day. Andrew's parents will drive him to work and pick him up until we find Bradley Sanford."

"Will the judge be okay?"

"We don't know yet." He narrowed his eyes. "Don't be reckless. Sanford is either desperate or crazed."

After he left, I leaned against the door and shook. Colonel nuzzled my hand, and I relaxed. "Thanks, Colonel." I glanced out the window and opened the door for the mayor as he hurried into the house.

"I think we need new hot pads." He grinned as he rushed to the stove.

Barbara carried a large tote. "Salad, rolls, and dessert. Do you have notes for our write-up?"

"Sure do. I'll catch you up."

"After dinner," the mayor said.

Barbara placed the salad and dessert in the refrigerator. "Never knew that rule would come back to bite me," she mumbled.

"How long until we sit down?" I set the table and poured out iced tea.

"Fifteen minutes," Barbara said.

"I can give you the five-minute version then we can talk after dinner." I told them about Darlene and the judge and showed them the picture of Darlene's injury.

Barbara set the salad, rolls, and chicken pot pie on the table, I poured tea, and the mayor let the dogs outside. After we finished eating, Barbara and the mayor cleared the table, and I loaded the dishwasher. Barbara refilled our tea before we went outside.

"When do you expect Darlene to be released from the hospital?" I asked.

"I suspect it will be before lunch," Barbara said. "Emma is going with me to pick her up. Emma said she and Darlene have some scheme to talk over."

"Gee suggested we close the shop. What do you think?"

"I wondered how we would manage everything," Barbara said. "I don't think we have a choice."

"I'm ready for your details, Karen," the mayor said. I told them what I knew about Andrew, Maisie, and the judge, and explained my idea to use the assault on Darlene for our case study for the sheriff.

"I'm glad the experts will brainstorm," the mayor said. "My brilliant idea fountain ran dry."

Barbara rubbed the mayor's shoulder. "You are awesome. Nobody can turn a phrase or tell a story like you."

When we went back inside the house, my phone had a text.

Jack: "Call when you can."

I showed my phone to Barbara and the mayor. "Not very personal, is it? I'll go out to the porch."

I sat on my rocker to call Jack and listened to the phone ring. He picked up right before it rolled over to voicemail.

"I'm having some problems," he said.

No kidding. I waited, and he cleared his throat.

"I need some time to heal."

When he didn't say anything else, I said, "Okay."

"I've put my house up for sale, and Roxie and I will travel for a while to see my family and Ava's family to reconnect."

Not much for me to say, is there?

"Thank you for telling me."

He hung up, and I stared at my phone before I went inside.

"What's wrong?" Barbara rushed to me and held my arm as she helped me to the sofa.

"Jack's selling his house and leaving town. He said he needs to heal."

"Are you okay?" Barbara asked as the mayor hovered.

"I'm sad, but I guess I'm not really surprised. He's been more distant the last few times I've seen or talked to him." I gazed at Barbara. "I thought we were growing close, but everything changed." Tears slipped down my cheek, and I accepted the tissue that Barbara handed me. "I don't know if I'm mourning the loss of a good friend or what might have been."

"Shall we leave?" Mayor asked.

"No. It was really a shock, and I do wonder if there were signs along the way that I missed, but it's not my style to wallow in regrets or guilt." I shook my head, and my mouth quivered into a weak smile. "It's good to have friends, and it'll take time for me to get over the hurt. Let's have dessert. Dessert heals."

"I baked a chocolate pie and piped whipped cream stars around the perimeter. Chocolate has magical properties."

"Certainly does. The pie is beautiful," I said.

Barbara plated our slices of pie.

In between bites of the silky chocolate dessert, I read my notes aloud while Barbara wrote a rough draft for our case study.

My phone rang. *Shirley.*

"Are you okay, Karen? Woody wants to know if you're okay. If you need us, you call. Woody said to tell you we love you." She choked before she hung up, and a tear slipped down my cheek at the kindness in her voice.

"I guess Jack has listed his house with Shirley." I sniffed back another tear and chuckled. "That was the sweetest, most awkward Shirley call I've ever gotten."

I told Barbara and the mayor what Shirley said, and Barbara hugged me. "It's amazing she didn't blurt out anything about Jack. Wonder how long Woody coached her before she called?"

"I'll bet he wrote a script," the mayor said, and Barbara and I giggled.

Barbara picked up my notes. "Give me a few minutes. I thought of a thing or two I want to add to our case study."

After she finished, I reviewed our draft and made a few editing changes.

"I suspect when I type this up, I'll spot a few more corrections. Are you okay with that?" Barbara asked.

"Of course."

"I'll bring a copy for you and one for the sheriff in the morning," the mayor said.

"I can make fast changes if you spot any errors. Call me, and I'll rush them to you right away." Barbara rubbed her neck. "I think I'm letting my perfection side leak out." She put her hands over her ears, and I smiled.

"Don't worry about it. The candidates will be stressing enough for you when they try to figure it out."

The mayor put our dishes into the dishwasher, and Barbara frowned. "We thought we'd leave after dinner, but we can stay if you'd be more comfortable."

"I'm fine. I've got my guard dogs."

After Barbara and the mayor left, I called Gee and told her about Bradley Sanford, the judge, Darlene, and the decision to close the shop for a while.

"I agree with closing the shop. I'm not sure I remember Bradley Sanford. Henry's cousin, you say?"

"That's what I understand, but I'd recommend not mentioning his name. Sheriff said he didn't know if Sanford was desperate or crazed."

"Got it. Summer came by to check on me. She offered to pick up Sandy and take him home with her. She took care of him when he was sick before I adopted him. She said she's inspired by his grumpy spirit." Gee snorted. "I'll call her after we talk. She offered to take Mandy too, but I told her the dogs are a team. Is that okay?"

"I agree completely. There's no reason to disrupt her any more than we already have, and she's a sweet, mellow girl."

I cleared my throat. "I have more." I told her about Jack.

"Are you okay?"

"I was a little blindsided, but I'll be fine."

"I'll keep my opinion of Jack to myself," she growled.

I told her about Shirley's call, and she laughed. "I agree with Barbara and the mayor. Woody's raising his mama Shirley right. Is there anything else I can do?"

"Get well, and get out."

"On my list."

After we hung up, my pen glowed, and I smiled as I held it and absorbed its warmth. *I'm not alone.*

I took the dogs outside before we headed to bed.

* * *

Refreshing night. I dressed and fed the dogs and Mia. Mia finished her breakfast and scooted into the pantry, and the shadows slid from the hallway to follow her.

When the dogs and I reached the donut shop, Andrew was inside, and his dad was parked in front of the door. Andrew's dad waved as the dogs and I went inside. He drove away after I locked the door.

"Good morning, Miss Lady. Maisie is with my mom. Maisie works at the hardware store," Andrew said.

"That's good. What's our plan for today?"

"Mama bought a bushel of apples at a farm yesterday. She sent a bunch for us. Want to see?"

When I looked into the box of apples that we had, I said, "We can do apple-something scones. Do we have a group?"

"We don't have a group today. Will the mayor be sad?"

"He might. Maybe he'd like the day off. I'll ask him when he comes in."

"The sheriff wants termite donuts with a side of worms."

"That's right. We haven't made classic strawberry donuts in a while, and what do you think about eyeballs to go with the termites and worms?"

Andrew laughed. "Josh at the gas station likes eyeballs. What kind of scones?"

"Apple cinnamon."

Andrew peeled and chopped apples for me. He had filled the large coffee machine with water before I arrived. I measured the coffee and started the machine and made coffee in the regular pot.

After I mixed the scone batter, I added the chopped apples. While I focused on the scones, Andrew drizzled strawberry glaze on the first batch of donuts and organized his eyeball decoration supplies and toasted coconut while his second batch of dough rose.

The mayor hurried into the shop as Andrew decorated eyeballs, and I wrote on the board.

"Termites and worms, strawberry glaze, and apple cinnamon scones." He frowned. "What are Eye-Full donut holes? Is that a French—never mind. I get it. Eyeballs."

"Yes. Eyeballs," Andrew snickered.

"Good addition to our termite donuts and worms. Who's our group today?"" Mayor asked.

"No meeting today. You can take the morning off if you like." I pulled out my first batch of scones and popped the second batch into the oven while Andrew fried his second batch.

"Oh, no. Emma and Barbara are rearranging our guest bedroom for Darlene. I don't care to join that particular party. I wouldn't mind doing a thorough cleaning of the meeting room. I'd like to pull out the chairs and sweep and scrub the floor and the baseboards."

"It's a good idea, but we can schedule a deep cleaning session for another time, and you can take it easy."

"Nope. Sounds boring. Here's your copy of the case study."

I sat at the counter. After I read the case study, I said, "This is actually pretty good, isn't it?"

"I thought so. Coffee?" Mayor poured a cup for me then headed to the meeting room to remove chairs.

The bell jingled, and the sheriff came inside and chuckled as he read the board.

"We made the termites and worms for you and the eyeballs for Josh at the gas station," I said.

The sheriff's eyes twinkled. "Yep, creepy."

Andrew poured coffee for the sheriff and plated a termite donut, worms, an eyeball, and a scone then set the plate on the counter.

"Thank you, Andrew."

I handed the sheriff my copy of our case study, and he read it while he ate his pastries.

"This is excellent." He swiped at the drizzle of strawberry he'd dripped onto the paper, but it smeared. "Is this my copy?"

The mayor said, "I have the copies for you to take with you in a folder. It is good, isn't it? When do you meet with your candidates?"

"They're scheduled to arrive at the office at eight. Tess will give them a tour then Jeff will meet with them at eight thirty in two small groups to cover the administrative stuff while I talk to each one individually before we attack the case study. I've already gotten a call from an applicant who accepted another position and won't be coming."

He glanced at the sheet of paper. "I can't wait to observe how they interact with each other and to hear their approach to the problem. Your write up is perfect. You've provided detailed, concise information without leading to any conclusions. I'll let you know how it goes."

Andrew boxed up the donuts, worms, and donut holes.

The mayor cleared his throat. "Maybe I will take the morning off, after all, Donut Lady. I remembered a meeting I have today at the sheriff's office at nine."

Sheriff laughed, and I said, "No, you don't, Mayor. If I can't go, you can't go."

"I want to go too," Andrew said, and the mayor chuckled.

.

"Nice try." Sheriff picked up his folder and headed to the door. "I'll see you later with a full report."

"Speaking of meetings," I said after the sheriff left, "We should cancel tonight's meeting."

The mayor nodded. "Overcome by circumstances. I'll call Barbara. What about Monica's personal chef?"

"I'll call Monica. Maybe the chef won't mind scaling back." My pen glowed, and I smiled as I headed to the storeroom.

Monica picked up the phone on the first ring.

"Plans changed for tonight," I said.

"No doubt. Dinner for two at your house at six?"

Monica always knows everything.

"Exactly."

The bell jingled as Shirley rushed into the shop. "Eye-full? Is that eyeballs? I'll need some for Woody."

I poured her coffee while Andrew sacked up her order. "Thanks, everybody."

She dashed out the door.

"Was she trying not to say anything?" I asked.

"Must have been, but I'll bet she manages to swing by the gas station," the mayor said while he swept the meeting room.

Our morning was busy with a steady stream of customers. Josh rushed in at eleven. "Am I too late? I couldn't get away."

Andrew pulled out the two boxes of eyeballs we'd saved, and Josh's eyes widened.

"Y'all are awesome. I love eyeballs."

After Josh left, Andrew said, "Josh loves eyeballs."

The mayor wiped down the chairs and returned them to the meeting room. "Ready for inspection, Donut Lady."

I strolled into the room. "It sparkles. I don't think it's ever been this clean. You even polished the table and the buffet."

"We should do this more often. The cleaning, not all that other stuff. We deserve a few normal days with no drama, except I've forgotten what normal is."

"Isn't that the truth?"

The bell jingled, and Andrew's dad strolled in. "Anything left? I heard Josh got his eyeballs."

"Hi, Dad. We have two scones left. Mama would like one."

"I'll take both of them. What are termite donuts?"

"Bugs." I winked at Andrew, and he grinned.

"Yes. Bugs."

"Give me some bugs and worms if there are any left."

While Andrew snickered and placed his dad's order into a sack, I asked, "Coffee?"

"Sounds good." He sat at the counter. "Okay if I hang around until you're ready to go, Andrew?"

"Yes, Dad."

My phone buzzed a text.

Sheriff: "See you at your house after lunch?"

Me: "That's great."

I showed my phone to the mayor, and he grinned. "Can I bring lunch to your house today, Donut Lady?"

I snickered. "Of course."

After Andrew and his dad left, the mayor locked the shop while I loaded the dogs then he followed me to my house. The dogs and I went inside, and the mayor honked twice as he drove away.

My phone rang. *Darlene.*

"I'm being released, and Barbara and Emma are on their way to pick me up. I'll have a new walker in a day or so. The physical therapist recommended a sturdier walker for me. Do you suppose I can deflect rocks with a sturdier walker?"

I snorted as she hung up.

I frowned as I examined the kitchen floor. "It wouldn't hurt if I swept and mopped too." Mandy trotted to the back door and whined, and we all went outside. "Or better yet, I'll rock and watch you all play."

I dozed off in my chair and woke when Colonel nudged my hand. "Mayor should be back soon." I opened the door, and the three dogs filed inside. I poured a glass of tea and read over the case study. "Sheriff will be mad. I thought of something else."

When the mayor tapped on the door, I let him in.

"So much for early fall. It's turning into a hot day." He carried in a sack from Gus's. "Drinks are too unwieldy to manage. I'll take whatever you've got." He set the sack on the kitchen table and pulled out sandwiches, potato salad, and cookies. "Today's special was a roasted chicken sandwich and potato salad."

I poured tea and pulled out forks for our potato salad.

As we ate, Mayor said, "I'm supposed to call Barbara with a full report after we talk to the sheriff. Did you get in touch with Monica?"

"She'll be here at six."

After we finished our lunch, the mayor asked, "Would you like to read and have a cup of hot tea with your cookies? I'll brew you a cup."

After the mayor placed my tea and cookies on the table next to the sofa, he took the dogs outside. I found my copy of Terry's notes about his associates. As I read, I took notes.

When the mayor came inside, he said, "I thought you'd read your book."

"I realized I didn't spend any time on Terry's notes except to read over what Jack pointed out. How can I feel all superior to the analysts if I haven't done any analysis myself?"

"Good point. It's Tuesday. I'll make the guest bed and read unless you come up with something else for me to do."

I listened for Terry's voice as I read, and every word dripped with contempt and derision.

After I read a half page, I finished my tea and ate a cookie. I paced then went outside with the dogs. *Feel like I need a shower.*

When I returned to the sofa, I read the first page and took notes. After I read the first page, I carried my cup to the sink and poured a glass of sweet tea. I drank half the glass and ate my second cookie.

"How are you doing?" Mayor asked.

"It takes me two cookies to read a page. I need more cookies and a diet plan."

Mayor sent a text. "Barbara's on it."

"I was kind of kidding, but no way am I turning down fresh-baked cookies. You did forget to mention the diet plan, didn't you? Suppose it would be okay if I call Darlene?"

"What diet plan?" The mayor chuckled. "I crack myself up. I'm sure Darlene will enjoy hearing from you."

When Darlene answered, I asked, "How are you doing?" "I'm in heaven. Emma helped me take a shower at the hospital before we left because they had a large walk-in shower. She brought girly-smelling soap and shampoo that annihilated the pervasive institutional odor. Barbara's baking cookies. I never realized how healing fragrances can be. I thought the fall had blinded me, but Emma cleaned my glasses, and my sight was miraculously restored. That's my full report." She chuckled. "What can I do for you?"

"Remember the name you're not to repeat? Is Senior alive?"

"He sure is, at least last I heard. He's in a nursing home. He was in his hometown for quite a few years, but his son moved him. Won't take much for me to find out where he is without asking."

"How do you do that?"

"According to Barbara, I have marvelous customer service skills. She said slick and devious, but I'm sure it was a compliment."

"You can nose around without anybody knowing who you're asking about?"

"Did you hear what I said?" Darlene cackled as she hung up.

"How's Darlene?" Mayor asked.

"In charge of the road to recovery."

He snorted. "I know exactly what you're saying." He glanced out the window. "Sheriff's here."

Mayor opened the door, and the sheriff sauntered inside and grinned as he sat at the table. Mayor waved the tea pitcher, and the sheriff nodded.

"Your case study was brilliant. My hat's off to you and Barbara, Donut Lady. Our applicants dove into discussion with each other, participated, listened, and bounced ideas around. It was amazing to see their willingness to support each other. All five would be stellar additions to the sheriff's department. In fact, and this is for you, Mayor, I intend to press the county commissioners for another deputy position. With three deputies, we can cover around the clock. With four deputies, we can plan for vacations and not require our deputies to work while they're sick."

"How will you pay your third new deputy while you wait for the county commission to approve the budget?" Mayor asked.

I held up my hand. "Before you two get into all the technical, administrative trivia, how did your applicants do with the bugs, worms, and eyeballs."

"They loved them.   Best ice-breaker in the world." The sheriff smiled.

"Back to the commissioners and the budget," Mayor said.

Sheriff nodded. "I'll use the money for a vacant position that I've been half-heartedly trying to fill for ages. After the commissioners approve the budget for the fourth deputy, I'll shift our deputy to the new deputy position. Now that I'm inspired by the quality of candidates that are available, I'm confident that I'll find someone for the position that I left open for too long."

"I'm interested in their assessment of Darlene," I said.

"After they read the case study, I asked them to decide whether to investigate or not to investigate. I reminded them we're a small department and have to be careful about where we spend our limited resources, but at the same time, we're here to keep our town safe. They handed in their slips of paper with their initial impressions and rationale."

"What did they think caused Darlene's wound?" I asked.

"They examined the wound carefully and compared it to similar injuries they found on the internet. After discussion and grilling me for information, they agreed it was a projectile like a rubber bullet. When we read their original decisions, the unanimous decision was to investigate. Their reasons were different, but essentially they all said one way or another that it was too early to walk away. See why I'd take all five of them?"

Mayor nodded. "So, who did you hire?"

"I won't share names or their current employment until after they sign and return their offers. I told our three we'd be sending them formal offers tomorrow. After they sign and return them, we'll work out start dates, and I'll make a formal announcement. I'm hoping they will be on board by the end of the month. I told the two we didn't hire how impressed I was and offered to help in their job search. I'm sure they'll find positions soon. As far as the position for our third hire, our new deputy will dispatch until the county commissioners approve a new deputy position." The sheriff shook his head. "I know. It's nuts that I forgot about that open dispatcher position."

The mayor rubbed his chin. "If I'm remembering correctly, the budget for your department personnel does not designate specific positions. We might want to check into that. If that's true, you could hire your three deputies and hit up the county commissioners for an additional dispatch position."

The sheriff's eyes widened. "I've always watched the bottom line and didn't pay as much attention to the line items as I should have. Can we look over my budget tomorrow? I'll pull together everything I can find this afternoon."

The mayor nodded. "If the budget isn't as open-ended as I think, I'm sure you can have your third new deputy assigned to dispatch a quarter of the time to split with Summer. That'll help Alana, and you can train all your new deputies at one time."

"I could even rotate the new deputies through dispatch as part of their training. Thank you, Mayor. Sometimes I forget I'm not alone. It's good to have friends."

The sheriff dashed out of the house, and the mayor beamed.

I stared at the mayor. "You are awesome."

He grinned. "Yes. See you in the morning."

Darlene called. "I have senior information, but it's not helpful. Stage three dementia. He's at Gee's center but in the memory section or whatever they call it these days. Interesting but irrelevant fact is that senior and junior have the same names except for the middle name. Junior's is West. It was his mother's maiden name. Doesn't flow, does it?"

After we hung up, a knock at the door surprised me. I glanced at the clock. *Not even close to six.*

When I opened the door, Amber stumbled inside and crushed me in a hug.

"We did it," she said. "Break out the champagne. The Ohio judge signed your appeal. The slate is wiped clean." Amber danced, I danced, the dogs howled, and Mia chased the dancing shadows.

"I've got lemonade." I hurried to the refrigerator and poured two glasses of lemonade. We toasted each other, the judge, our Ohio lawyer, the no-show lawyer, and the bailiff.

"Why the bailiff?" I gulped the last of my lemonade.

"I got carried away." Amber flopped down onto the sofa. "I ran all the way here. Will you give me a ride back to my office?"

"You ran in those heels?" I dropped into a chair and snickered.

She raised her feet and stared. "They will hurt tomorrow, won't they? All those closed doors are open, Karen. What will you do first?"

"I don't know. The smartest thing to do would be to tell Shirley."

Amber laughed. "Make a list. I'll tell Mom and Dad. I know you'll want to tell the Sheriff and Gee."

She patted her pockets. "Dang. I ran out without my phone. Would you mind texting Leah and tell her I'm here. I should probably get back to the office." She rose. "Ouch."

I texted Leah before I grabbed my keys and purse. The three dogs lined up at the door.

"I'm not sure we can get past them," Amber giggled.

After I dropped off Amber, I sent the sheriff a text before I left the parking lot.

Me: "Appeal approved."

Sheriff: "When's the party?"

Me: "The rest of my life."

Sheriff: "You're right. Congratulations."

After the dogs and I returned home, I poured myself another glass of lemonade, and the dogs and I went out back.

I called the mayor. "Are you home?"

"Yes, do you need me there?"

"No, put me on speaker phone. This is for Barbara, Emma, and Darlene to hear too."

"Okay, we're all here. What's up?"

"My appeal was approved."

I moved the phone away from my ear while my dear friends screamed, shouted, and laughed. I giggled at the tumble of excited questions.

After they settled down, I said, "I'm still processing. I'll call Gee and Shirley. Can you think of anyone else?"

Emma asked, "What about Grady?"

"I texted him first."

"Monica?" Darlene asked.

My pen glowed. "She may already know, but you're right."

"When can we have a party at your house?" Barbara asked. "Do we wait a bit for other things to settle down?"

"I'd like that."

I hugged myself with excitement and sent a text to Monica.

Me: "Appeal approved."

Monica: "Yes. See you at six."

I knew she knew.

I called Gee. "My appeal was approved."

"I can't believe it. We've waited so long. It's almost unreal, isn't it?"

"You're right. Unreal. That's it exactly."

"What will you do now? Where are you going?"

"Where would I go?"

"I don't know. I'm so excited I'm not thinking straight, but if you go somewhere, I'll go with you." Gee smiled.

"Deal. I'll talk to you tomorrow. I'll call Shirley."

"That'll save you a lot of calls."

"Sure will." I snickered, and we hung up.

I rose and strolled to the back fence, and Colonel stayed by my side. Pepper pounced on her ball and dropped it in front of Mandy. Mandy picked it up and tossed the ball into the air, and Pepper raced around the yard before she snatched up her ball.

Mandy padded to join me and Colonel. I stroked her head. "Good girl, Mandy."

A car drove by the end of the alley, and I narrowed my eyes. After a closer look, I relaxed. "It's the neighbor down the street."

When I went inside, the dogs followed me. I fed them and Mia and called Shirley.

"The judge in Ohio approved my appeal."

"It's all over? You're cleared? No more court? You can teach school or foster children or anything you want? I'm so excited. I have to tell Alfred and Woody. They're working on a project outside. You aren't selling the donut shop are you? Is it okay if I tell Alfred and Woody? Don't sell the donut shop."

"I have no plans to—"

She hung up.

"I'm not selling the donut shop, Colonel."

Colonel licked my hand, my pen glowed, and I rose from the sofa and opened the front door.

CHAPTER THIRTEEN

Monica breezed into the house. She wore a long, flowing orange skirt, a bright blue blouse with puffy sleeves, and dark purple ballerina shoes. Her dangly silver earrings jingled like tiny fairy bells, and she wore a silver tiara with green jewels in her short, coal-black hair.

She reached into her messenger bag and pulled out another silver tiara with pink jewels. I grinned as she placed the pink bejeweled tiara on my head.

"We are celebrating." When she twirled her pen, the living room sparkled with tiny white lights.

A young woman in a black chef's jacket came in behind Monica carrying a large, insulated tote and a canvas tote. She had wrapped a silky, red scarf around her short, black hair and tied the scarf at the back of her neck. As she came inside, she bowed, and I bowed in return.

"Karen, this is Chef Noriko. She has prepared a splendid Japanese meal for us. She understands English, but is still shy about practicing around people she doesn't know well. We should give her some space and privacy to work."

"Of course. We can relax on the back porch."

The dogs followed us outside, and after we sat, Monica asked, "Are you still in shock?"

"I think I am. I never thought much about what it would be like to have my conviction appealed, but a huge invisible burden I didn't realize I carried is gone."

"The invisible ones are the heaviest."

While we rocked, Monica told me more about her grant, and the interest the library system for the state of Georgia had in the results.

Chef Noriko stepped outside. "Ms. Monica, your dinner is served."

Monica and I followed her inside, and the dogs stayed outside.

My eyes widened at the red placemats, bamboo soup bowls, intricate golden characters painted on the deep brown chopsticks, and the gleaming white individual dishes. "The table setting is beautiful."

After we sat, Chef Noriko poured our hot tea into white ceramic, Japanese style tea cups with delicate, hand-painted pink cherry blossoms.

"I have prepared for you miso soup, grilled mackerel, meat and potato stew, cucumber salad, and brown rice. Enjoy."

We picked up our chopsticks, and Noriko giggled as Monica tried to show me how to hold them.

"Allow me," Noriko said. She massaged my hand then placed the chopsticks between my fingers and thumb.

"Very comfortable. Thank you."

Monica and I talked about the barriers nonreaders faced, including their own shame and loss of self-esteem.

After we finished our leisurely meal, Noriko said, "I have a special treat for you. Japanese cheesecake. Not like American. Enjoy."

"Mmm." I said after my first bite. "Very light and airy. Delicious."

Noriko smiled and bowed.

After we finished our desserts, Noriko placed the dishes into her canvas tote, and Monica accompanied her to the door. I peeked out the window at the young man who waited at the curb in a small, red car, and he grinned when he saw Monica. He jumped out of the car, took the totes from Noriko, and opened the car door for her. After the three of them had a short discussion, the young man hurried to the driver's seat and drove away.

Monica smiled when she came inside. "We were Chef Noriko's first clients in Georgia. She and her husband will open a restaurant in Macon. They plan to Americanize their menu and servings sizes, but Noriko enjoyed preparing and serving a more traditional meal."

"It was absolutely marvelous."

"I agree. They promised if we visit their restaurant, we will be served traditional meals."

"Wow. What an honor. The serving sizes were perfect for me."

"Now that you no longer have a felony conviction, did you know you can travel to Japan? We'll plan a vacation. In between adventures and projects, of course."

I let the dogs into the house, and they scoured the rooms. "They're looking for Chef Noriko and the grilled fish."

"Smart dogs. You never know if you don't look," Monica said.

"That's for sure."

"I'm calling it a night. I'm tired, and you must be too. Sleep well." She waved her pen, and the dark gray shadows lightened to a pale, shimmery silver then she snapped her wrist. "No nightmares."

My eyes widened, and her eyes sparkled as she smiled. "You deserve some rest. Good night, Karen."

After she left, I brewed a cup of peach tea and relaxed with my book. When I finished my book, I patted the last page. "Knew it all along."

After the dogs had their outside break, I locked up the house and padded off to bed.

* * *

I smiled when I woke. "Another good night's sleep, Colonel." I hummed as I sauntered to the kitchen and opened the back door for the dogs. While they frolicked, I made my coffee and dressed. I stepped outside and breathed in the fresh, night air.

After I fed Mia and the dogs, Mia stayed home, and I loaded the dogs into the van. When I opened the door, Andrew said, "Good morning, Miss Lady. Historical society today."

I hurried to measure my flour for the scones. "We should do something new that is old."

"Yes. Mr. Otto made sweet plantain donuts. Did you know that? Plantains sound like plantation to me. That's old."

"Brilliant, Andrew. We're surrounded by old, abandoned plantations, and sweet plantain donuts would be new for us to make. I can dash to the store to buy sweet plantains as soon as they open."

"Is it okay that Mama and I did that yesterday?" Andrew frowned. "We saw them, and they were on sale. Mama said she heard Mr. Otto made sweet plantain donuts one time. She brought me to the shop this morning, and we found the recipe."

"I can make shoo fly scones. That's easy. Shoo fly pie is made with molasses. I'll add vanilla drizzle and raisins for the flies, and we should have pink-sprinkled donuts because they are our old standby."

"Yes."

"I'll mark the board and check Mr. Otto's recipes. I'm sure I can find something close to shoo fly pie."

I tried to flip from page to page, but I kept getting caught up in reading interesting recipes. I stopped reading and grabbed the molasses off the shelf.

"It doesn't take much molasses for flavor. I'll make plain scones and add molasses. It'll work."

"I don't like molasses. It's too strong," Andrew said.

"I agree with you, but some people like it." I wrinkled my nose. "Should I do something else?"

"No, Miss Lady," Andrew said.

After we'd made coffee and decorated our donuts and scones, the bell jingled, and the sheriff strode in.

I poured his coffee, and he read the board. "Plantation donuts, pink sprinkled, and shoofly scones. Historical society today?"

"Yes."

The mayor rushed into the shop. "Sorry I'm late. Can I come to your house in the mornings and take a shower, Karen? Better yet, can I sleep on your back porch?"

Andrew snickered as the mayor checked the board and mumbled, "Historical society."

I served the sheriff his donuts and a scone.

"Shoo fly pie is made with molasses. I loved it when I was a kid." He shrugged when I widened my eyes. "It's an acquired taste."

I refilled his coffee, and he finished off his scone.

"Karen, Henry Worley regained consciousness last night. He's still in critical condition, but he named his attacker: his cousin, Bradley Sanford. The Georgia Bureau of Investigation has taken over."

He ate his pink-sprinkled donut. "There's more. Bradley Sanford is nowhere to be found."

Mayor stepped out of the meeting room and joined us at the counter. "Does that mean Karen's out of danger?"

"I'm not sure. You'd think he'd be smart enough to stay away from here."

Mayor shook his head as he headed back to the meeting room.

The sheriff finished off his coffee. "I'm not convinced he's gone for good. I think there's still something he thinks you know, and he is obsessed with silencing you."

I raised my eyebrows. "Wish I knew what I'm supposed to know."

He nodded. "Congratulations again on your conviction appeal. It's been a long road for you, but your journey brought you here, and I'm glad about that. Can I have a coffee to go and another scone?"

I handed him his coffee, and Andrew placed a scone in a sack. On his way out, he stopped to hold the door for the historical society arrivals, and Shirley bustled in after he left.

"I'll take whatever I'd like. Have you seen Jack's place? He really let it go. I've got a call in to him to see if he'll hire Alfred's boys to do his landscaping for him, and the inside of his house hasn't been cleaned or decluttered in years. Looks like one of those TV shows. I recommended an agency that clears out trash, and he can hire a local company to clean. I can't show it in its current condition, and just as bad as the mess, he turned off his utilities. That house will be overrun in no time by roaches and mice if it isn't cleaned up and by mold without air conditioning and the dehumidifier. This is south Georgia, for goodness sake. What was he thinking?"

Mayor slipped out of the meeting room to listen as Andrew carried in a platter of donuts.

Shirley glared and held up one finger for emphasis. "I've given him one week to clean it up before I cancel his contract. I had a buyer all lined up. I'm glad I decided to do a quick walkthrough first. I'll scope out some other houses today. Did you know the sheriff is hiring three new deputies? Or maybe two. I sometimes get numbers mixed up. I'm sure they'll be looking for places to live. It would be nice if we had something for them. I don't know what they might want, so I'm looking at everything. I have to run."

After she left, the mayor shook his head. "When does she breathe?"

I frowned. "The last time I went to Jack's house, the driveway needed to be cleared, and the weeds had taken over the yard, but I've never been inside his house. He talked a few times about inviting me to dinner, but he never did."

Mayor poured me a cup of coffee. "Ready for more shocking news that is actually exciting?"

I perched on a stool and sipped. "I'm always ready for exciting in a good way news."

"Darlene decided she's well enough to go home. I think she's worn out by the attentiveness of her caretakers. She said she needs a dog and a grumpy cat. She loves Pepper, but she wants a big dog that she can see and not fall over."

I laughed. "I think it's a great idea, and I'm sure Alana can help her, but what brought that on?"

"All she talked about last night were the dogs and Sandy and how much she missed them. She was worried about Maisie, but we assured her that Maisie and Andrew enjoyed their walks together. She said she needed a dog to talk to and to let her know if someone's around and a grumpy cat to remind her how much people annoy her."

"I'd forgotten she was around Colonel and Mia at the shop when Mr. Otto owned it. Of course, she needs a sweet dog and a grumpy cat. She'd just forgotten."

When all the donuts and scones were gone, I locked the front door and glanced out. "Andrew, your mother is here. Please thank her and tell her how successful the plantain donuts were."

"Yes."

After Andrew left, the mayor asked, "Do you have the bank deposit ready yet? I'll drop it off."

"Won't take me long."

I prepared the deposit and handed him the bank bag. "I've been really shaken up the past two days, but I just realized something. I've been angry beyond words at Terry since the first time he made fun of me and made me doubt myself. The more he tortured me and laughed, the more I hated him but wouldn't admit it. I hated him for targeting me in the first place. He knew I wanted to come back here to teach. I grew up around people who were nice, and he was not. I'm angry at him for jumping in front of my car. I hate him for dying. I'd run over him again in a heartbeat, except earlier, like the day I met him in the library." I clenched my fists and took a breath. "Allegedly."

The mayor blinked. "Yes."

I snickered. "Sometimes Andrew is the smartest of us all."

"Let's sit." He pointed to the reading table. "What about Jack?"

"I'm angry at Jack. It wasn't necessary for him to pull me into his problems, and they are his problems, not mine. I don't hate him, but I'm the forgive but don't forget type."

"Well said. Do you think Bradley Sanford's still around?"

"He may have left the area for a while, but he'll be back, and I'll be ready."

"What is our plan?"

I grinned. "I can't slip anything past you, can I?"

"Nope."

"I'll spend this afternoon on the documents. I made the mistake of believing Jack when he said he'd be thorough."

"Call me when you're ready to brainstorm."

He rose and headed to the door, and the dogs and I followed him.

When we arrived home, the dogs ran into the house and to the back door. As I reached for the doorknob, Mia crept out from under the sofa and stalked Pepper. She pounced as Pepper dashed outside. Mia remained splayed on the floor as she hissed at the door.

"I don't think it's the door's fault, Mia."

Mia scrambled to her feet and marched to the hallway. The pale shadows gathered then followed her, and I shook my head. "We've all got our people, haven't we, Mia?"

I poured a glass of tea and grabbed a small carton of yogurt. I let the dogs back inside and filled their water bowl. After I pulled out my folder with all of Terry's documents, I took notes. When I shuddered at the sound of Terry's voice as I read, I held my pen. "Forget it, Terry. I have friends."

I reread a page with a new perspective. *He hated the counterfeiter as much as he despised me. I'm not sure I knew that.*

By midafternoon, I'd read almost half of the documents and had six more pages of notes. I added ice and more tea to my glass and gulped down half of my cooling, sweet drink. "I was thirsty. Anybody going outside with me?"

Mandy remained asleep under the kitchen table on the cool floor, Colonel lumbered to the door, and Pepper nosed the pantry door.

"Did you close the door on Mia again?" I opened the pantry door, and Mia licked her paw and swatted Pepper. Pepper dropped onto the pantry threshold in a dramatic thud, and Colonel and I went outside.

"So much for our early fall. We're back to our hot and humid afternoons, Colonel. That little breeze is a lifesaver, isn't it?"

Colonel raised his head and flipped his tail.

The neighborhood birds darted to the birdfeeder then to the birdbath for a sip, and a kaleidoscope of butterflies decorated the yard as they descended onto my yellow flowers.

I need an outside project. I wonder if Alfred's boys would help me put in a small fall vegetable garden?

The dark clouds in the west hinted of rain later in the day. "I always think the rain will knock down the humidity, but it never does." Colonel gazed at me, and I rose. "Back to reading."

When Colonel and I went inside, Mandy was still asleep, and Pepper and Mia were curled together on one of the soft chairs.

I dove into the documents and took notes.

When I came across ten pages of real estate listings, I leaned back in my chair. "This is interesting. I never knew Terry was interested in real estate." I jotted down the addresses and set the listings aside while I did more research.

"Ah. I've got it." I checked social media. "Bingo."

I picked up my phone and called the sheriff. "Sheriff, I assume the Georgia Bureau of Investigation is searching Bradley Sanford's house in Conway. He owns another property that may be the base for his operation. I'll give you the address."

He repeated it back to me before he hung up.

At five, I'd reached the last page and had twenty pages of notes. I paced the kitchen then called the Mayor.

"You're inviting us to dinner, right?"

"I have twenty pages of notes, and I counter your offer to brainstorm with an invitation to dinner. Is this short enough notice that I can order the specials from Ida's Diner for us?"

"Darlene abandoned us, and Emma went home too. You could call Ida's if you like, but Barbara would throw out tonight's dinner and be mad at us for wasting food."

I chuckled. "Sometime we should plan ahead so I can hire Monica's chef. I know Barbara will be insulted at first, but she'll be impressed by Noriko's culinary skills."

I set the table, fed the dogs and Mia, and picked up my notes to reread them but decided I needed a break. I researched fall vegetables for small gardens in the south until the mayor knocked on the door. *That was a fast hour.*

Mayor carried in a casserole and placed it on the stove. "Be right back." He brought in another casserole dish covered with foil and a tote bag.

Barbara carried in a covered dessert dish. "Congratulations, again. I'm so happy that's behind you. We can eat right away so you two can brainstorm. I brought my book, so I can pretend I'm not listening."

I poured sweet tea while Barbara set our dinner on the table. "Ham, sweet potatoes, mustard greens, and rolls. I decided we needed a southern supper."

She placed a bottle of hot pepper vinegar on the table for our greens. "Homegrown chili peppers. I planted pepper seeds in two pots on our deck last spring. I was surprised at how well they did. I have pepper jelly too if we ever decide we need a topping for our crackers and cream cheese appetizers, and if we ever slow down enough for appetizers. Let's eat."

After I ate half of my dinner, I placed my fork on my plate and sipped my tea. "This is delicious, Barbara, and perfect for an early fall that fell back into late summer."

She smiled. "Isn't that the truth?"

As Barbara cleared the table, she asked, "Dessert now or in a bit?"

"Hard choice." Mayor narrowed his eyes. "Now, because it would be tragic if we're heads down and forget to have dessert."

"Not likely, but now it is."

Barbara served us generous slices of lemon meringue pie. I ate half my pie. "I'll have the other half later."

Mayor stared at his empty plate. "I'll have a second piece to keep you company."

Barbara grinned as she cleared and wiped it off the table. "All yours."

"Whatcha got, Donut Lady?" Mayor asked.

"Lots. For starters, I understand why Terry called the counterfeiter *Pear*. Wished I'd figured this out sooner. Bradley Sanford. Brad-ford."

"Pear." Barbara said.

"Correct."

Mayor gazed at us with his brow furrowed.

"Bradford is a variety of pear, David," Barbara said. "It was quite popular for a while, but it turned out to be peskier and more stinky than people thought. It's probably considered an invasive species because it cross-pollinates with other pear trees with undesirable effects including producing large thickets and crowding out native plants."

"How appropriate for Bradley Sanford." The mayor frowned. "Even if someone figured out the Brad Sanford reference, who would know how obnoxious the term was?"

"Right. That was my first hint of what Terry thought of Sanford. It shed new light on the rest of the documents which brings us to the real estate listings." I handed the stack to the mayor. "Read these."

The mayor flipped through the pages and returned to the first page. "Do you have some paper? I might need some notes to keep a few things straight."

Barbara handed him a pen and the notebook she'd brought. Mayor wrote a few lines and continued to the second page of real estate listings.

"While he's doing that, want to go outside for a bit, Karen?" Barbara asked.

When I opened the door, the dogs rushed out, and the neighbor's cat scampered home. We relaxed in our rockers under the clear night sky.

"I expected rain earlier," I said.

"It turned north. Tell me about Monica's personal chef."

"Noriko and her husband may open a Japanese restaurant in the area. They plan to adapt their recipes to American tastes and portion sizes, but she served us a traditional Japanese meal, and it was amazing."

"Maybe we can hire her for another traditional meal. There may be a market for authentic Japanese food. After all, you can get Americanized

Chinese, Cuban, Mexican, Italian-type meals that have lost their cultural roots, and people may be tired of that."

"That's a good idea. Would you and I freak out if we hosted a large crowd for a celebratory dinner?"

"Of course, we would, but we'd get over it." She giggled. "Want to check on David?"

We went into the house, and the mayor glanced up from the table. "I give up. How did you make sense out of this?"

"One point that might make sense later is that I learned Bradley Sanford has the same name as his father except for the middle name. The younger's middle name is West."

"Aha," the mayor said. "Just kidding. Didn't help at all."

"Right. What if we're looking at the documents in the wrong sequence? What if Terry first tried to find the counterfeiter he'd heard about?"

"Why did Terry think the counterfeiter was in Georgia?"

I rubbed my forehead. "Maybe I forgot to tell you. Lloyd told me the only reason Terry married me was because he found out about a bigtime counterfeiting operation near Conway, Georgia. Terry assumed I'd know something about it because he'd heard people from small towns know everybody's business."

The mayor frowned and titled his head. "That does explain Terry's real estate search, but all these are for sale."

"Look again. All the listings were recently sold, at least when they were printed twenty years ago."

Mayor frowned at the pages again. "You're right. I overlooked the dates and the fact they were sold and focused on the similarities of the properties—geographic location, lot size, number and types of rooms, and the other typical details people look for in a home to buy. Did Terry use the familiar to hide details often?"

"Frequently. It's how he got away with his victim scheme. He'd fake an injury and call the police who saw an injured, aggrieved, and apologetic man and an uncooperative wife who denied everything with wild accusations. You could see the boredom in their faces when I tried to explain. I think Terry was always irritated he couldn't convince or taunt me into having a glass of wine or a sip of beer, but I never acquired the taste for alcohol, and it was the one thing under my control, not his."

Barbara glanced up from her book. "Good girl. Sorry, I'm supposed to be pretending to read. Broke my cover again."

I smiled. "Now we can talk about geographic locations."

"I know the answer to this one. All the properties are in the northwest quarter of Georgia and are fairly rural and near mountains. Terry must think the counterfeiter bought property in the area and had an idea of what the counterfeiter's requirements for the property were. How did he know that?"

I sorted through the documents and handed the mayor three more sheets. "He asked around. Terry used Lloyd's associates."

I pulled out another sheet and handed it to the mayor. "Terry refers to his family's dog and the dog's friends at the dog park. Terry's mother was terrified of dogs and allergic to cats. The Ahrens would not have had a house pet."

"An analyst might come to the conclusion that Terry was describing a person, but it would only be a supposition with no facts." The mayor read the sheet. "The dog's name is Lucky. That doesn't sound too bad."

"Right, except Terry said anybody who believes in luck is a loser. If you read the descriptions of Lloyd's associates carefully and check public criminal records, you'll see that most of them were associated with counterfeiting. Good contacts for Terry."

"So dog park was Terry's word for prison, and he described his younger brother as a loser?" The mayor shook his head. "Not that I disagree about Lloyd, but don't most older brothers look after the younger ones, or is that a country folk thing?"

I chuckled. "Maybe. Terry would be incensed if anyone accused him of being country. He bragged about his street smarts. I'll save you all the details of my real estate searches, but I found the house that Bradley Sanford bought. Like everything else, it wasn't straight forward because he didn't purchase it as Brad Sanford."

"Isn't it impossible to complete a legal transaction without using your legal name? My head hurts."

"Yes, but—"

"We need a break," Barbara said. "Time for second dessert. Coffee, tea, sweet tea, water?"

I rose. "I'd like hot tea. Would it be okay if I stand for dessert?"

"Good idea, and sweet tea for me," Mayor said.

Barbara placed our drinks and desserts on the kitchen counter. As we enjoyed our pie, she snickered. "I feel like a kid sneaking the last piece before someone comes in and catches me."

"That's sad. So do I." I finished off my dessert. "Should we sit on the sofa? It might be more comfortable than the dining chairs."

The mayor moved my side table to the front of the sofa for the documents.

I set my cup of tea on my side table. "Bradley Sanford is a radiologist but also wrote romance novels under Bradford West. He went farther than many authors because he created a legal entity, a partnership named Bradford West."

"Where do you see that?" Mayor shuffled through the pages.

I chuckled. "I searched the internet earlier for Bradley Sanford. I expected to find he was part of a radiology practice in addition to working at the hospital and found his partnership. I checked social media and found the romance writer, Bradford West. I found it interesting but not related to anything going on in Asbury."

"So he purchased one of these properties as Bradford West. That couldn't have been a difficult search."

"It wasn't."

"That's where Terry got *Pear* from." Barbara bit her lip.

I nodded. "I'll bet he laughed over what he perceived as the ignorance of a writer using an invasive tree for a name."

"Do you think the northern property is the base of Brad's counterfeit operations? Do you think that's where he went? Should we call the sheriff?"

"Yes, to the base of operations, but Sanford doesn't know it's no longer hidden, and I don't think he wanted anyone to follow him there. I called the sheriff, and he will alert the Georgia Bureau of Investigation."

"But we're not done," the mayor leaned back.

"No. I think he's nearby and has to stop me before I realize what I know."

"What do we do?" Barbara asked.

"Now, we brainstorm," the mayor said. "We don't want to set a trap. We're too fond of the bait. What do we want to do? I think our best action is for you to hide, Karen. We can brainstorm the best place. Maybe we send you to Savannah, and you stay with Roger and Tiffany."

"Bad idea. I don't want to bust in on newlyweds." I frowned. "Divert, hide, trap, ambush, track, what else?"

CHAPTER FOURTEEN

Barbara set down her book. "Seems like to me it would be useful to know where he is. Is that track? I'm sure the investigators are looking for him, but Karen, you have special insights, and that's something we can do in safety. If we find where he is, you can tip off the sheriff. Is that the right word? We don't actually have to follow footprints in the snow. That would be too cold."

My pen blinked in my hand, and I smiled. "Hide and track then tattle? I kind of like that."

"You two make it sound so simple, and I hate that I like it," the mayor said.

"I think we maintain our same routine. We go to work as usual, and Andrew's parents are driving him, so he'll be safe."

"How do we track him?" the mayor asked.

"I'll reread the documents. There may be something I missed because I wasn't focused on where he could hide in Asbury."

"Dinner tomorrow. Six o'clock. The same routine." Barbara grinned.

"Why do I feel there was a huge argument, and I lost?" Mayor chuckled as he rose. "Good night, Karen. Hide safely. See you in the morning."

My phone rang. *Sheriff.*

"I forgot to ask. How did you find that address?"

"Bradley Sanford is a romance writer. He writes under the name Bradford West. The house was purchased by Bradford West."

"Of course." The sheriff hung up.

"Anybody want to go out?" The dogs rushed to the door, and we went outside.

A car pulled into my driveway, and I peeked around the corner. *Sheriff?*

"We're back here, Sheriff."

He strolled to the backyard. "Barbara told Emma she gave you some pepper spray."

"It's not illegal, is it?"

"Do you have it on you? Do you have any paper plates?"

I patted my pocket. "Sure, do you need paper plates?"

"Bring out one or two, and take the dogs inside."

My eyes widened, and he chuckled. "We'll do an experiment. Won't take long. You might turn on your porch light before you come out."

The dogs went inside with me. I grabbed the paper plates and flipped on the porch light.

The sheriff waited for me at the back fence. I handed him the paper plates, and he pulled duct tape and a black marker out of his back pocket. He drew a smiley face on the back of the paper plate and made the eyes large and dark. He taped the paper plate to the top of the fence and took two strides away from the plate.

"Stand here. I know he's a little short, but if your bad guy was even this close to you, he could grab you in one stride. Let's back up one more stride." I stepped back, and he chuckled. "Mine. Not yours."

I stepped back the length of the sheriff's long-legged stride. "Aim your pepper spray at his eyes. You should never use a weapon if you haven't practiced with it first."

I frowned. "It's pepper spray, not a weapon."

"If it's what you have to fight a bad guy, it's a weapon. Quit stalling. Get his eyes. I'll step away in case there's a wind drift."

What about me?

I held my breath, aimed the pepper spray at my attacker, and sprayed the grass in front of him.

"Step closer. Except remember every inch you are closer to him makes him twice as close to you because of his reach."

I stepped closer and held the pepper spray higher before I sprayed. I sprayed the middle of the fence a foot to left of the bad guy. The sheriff stood with his arms crossed. I walked up to the plate and sprayed it four inches away, and the sheriff guffawed.

"Got him." I blew across the top of the pepper spray.

On our way to the porch, the sheriff held out a plastic bag. "Drop it in here, and go inside and wash your hands. Don't touch your eyes, and don't let the dogs out."

After I scrubbed my hands, I returned to the porch.

"I don't have much faith in pepper spray as a defense against a human with bad intentions," he said. "The best pepper spray is a spray, not a stream like this is supposed to be, and the better, more expensive sprays are intended to stop an attacking dog, not a thug. I'll take the paper plate with me. Water the yard tonight so the dogs don't get into the residual, and I suggest you take a shower and wash your clothes."

He pulled the plate off the fence, dropped it into the sack with the spray, and waved as he strode to his car. I moved my sprinkler to the back fence and turned on the water for an hour.

Smarty pants sheriff.

After I went inside, I showered, put on my pajamas, and tossed my clothes into the washer. I held my pen while I brewed a cup of tea.

"Don't tell the sheriff, Colonel, but that was an effective lesson."

I sat on the sofa with my tea, pen, and notebook as I pored over Terry's notes to discover where Bradley Sanford hid out.

* * *

The next morning, I hurried to make sure the sprinkler hadn't flooded the yard overnight. When I opened the door, the dogs headed outside. The thick fog and cold morning air sent a chill through me, and I shivered then frowned. *Temperatures weren't supposed to drop until next week.*

I dressed before I called the dogs in for breakfast. Mia and her shadows stayed in the pantry. *I'll get coffee at the shop.*

"I'm not chasing you around to feed you, Mia. Here's your food. If you don't eat it, Pepper will." I set her dish down, and Mia dashed out of the pantry. The dogs sat for their food, and I placed their dishes in front of them. While they ate, I searched through my closet for a sweatshirt and my fall jacket. After they took their break outside, the dogs came in and stood at the front door. I put on my pink sweatshirt and grabbed my jacket.

After we left the house, I squinted through the windshield as I crept to the shop, but when I parked, the shop was dark. *Did we have a power outage?* My phone rang.

"Ms. Karen, this is Summer. Tess asked me to call you. Andrew has been missing all night. He and Maisie went for a walk and didn't come home. His parents are frantic. Call Tess if you see him or Maisie."

After Summer hung up, I called the Mayor. "Sorry for the early call, but Andrew is missing. I can simplify the menu to one I can manage alone. Just wanted you to know."

"We'll be there a little early."

After we hung up, the dogs and I went inside, and I mixed the first batch of donuts. I checked the calendar and sighed with relief. *Only one group, Amber's book club.*

While the dough rose, I mixed the ingredients for scones, prepared my baking pans, and turned on the mixer and the fryer.

After the dough doubled, I patted it down then cut out my donuts and dropped them into the fryer. *Did I forget a step?* I shrugged and lifted the donuts to the draining screen. I cut the scones and popped them into the oven. I rushed to the storeroom to gather the ingredients for the toppings.

When the oven timer dinged, I pulled the scones out of the oven to cool and scanned the kitchen. *What do I do next? I am definitely out of practice for this solo stuff.*

The mayor and Barbara hurried into the shop. She wore jeans and western boots and had covered her curly gray hair with a pink bandana biker-style. Barbara breezed past me and returned with her apron. "Where are we in the process, Karen?" she asked.

"I've got donuts and scones ready to be decorated. I can do that. Today's donuts are pink-sprinkled and maple, and the scones are cranberry-orange. Would you take over the second batch of donuts? I'll focus on the decorating and the scones."

"What do I do with the scrap dough?" Barbara asked.

"More donut holes. We sometimes even make a third half-batch specifically for donut holes because the book club members claim they don't like donuts, but donut holes aren't donuts."

Barbara's eyes widened, and I laughed. "I gave up understanding the logic long ago."

"Do I leave the donut holes plain?"

"Roll a few in sugar after they cool a bit but are still a little warm. The sugar isn't sugar but clear sprinkles, but leave most of them plain. They're the darling of the book club crowd, especially if they're reading a steamy romance novel. They call them bare-naked."

Barbara chuckled. "Thanks for explaining the rules to me."

While we worked on the pastries, Emma tapped on the door, and the mayor let her in.

"I heard about Andrew and came to help. I can help wait on customers," she said.

I smiled and waved to the storeroom. "Glad you're here. Let's get you an apron and a ballcap."

While I pulled out the box with aprons and caps, Emma joined me in the storeroom and closed the door.

"Grady told me he gave you a pepper spray lesson last night. My dad gave me the same lesson when I was in high school. When I asked him what I was supposed to do to defend myself, he told me I was smart and I'd figure it out. I was mad at him for an entire day. I called Barbara last night after I heard about your lesson. Please don't be mad at Barbara or me, but you can be mad at Grady, if you want to."

I handed Emma the apron and cap. "I was mad at him last night, but this morning, I decided it was better to be mad and embarrassed than badly injured or worse."

After I opened the storeroom door, Emma put on her apron and cap then hurried to take over the scones and to help Barbara with donut holes.

While I worked on the decorations, I asked, "Emma, were you ever in a situation where you would have used pepper spray if it had actually worked? What did you do?"

"I sure was. I should tell the mayor about it so he can turn it into a great story. Bottom line is, I died." She smirked, and Barbara and I giggled.

"Seriously, I had left myself a way to escape the situation and got away."

"Thank you for coming to help us, and for telling me about your dad."

After we mixed, baked, fried, and decorated all the pastries, Barbara, Emma, and I hugged.

"Do I get a hug too? I made the coffee, and the room is ready for the book club." Mayor feigned a downfallen expression.

"You poor thing." Barbara rushed to the mayor and hugged him. He wrapped his arms around her and swayed.

"Back to work." She kissed his cheek, and he unlocked the front door.

The bell jingled, and the sheriff strode in and read the board and smiled. "Good to see the whole gang is on duty. I need a to-go coffee and two pink-sprinkled donuts. Do you have enough for me to take a dozen bare-nakeds to the office? I've got a staff meeting in ten minutes. Maybe two dozen? I just heard back from our three prospective deputies, and all three accepted our offer. They'll mail their signed letters today, but I called a quick meeting with the staff to give them the news and a little background on each one. It may be Monday before I can make a public announcement, but I wanted the department staff to have the inside scoop before the gas station has the news."

"Congratulations." I handed the sheriff a large to-go cup of coffee.

"This is exciting news for the town," the mayor said. "You're right about the gas station. There's no way to keep this quiet. I'm having lunch today with a close friend who is also one of the sympathetic county commissioners. He and I will discuss the best way to approach the other commissioners with the need for a second dispatcher."

"Thank you, Mayor." The sheriff saluted as Emma gave him his bare-nakeds, and Barbara handed him his sack of donuts.

While Emma and Barbara placed pastries onto the display trays, the mayor carried a platter of bare-naked donut holes to the meeting room. I sipped a cup of coffee and held onto my pen. On my way to the storeroom to get the change for the cash register for Emma, my pen glowed and a strange warmth surged through me. *Andrew is lost. I can find him.*

I handed the money to Emma and poured myself a to-go cup. "I just remembered something. Can y'all hold down the fort until I get back?"

"Of course," the mayor said. "Take Colonel with you."

Colonel waited at the front door. "Evidently, he agrees with you." Emma chuckled.

When I stepped outside, I was relieved the fog had lifted, but without the blanket of clouds, it was colder. I zipped my jacket. After Colonel jumped into the minivan, I left the door open then headed to the house. "Remember when Woody was missing? Let's pick up some supplies."

While Colonel waited, I ran inside, changed to my western boots, and stuck dog treats into my jeans pocket. I pulled out a backpack and stuffed in a blanket, a bottle of water, and an energy bar then threw another blanket over my shoulder.

When I pulled out of the driveway, I headed to the river.

"I have a feeling Maisie went to the river to look for the judge, and Andrew followed her."

I slowed when we arrived at the culvert where the judge had sought refuge and scanned the surrounding area. I spotted a cleared, level area across the road from the nearby river. I pulled in and turned the minivan around to face toward the road then backed up to the barbed wire fence.

I tied my jacket arms around the backpack, stuck my purse into a backpack pocket, and grabbed a flashlight. I slipped on the backpack and clutched my pen with one hand while I scanned the ground across the road with the flashlight.

The gravel shoulder was barely wide enough for a car to pull off the road. High grasses and weeds grew alongside the shoulder and down the riverbank, and the mucky odor of decayed vegetation permeated the air. The water was dark and hid its depth. Frogs croaked a chorus and were answered by crickets and katydids, and the rolling buzz of the cicada community drowned out them all.

I shuddered. "I have no idea what I'm doing, Colonel."

We crossed the road. When Colonel trotted away from the culvert, I followed him. After fifteen minutes, we came to a wooden swinging footbridge. It was four feet wide and had posts with braided cables strung as handrails on each side. Colonel trotted onto the bridge and turned to stare at me.

"We're crossing that rickety bridge?" My pen glowed in my front pocket, and I steeled myself to follow Colonel.

When I stepped onto the bridge, I lost my balance in the sway, clutched the nearest post with both hands, and hyperventilated.

Colonel increased his pace.

"Wait up," I called.

After I slowed my breathing, I grabbed the cables and strode across the bridge like a fearless cross-country skier with the soul of a terrified mouse.

Colonel waited on the other side for me. I stepped off the bridge and fell into the weeds and thickets.

"Guess I can't glide through high weeds," I sputtered as I cleared the grass and weeds from my mouth.

Colonel nudged me, and I sat up and pulled my jacket away from the sticker bush. After I caught my breath, I slid off the backpack. I pulled my gloves out of my pocket and struggled to my knees. I dragged my backpack as I crawled to a nearby river birch tree and pulled myself up.

"I'll be sore tomorrow." I spotted a downed branch. *Better not be a snake. I'll have a heart attack.*

I held my breath as I picked it up. When it didn't wiggle or hiss, I breathed a sigh of relief. It was sturdy and not too curved. *Good walking stick.* I grunted as I slid the pack onto my back.

"Ready, Colonel. Which way are we going?"

Colonel headed back through the weeds into the brush and forest.

I tapped the brush ahead of me with my stick. *Sure am glad I wore my boots.*

Colonel ran back to me and crashed through the brush toward the culvert. I picked up my pace to keep him into sight but still listened for rattles. When we were almost halfway to the culvert, my pen buzzed and blinked, and Colonel stopped. He yipped and was answered by a whine.

He headed away from the river into the brush, and I tried to go through the thicket but couldn't find a way in.

I crouched and peered through the brush and called out, "Andrew? Here, Maisie. Come on, girl."

Dry leaves in the thicket rustled then Colonel crawled out of the brush, and Maisie appeared behind him. When they reached me, I rubbed Maisie's face and gave them treats.

"You're all wet, sweet girl."

Maisie darted back into the thicket, and Colonel followed her. The rustle of leaves helped me to follow their progress.

"Andrew? Are you there?"

"Is the bad guy gone?"

"He's gone. Not around anywhere."

"Me and Maisie hid."

"Are you okay?"

"I'm okay. I got scratches."

Birds chirped and called from the trees, but I didn't hear the dogs anymore until Colonel yipped.

"Maisie came back, and Colonel is here," Andrew said. "I can follow them."

In a few minutes, I heard the rustling of leaves, and the snapping of brush and twigs then the thrashing of brush. Colonel and Maisie slid out from under a thorn bush. Andrew broke through into the clearing. His clothes were wet, and his hands and lips were blue. I cringed at the sight of the bug bites and scratches on his face, neck, and bare arms. I jerked the blanket out of my backpack and threw it over his shoulders.

"How did you get so wet?" I asked as Colonel led the way back to the footbridge.

Andrew shivered, and his teeth rattled as he tried to speak.

"Can you follow Colonel?" I asked. "Let's get to my car, and you can tell me what happened."

It was easier going back to the bridge because this time, I knew where I was going.

"Hold onto the cables," I said. "The bridge sways."

Colonel led the way, and Maisie was cautious at first, but trotted along behind him. Andrew held onto his blanket with one hand and onto a cable with the other as he crossed the bridge. Colonel and Maisie headed down the road to my minivan, and Andrew followed them as I crossed the bridge more slowly than they did, but much faster than the first time I had crossed.

When we reached the minivan, I started the engine and called nine-one-one.

"Tess, I found Andrew and Maisie. They were in the woods not too far from the culvert where the judge hid. We're on our way to the hospital. Let Andrew's parents know. Can you call Tammy's kennel to see if they can clean up Maisie? She has burrs and stickers in her hair and needs to be fed, shampooed, and brushed then checked out by the vet."

On our way to the hospital, I asked, "What happened, Andrew?"

"The bad man we don't like tried to take Maisie, but she got away and ran down the road. I knew where she'd go and walked to the river. I guess the bad man followed me."

The engine warmed up, so I turned on the heater, and Andrew held his hands near the vents.

"He tried to hurt me, but Maisie bit his leg then he kicked her. I threw a rock at him and hit him in the head, and he fell down. My dad taught me to pitch a baseball. I can throw fast and hard."

My phone rang. *Tess.* I pulled over.

"Andrew's parents will meet you at the hospital. So will the sheriff. You know he's mad, right? Tammy's kennel is waiting for you."

I hung up and continued to the hospital. "Not nice to hurt a dog."

Andrew echoed, "Not nice to hurt a dog."

"How did you and Maisie get so wet?"

"The bad man got up and ran after Maisie, and she jumped into the river. I jumped in to save her, but it was deep and cold."

"It must have been hard to swim in the icy river."

"I don't swim so good. Maisie pulled me to the other side."

I shuddered at his big-hearted bravery to save Maisie. "Why were you so far into the brush?"

"The man shined a flashlight to find us, and Maisie and I crawled where he couldn't see us. I heard him walk up and down the road. I held Maisie and stayed awake all night. I was afraid the bad man would come back."

"You kept each other warm."

He nodded. "It was cold."

When I pulled into the emergency entrance, Andrew's parents stood at the driveway. Andrew's dad jerked open the passenger's door, and his mother gasped then rushed to grab a wheelchair.

"He and Maisie jumped into the river to get away from the attacker. They spent the night in the woods. I'll take Maisie to the kennel."

His dad helped Andrew to the wheelchair, and they hurried inside. Before I pulled away, the sheriff tapped on my window.

"We'll talk later," he growled and headed into the hospital.

"Thanks for the warning," I mumbled as we drove to the kennel. A groomer hurried out when I parked.

Colonel and Maisie hopped out of the van, and the groomer slipped a leash onto Maisie's collar. "Let's get you cleaned up and fed, Maisie. We'll call you later, Ms. Karen."

Colonel hopped into the van, and I called the mayor. "Sorry I was gone so long. Colonel and I found Andrew and Maisie. I'll be there in a few minutes."

I hung up before he could say anything and drove to the donut shop. "We'll be in trouble there too, Colonel."

When we went inside the shop, Barbara said, "You're a mess."

I frowned at the mud and debris on my jacket and pants. "I guess I am. I should wash my hands."

"You can have coffee," Emma said, "but we need details."

After I washed, I sat at the counter, and Colonel flopped at my feet. Emma stood on the other side of the counter, and Barbara and the mayor sat on either side of me. Amber came out of the meeting room and stood next to Emma. I told them I realized I could find Andrew, and Colonel and I went to the river near the culvert where Maisie found the judge. I told them about the bridge, the thicket, and Colonel leading Maisie and Andrew out of the thick brush.

Emma refilled my coffee, and I told them about Andrew, Maisie and the river.

Emma's face paled. "He could have drowned or died of hypothermia."

"I know." I shuddered. "I had to focus on my driving, or I would have fallen apart from thinking about it."

"What about the bad man? That's Bradley Sanford, right?"

"I think so. He should be easy to spot. He most likely has a knot on his head and a dog bite on his leg."

"Does the sheriff know that?" Mayor asked.

I frowned. "I didn't have a chance to tell him. He went into the hospital to see Andrew."

Amber nodded. "Here's your chance."

She returned to the meeting room, and Emma and Barbara hurried to the sink to wash dishes. The mayor poured a cup of coffee and set it at the sheriff's usual place. He sauntered to the utility cart, picked up a platter, and took donut holes into the meeting room.

When Colonel rose and flopped next to Mandy and Pepper near the meeting room, I grumbled, "Fine team you are."

"Did you say something?" Barbara asked.

"No." Emma snickered.

The bell jingled, and the sheriff stomped inside and sat on his stool. He glared as he sipped his coffee. "You saved Andrew's life. He was tired and falling asleep in the woods, but he never would have woken up. I'm still mad. Tell me something that will make me happy."

"Did you talk to Andrew? Bradley Sanford probably has a dog bite on his leg and a knot on his head."

"Really? Tell me more."

His cup was empty, but before I could pour a refill, the mayor came out of the meeting room and refilled both our cups.

I told the sheriff about Bradley Sanford following Andrew to the river and his failed attack on Andrew and Maisie.

"Be right back." The sheriff stepped outside and spoke on his radio.

When he returned, I told him about Maisie and Andrew jumping into the river, and Maisie saving Andrew. He shook his head.

"Andrew's parents and the doctors thought he was wet from the fog and dew. Give me a minute. The hospital needs to know they have a hypothermic, near-drowning patient."

CHAPTER FIFTEEN

While the sheriff was on his phone, Emma slipped a plate with a pink-sprinkled donuts and two bare-naked donut holes onto the counter in front of him.

I raised my eyebrows. *Peace offering? Might work.*

The sheriff popped a donut hole into his mouth. "Anything else? How'd you find them?"

"Colonel found a footbridge that went over the river and led me to where they were. I couldn't get into the brush, but he did and led them out."

He nodded. "I think I know that footbridge. I thought it fell apart years ago. It's a wonder it didn't drop you into the river."

"Now you tell me," I muttered, and the sheriff laughed.

"You finally told me something that made me happy."

He picked up his pink-sprinkled donut and strode to the door. He stopped and shook his donut at me. "I'm still mad, though."

"That went well." Emma giggled.

"Why is that? He's still mad."

Emma smirked. "He's not mad at me."

I rolled my eyes. "You all can close up. I have to go home and shower."

"Dinner at your house at six," Barbara said as the dogs and I left.

After the dogs and I were home, I took a shower and dressed in warm clothes then brewed a cup of tea.

I threw on a sweatshirt and took my cup of tea out back. Mandy and Pepper romped in the yard, but Colonel stayed close to me.

"I will be cold every time I think about Andrew and that icy river." I rocked and scanned my yard. "I'd like more flowers for the butterflies. I'll see what the nursery has. If the hardware store is open, I could get a good shovel, a trowel, and gardening gloves."

After I finished my tea, the dogs went inside with me. When I headed to the front door with my keys, not even Colonel budged. I shrugged and left.

I stopped at the hardware store and read the handwritten sign taped to the door: *Closed for the rest of the week.*

I continued to the nursery and wandered through the flowers as I pulled the small wagon the nursery provided at the entrance. I honed in on the perennials and read the planting instructions and generic descriptions. I decided on an orange flowered plant and a yellow flowered plant. They filled the small wagon.

The garden wagons were on sale, so I selected a green one and moved my plants into my new wagon. I dropped two bags of soil next to the plants and chose a pair of pink gardening gloves. After I picked out a shovel and a trowel, I rolled to the cashier's desk to pay. One of the workers pulled my wagon to the minivan and loaded my purchases into the back.

I hummed on the way home. *Feels good to do something I can enjoy for a long time.*

After I parked in the driveway, I unloaded my wagon, filled it with my other purchases, and wheeled to the backyard. I dropped the soil next to the spot where I planned to plant the flowers then set the pots and trowel next to the soil.

As I lifted out my shovel, I heard something behind me and turned. Bradley Sanford limped toward me. He had a lump the size of a golf ball over his right eye and his lifeless eyes were blinded by fury and hate.

"You're a dead woman," he growled as he lunged.

I swung the shovel with all my strength and struck the right side of his head, and he howled in pain and clutched his head but kept moving. I swung again and slammed the shovel against his leg where his pants were torn, and he went down. I ran with my shovel to my car and jumped inside then locked the doors and called nine-one-one.

"Tess, Bradley Sanford came to my house, and he's in my backyard on the ground."

"Sheriff was on his way the second I saw you were calling. Are you hurt? Are you in a safe place?"

"I'm fine. I'm in my car in my driveway, and the doors are locked."

"Does Sanford need medical?"

"Yes."

"You are my hero, Donut Lady. I'll stay on the line until the sheriff shows up. I can't wait to hear the details. Are you sure you're not injured at all?"

"Not at all, unless almost scared to death counts."

"Sheriff's there." Tess hung up.

The sheriff tapped on my car window, and Jeff eased to the back corner of the house with his weapon drawn.

"You okay?"

"Yes."

"Stay in your car."

He shifted to back up Jeff. After Jeff rounded the corner, the sheriff followed him, and the ambulance pulled in front of my house. Carol stopped by my van, and I pointed to the backyard. She strolled toward the back of the house and peeked around the corner before she returned to the ambulance. Her driver pulled out the cot and rolled it along the driveway to the back.

Carol tapped on my window. "You don't know this, but the man on the ground claimed you attacked him. I'm ashamed to admit I laughed. Shh." She put her finger to her lips, and her eyes twinkled. I giggled.

Carol joined her driver, and they continued to the backyard.

The sheriff passed them on his way to my car.

"Let's go inside. The ambulance crew is taking Sanford to the hospital. Jeff will stay with him until we can put him in jail. This is exactly why having only one deputy available per shift puts us in jeopardy." He glanced at the back seat. "Is that the alleged weapon?" He rolled his eyes.

When we went inside, he said, "I'll take the short version."

"I bought flowers and supplies at the nursery and was in the backyard unloading my purchases. I heard something behind me, and Sanford told me I was a dead woman then jumped to grab me. I kind of aimed at his head and swung the shovel. He kept coming at me, so I hit him in the lower leg and ran to the front yard. After I jumped into my car, I called Tess." He headed to the door. "The donut shop is closing soon, and the crew will beeline it here if I call them. You might want to call them yourself." He chuckled as he left.

I called the mayor. "You ready to close?"

"Just about."

"Good. The sheriff said you all should come to my house to get the story from me."

The mayor laughed. "Just a second. I'll turn on my speaker so everybody can hear why we should come to your house."

"Okay, Karen. We can all hear," Emma said.

"Sanford attacked me in my backyard, and he's on the way to the hospital."

"What? We'll close up and be right there. We need details," Emma said, and the mayor hung up.

My phone rang. *Amber.* "Dad called me. I'll hang out at the hospital for a bit. Maybe I can get a clue on why he was so obsessed with you and, in particular, your demise."

After I poured myself a glass of tea, the dogs followed me to the backyard.

I set my glass next to my rocking chair. "Be right back. I forgot my shovel is in the minivan."

I returned with my shovel and dug the first hole. I stood back to examine my work. *Two inches deep won't work.*

I loaded my plants into the wagon and rolled it to the back porch. I placed the plants on the ground along the porch and felt their soil. "You all are dry."

I watered them well and lifted the bags of soil into the wagon.

I heard the knock at the front door and hurried into the house to answer it. The mayor and Barbara carried in bags of food. Emma parked and joined us.

"We have make-your-own subs," Barbara said. "Eat first."

We sat at the table and passed around meats, cheeses, vegetables, pickles, and condiments.

"Sub, hoagie, hero, grinder. Don't matter what you call it, nothing's finer." The mayor said in a pseudo-rhyming rhythm and rose and bowed. We laughed and applauded.

After we ate, Barbara said, "Now. Tell us about Sanford."

"Better yet, show us," the mayor said. "Backyard, right?"

We all headed to the backyard, and I grabbed my broom on the way out. "You know the rule, never point a weapon unless you plan to use it."

The dogs ran around the backyard and flopped down on the porch. I raised my eyebrows. *Here for the show?*

"I'll be the thug," Emma said. "I always wanted to be a thug. Don't tell Grady."

"Stand over by the gate, and creep up on me," I said. "Okay, I unloaded my new wagon, and I picked up my shovel."

I held up my broom. "When I heard something behind me. I turned around. Come a little closer, Emma, and look fierce. Sanford said something like I was a dead woman. Did I tell you Andrew hit Sanford in the face with a rock? And Maisie bit his leg."

Emma sneaked closer and growled, "You're a dead donut."

Mayor laughed, and Barbara said, "Hush, David. The bad guy might hear you."

"I swung my shovel and smacked him in the head."

I pulled my broom back and held it close to Emma's face. "When I hit him, he grabbed his head."

Emma grabbed her face, swayed, and moaned.

"I swung my shovel again and hit him in the leg where his pants were ripped."

I tapped the broom on Emma's lower leg, she collapsed in slow motion onto the ground, and we laughed.

"Just like that. I ran to my car in the front." I feigned running to the fence.

"Karen?" Shirley called out as she and Woody hurried from the front yard to the back. "We heard a man tried to hurt you. We went by the shop, but no one was there, so we came here. Can you tell us what happened or is it a secret you can't talk about? That's okay if you can't. You're okay right?"

"I'm fine. I showed—"

Barbara interrupted. "My turn to be the bad guy."

"I'm Karen," the mayor said.

I rolled my eyes. "Before they start, here's some background. Andrew hit the bad guy in the forehead with a rock last night, and it raised a knot over his right eye. Maisie bit him on the leg and ripped his pants. I unloaded my garden wagon but still held my shovel. The mayor is me, the broom is standing in for the shovel, and Emma is the bad guy. She is creeping up on the mayor. Okay, action."

The mayor swung his hips as he carried the broom to the wagon.

"I do not walk like that." I put my hands on my hips.

The mayor narrowed his eyes. "I'm a method actor. I'm getting into the mood."

He stood next to the wagon, and Barbara crept up on him.

"Watch out, Miss Lady," Woody shouted, and when we all laughed, he bowed.

"Shuffle, shuffle," Barbara said.

The mayor put his hand behind his ear. "Hark. Do I hear a creeper creeping?"

He wheeled around, and Barbara assumed her fierce thug look. "You're a dead sprinkle."

The mayor swung the broom and stopped near Barbara's head.

"Ow. Ow. Ow. You hurt me." Barbara clutched her head.

The mayor swung the broom and tapped Barbara's lower leg. Barbara swayed and reeled then sat down on the ground. She flopped onto her side. After a short pause, she kicked out her legs.

The mayor tossed his head and sashayed to the gate.

We all laughed and applauded. The mayor helped Barbara up, and they bowed.

"Why did you have such a good swing to hit him like that?" Emma hefted the shovel. "This is good quality. Heavy."

"I know why," Shirley said. "Karen and I played softball when we were in high school. I was the best pitcher in the county, and Karen was not only our best hitter but also was the only switch hitter in the state. I can still pitch a ball straight and hard and slam it into a target. I'm sure she gave the shovel all the power she put into hitting a home run."

"You're awesome, Miss Lady. And you too, Mama Shirley."

Shirley's eyes misted. "Thank you, Woody."

"We'll see you later," Barbara said. "I've got a busy afternoon."

Everyone left. I carried the broom back into the house and straightened the kitchen. I settled down on the sofa and propped up my feet. *Busy day.*

When my phone rang, I woke. *Amber.*

"Did everybody leave? Are you alone?"

"Just the dogs," I said.

"Good. I'll be right there."

Five minutes later, Amber knocked on the door. She smiled when she came in and flopped onto the sofa. After I poured two glasses of sweet tea, I joined her.

"I hung out at the hospital for a while. The Georgia Bureau of Investigation searched Sanford's northern property and found what we expected. They had already cracked the code on the financial side of Sanford's business for both generations. Sanford has been after you because Lloyd said only you could decipher Terry's code about the counterfeiting activities."

I frowned. "I don't think Terry believed that though. He didn't think anyone was as smart as he was. I suspect he intended for the counterfeiter to focus on me as a distraction while Terry pursued his leads without detection."

Amber sipped her tea and nodded. "Sanford tried to implicate Terry in his ranting explanation, but in the process, he identified himself as the leader of the counterfeit ring. He has been obsessed because Lloyd told him Terry's search led him to Georgia, but Terry didn't know who the counterfeiter was."

"Did Sanford expect me to pick up where Terry left off?"

Amber raised her eyebrows. "Appears that way. It's clear to me that Terry planned for you to be a diversion. It's in line with his claim that you would know who the counterfeiter was because you grew up here, and people in small towns know everything about everyone else."

"So, Terry set me up?"

"I think so. I am so relieved that your appeal to the conviction was approved. For the record, and I'm serious, I'd run over Terry in a heartbeat if he was even close to this town. I'd hunt him down and run over him then back up in case I missed his lying tongue. But we have lawyer-client privilege or something like that, right?" She winked, downed the rest of her tea, and left.

Sure am glad I ran over Terry.

ACKNOWLEDGEMENTS

Huge thanks to my husband for being my silver pen when times are bumpy, and my constant source of joy all the time!

Thanks to my family and friends for their support, and to my beta readers and fierce editor.

Thank you for reading. You've read four of the Donut Lady Books! You are awesome!

If you're so inclined, tell a friend how much you love Donut Lady and a leave a short review. Authors can always use a few sparkles in reserve to brighten the gloomiest of days.

WHAT'S NEXT?

Dive into a unique mystery/thriller with intrigue and twists!

MAGGIE SLOAN MYSTERY SERIES, BOOK 1

I ALWAYS WANTED TO BE A SPY

Will the librarian with the soul of a spy and the unusual security team stop the desperate criminals or will she become the latest victim? It all comes down to kill or be killed.

ABOUT THE AUTHOR

Judith A. Barrett, award-winning author, lives in rural Georgia on a farm with her husband and two dogs. She writes thrillers, post-apocalyptic science fiction, and cozy mystery novels. Stories with a twist!

When she isn't writing, Judith is working in her garden, hiking with her husband and dogs, or rocking on her front porch while she watches the sunset.

Website   www.judithabarrett.com/

SUBSCRIBE to the newsletter!

Join her e-newsletter readers to be the first to know about the schedule and progress for new books, the latest monthly promotion, and other exciting news!

FIND the SUBSCRIBE button on www.judithabarrett.com

Let's keep in touch!

www.ingramcontent.com/pod-product-compliance
Lightning Source LLC
Chambersburg PA
CBHW030406030726
47497CB00002B/496